FIREBIR　　　　　　　*BOOK TWO*

THE GIRL WITH FIRE IN HER VEINS

DAWN FORD

Expanse Books

Published by Expanse Books,
an imprint of Scrivenings Press LLC
15 Lucky Lane
Morrilton, Arkansas 72110
https://ScriveningsPress.com

Printed in the United States of America

Paperback ISBN 978-1-64917-284-6

eBook ISBN 978-1-64917-285-3

Editors: Erin R. Howard and K. Banks

Cover design by Linda Fulkerson - www.bookmarketinggraphics.com

To my husband and family. You are the stars in my night's sky. I love you more.

A

TRELLER TERRITORY

KINS

DU

GOLDEN BEACH

RIN

MAJESTIC GREY MOUNTAINS

MERIDIAN PEAKS

armara

THORN FOREST

Anatolia

AINS

•Lowborn

BETWIXT

ERLANDS

DUNDOVER LAKE

UNKIN GRAVEYARD

HINTELAND DESERT

ZOE TREE

ACKNOWLEDGMENTS

As a writer, I must thank God first and foremost for gifting me with this story and then trusting me to play it all out. It was He who placed the characters and their story in my heart. I was immersed into this fairytale land from the beginning and each time after as I worked with Tambrynn to bring her story to life.

For my readers, it has been a wild ride with many ups and downs. For those of you who sent me comments about how much you enjoyed The Girl With Stars, you lift me up higher than I thought possible. You make my journey worthwhile. I am humbled by your words of encouragement. I hope The Girl With Fire In Her Veins, takes you on a deeper journey with Tambrynn and Lucas, along with Bennett, Audhild, and Rekspire. I pray it's worth the time you spend with them. As always, if I have managed to pull you in for the ride, my job as an author is successful.

For Jennifer Rupprecht, thank you for taking the rough diamond and making it shine. You rock!

And to Linda Fulkerson and all of the staff of Expanse Books and Scrivenings Press, I am humbled by your belief in me and this story. It is a part of my heart and soul, something I trust to very few. You all are incredible and amazing, and I'm so glad to be on this journey with you.

PART ONE

1

A bright midday sun breaks through Anavrin's overcast sky, revealing a rain-washed landscape. Wind ruffles through my damp feathers, cooling my inner fire.

"Tambrynn. Don't fly so fast and far ahead. You never know what dangers are lurking." Trepidation fills Lucas's voice as he 'mindspeaks' to me, a term my grandfather has given to our mind communication.

Shadows race across the lush pasture chasing Lucas and me as we fly. It had been two, long storm-drenching days with the three of us cooped up in a mountain cave staying dry.

"I can't help it. This feels glorious!" I reply and stretch my long wings. I'm overjoyed to get out and move around. With a taste of freedom in this new kingdom, despite all the perils we've been through, I'm itchy to explore more. And to find our lost belongings.

"It does feel wonderful." Lucas's magpie form sails in and out of the wind currents like a dance. There's a sense of watchfulness and disquiet in him.

I twist my head his way, wishing I could navigate the

breezes so easily. Though I'm bigger and stronger than he, Lucas is far more adept in his bird form.

Normally he's the one pushing to go further. However, our harrowing trek and my father Thoron's evil hexes have taken a toll on my beloved. My heart pinches at his abnormally hesitant attitude. *"Are you worried about something?"*

"Do you recall the snowstorm on Tenebris?" he asks.

"Vividly." I could still feel the lashing snow, blinding in intensity in my mind.

"That's what this is like. I don't recall Anavrin being this rainy. Something ominous is coming. I can feel it in my bones." He dips down and bobs back up on a cold gust, his inky black wings spread wide.

"But we know Thoron is already here. What could it be?" I reexamine the biting sensations I've been having. At first, I thought I was simply acclimating to this new kingdom and my firebird abilities.

"I'm unsure. Just—just don't stray too far from my sight." He darts left. *"And keep an eye out for anything shiny."*

My silver ring, the key to the Zoe Tree which connects my old kingdom to this one, is missing. My stomach sours again at the thought of Stiltworth, the froggen, finding it. *"I noticed it was gone after we found Grandfather, but truly it could be anywhere between where I happened upon the nomad women and where I jumped off the cliff from the eldrin's sanctuary."*

I picture it in my mind. A large ring with a sprawling tree carved into the metal band. It only takes one to open the hidden doorway in the Zoe tree, and even though Lucas still has his, it's alarming that mine is gone.

Puddles the size of ponds dot the land below us. The rain had been significant. Floods surrounded the pastures that days before had been lush and overgrown with flowers and grasses.

Now only the tips of weeds and tops of brush can be seen above the glistening surface.

I drop down and teeter against a gust as the realization hits me. *"We'll never find it."* My thoughts turn to the smallish people whom we'd met only a few days ago. *"Do you think the nomads are safe?"*

Lucas flits gracefully past me and down toward the curving ribbon of rushing water. *"Nomads are very resourceful. I'm sure they're safe in their kinstone mountain."*

We fly above the pasture not far from that same mountain. The stream where I'd found the women is now burgeoning, the ground around it saturated. Water and drowning grassland are all I see.

No, that's not all I spot. My pulse quickens.

I swoop around in a circle. Reflective eyes gaze upward while darker bodies slither around each other below the surface of the river. I catch a murmur from the water, like muted voices that make no sense, much like the bubbles in the stream around the froggen's castle.

Could it be them?

I sail higher, far out of reach in case any of them have plans to snare me again. *"Do you see them?"*

"I do."

His concern and fear creep along my nerves and join my unease. *"We're not safe here."*

"No. Let's head to the nomad's mountain. I hope you lost it there while battling your father. It would be easier to find among the rocks." He tilts his body northward.

I follow closely behind him, heartened that he remembers this area enough to lead. We'd traveled there by foot. It's not as far by air. But strangely, it's deserted. There's not a small, plump, or bearded nomad in sight. The bushes along the perimeter are no more. Only a smashed and soggy waste remain. It's a chilling reminder of Thoron and the eldrin who'd been turned into a beast in front of my eyes.

Images of Garrett changing to a beast while I looked on helplessly play in my mind. I don't want to relive it. I wish I didn't remember it at all. I swallow and push the horrid memory away.

"If only I remembered more about that day." Regret laces Lucas's words. He lands close to the stony perimeter of the kinstone.

"I'm glad you don't." I lightly land beside him, my wings caressing his sleek head as I return to my girl form mid-drop. Though Lucas is graceful, I settle on the tips of my toes. Luckily, he is there to stop me from tumbling to my knees. "Thank you," I tell him. "I may never get the hang of this."

Lucas's grin sets my heart racing, distracting me from my unease. He grabs my hand in his warm one, kisses it, and places it on his chest. "You're doing a wonderful job, my lady. You've only been a bird for a short time. And your firebird form is much larger. It took me weeks, maybe months, to successfully descend."

I brush back a dark lock that's fallen across his forehead. "If you say so." I wasn't so sure. I rub my palms down my slick eldrin clothes to ease my nervous energy. I anticipate Nobbert or another of the nomads storming out of the new crevice opening to greet me in their blustering, oh-so-welcoming way.

There's nothing but silence.

We turn and step across the bush border and onto the nomad's rocky soil. Washed clean, the gray stones are marbled with kinstone, a metal that suppresses magical abilities. The non-magical nomads form it into shackles, enabling them to stop magical beings from using magic against them. It's what has kept the nomads safe, at least until I came.

The crevice opening, which had been blown apart by one of

Thoron's spells, is now neatly reshaped so only the smallest of bodies could squeeze by to get inside the mountain. "Do you think if it were here, the nomads would've found it by now?" I search the outer base.

"Maybe. I'm sure Arrin would tell you. The others, I'm not so sure about. I wonder where they are." Lucas's footsteps scrunched against the ground. "They found all the maps and papers in the bushes, correct? Do you know if they gave them all back to you?"

"From what Nobbert said, yes. Since he can't read, I don't expect him to have lied about it." I explore wider, around the scraggly-looking foliage. Had it been this bare and dead-looking before? Most of that night is a confusing blur. Only a few things are clear, and those are the details I wish weren't burned into my memory.

We both explore the rocky expanse for several minutes and find nothing. The nomads may not be magical, but they are tidy. "I don't think we're going to find it here. Maybe it will be by the sack Arrin gave me."

We fly for several hours in the direction I'd flown when I left the nomads across an endless damp landscape. It's so different from Tenebris where small villages and farms are a simple carriage ride away from each other. My wings tremble when I hear the howls of my father's beasts splashing around in the forests. They're on the search for me, no doubt.

"Why are there no villages here or by the mountains?" I duck beneath the branches of a tall oak tree. The shade's coolness is a welcome change from the sun's heat.

Lucas is quiet for a few moments before he answers. *"The eldrin's law forbade living freely between areas, and so you normally find only travelers where there are no townships or villages. So, the voyants dwell in the east Meridian Peaks and the Majestic Grey Mountains. The djinn live in the towns along the streams and lakes, co-existing among the many different kinds of people. There are forest dwellers called trellers who live among the Great Northern Timberlands. Their job is to fell the trees for the wood used to build houses and businesses. And, of course, there are all of the fishkin, finfolk, and merpeople who live in the water. You know about the eldrin who live in the Sanctuary's holy mountain. I recall tales of other races that dwell in the deserts and the marshes, but I never knew if they were true or not."*

I'm amazed at all the different kinds of people who live in this kingdom. On Tenebris there were only the nomad non-magical people. *"If dragons exist, I'm sure the tales you heard are at least in part true."*

"After having seen Audhild, I have to agree with you."

Below us, the landscape grows familiar. Another stream burgeoning at its banks meanders through a meadow dotted with trees. A low hum, almost singing, whispers among the sound of the rushing water. We follow it down to a crooked bend that I stopped near before I took my ride to the froggen's castle.

I spy no dark, slithering bodies or reflective eyes glancing my way. Some of the tension I've had since the meadow eases from my shoulders.

"Tambrynn, you explore left. I'll take the right." Lucas's words flow easily into my mind. Possibly he's feeling the same relief as I am.

Unfortunately, the bag the nomad woman, Arrin, had given me was made of dark fabric. It would be hard to pick out in this landscape even now due to it being soaked.

Desperate, I ask Lucas, *"Did you see a water creature take it?"*

He dips down. "My memory is foggy, though I recall panicking when you disappeared into the water."

We search but find nothing again. Thanks to the storm,

there is no trace of where we'd been. *"It's too hard to see up here. I'm going down."*

"I'm going to make one more swing over the water," Lucas replies. *"Be careful."*

"You, too." I pick a spot by a tree on an incline, close but not too close, to the gushing stream. As predicted, I tip forward and have to brace myself against the trunk so I don't fall over. I lean gratefully against the bark to rest my weary arms. A lilting song carried by the wind shifts into the hiss of near-boiling water. Yet even with the sun so hot, it is an impossibility. I brush the thought off as nothing more than irrational fear.

After a moment of rest, I push off the tree and begin my hunt. The sun is bright and I have to squint against it to get a good look around me. I turn away from the water so I can see better. My necklace warms against my skin.

Suddenly, there's a cold hand on my shoulder, bringing pinpricks of ice across my arm. "Silver mage?" a strange voice croaks out.

2

I swing around, heart pounding, and my arms alight with blue energy. I instinctually swing my hands up to shield my face. "Stop!" I push my ability into my voice.

It's a female. Her shape does not resemble Siltworth the froggen, the only other one to call me 'silver mage.' She's not pot-bellied with long limbs. However, her hair and pale skin have a distinct greenish tint to them.

Like a froggen's.

Her wide eyes move back and forth, though her body remains frozen.

"Tambrynn, who is this?" Lucas flutters down beside me and changes back.

"Do I know you?" I ask the creature through gritted teeth.

Her mouth moves only slightly as she tries to speak, but is unable to.

"Return," I state, letting her go.

She sucks in a great swallow of air and bows.

"Who are you?" Lucas orders. His immediate anger and suspicion set my frazzled nerves snapping.

11

The girl raises her head. Her glance darts from me to Lucas. There's a calculating sharpness to her gaze. "My apologies for the misunderstanding. I saw you land and thought you'd heard me—"

The clouds move and light spreads across her face. She has large, deer-like eyes, pale skin, and her clothes are worn and shabby—dripping from the stream.

I inwardly groan. I should've known better than to land near the water. Especially the same one where I was dragged up to Siltworth's castle. But, what did she mean by *heard* her?

"What misunderstanding?" Lucas steps toward her.

"I was too eager. I shouldn't have touched you without announcing myself first." Her mouth is wide with an overbite and the sun reflects off a scaly, multi-colored patch of skin at her nape. She bows her head again.

"You shouldn't have touched her at all. What is your business with us?" Lucas's tone is demanding, inserting himself into the situation without hesitation.

I'm relieved he is asking the questions for the moment while the shock of surprise wears off and my heartbeat returns to a normal pace.

"I only wish to thank you for breaking the spell that has held me captive." If possible, she bends lower, her stringy hair grazing the wet ground.

Lucas and I both stiffen.

"It may be a trick, my lady. Be careful what you say." Lucas's warning beats like a drum in my mind.

"I'll be careful," I assert, though I'm confused. I want to be sure of what I'm dealing with. "I don't know what you mean," I say.

"His talisman. The pearl you broke," she states tartly as if I should've known.

And though Bennett told me as much, it is quite

disconcerting to discover it's true. "His necklace," I murmur, my mind rolling in thought. There had been hundreds of froggen at the castle. I hadn't stayed around to see what happened. What horror had I unleashed after I broke Siltworth's prized jewelry?

"Yes. When you broke it, the spell on us was destroyed. Well, most of us." She waves a hand as if that's of no consequence. "I am ever so grateful and wished only to thank you in person. So, when I spotted you in the air, I called out to you." She moves forward, her hands outstretched.

Lucas reaches in front of me and pushes me back a step. "How did you recognize us?" His voice is tight. I can't blame him. My throat constricts as well. *"Did you hear her?"* he asks in my mind.

"No. Though I did hear some sort of hissing the moment I changed—"

Her wide eyebrows scrunch together. "Is there another silver bird that burns bright like fire?"

I narrow my eyes at her. There's a hunger beneath her intent that seeps out of her like steam above a boiling pot. My necklace is warm against my collar, my hands covered in crackling blue magic. If she were truly wishing me well, the magic and my senses wouldn't be on alert.

Lucas lets out a low groan. "Are you fishkin or finfolk?"

She blanches. "I am Shellsea of the Bay of Hargough. I do not claim those titles of which you speak. I am merfolk, though our coral crowns are gone and our king's trident is missing."

Lucas shifts beside me. "Coral crowns and trident?"

She makes an annoyed gurgling noise in her throat. "Our crowns are what enable us to turn back into our water bodies. The trident is the power we use to protect our underwater cities."

I'm confused by the whole lot of it. "Where are your crowns and trident?"

Shellsea's face twists into an ugly grimace, making her eyes bulge more. "They were excised when we were taken." She moves a hand from one scar on her forehead to a matching one on the other side. "We searched *his* castle when you broke the spell, but they weren't there." For someone who's here to thank me, she seems irritated instead. "Siltworth's hiding them, probably among the deep canyons in the sea. None of us can return to the water properly to search for them."

Lucas crosses his arms over his chest.

I squint at her, not believing her claims. "But you came out of the water."

She shrieks, her eyes taking on a dangerous glint. "Any creature can swim in shallow water. Tell me, how long can you hold your breath, oh daughter of the death mage? Can you swim to the bottom of the sea without oxygen, half-djinn Watcher?"

Her acidic tone reminds me of Adelia, the maid who lied and got me dismissed. Anger flares in my gut, hot and liquid. It spills into my temper and ignites it. I raise my hand and clutch her throat with a blue magical hold. "Don't get snotty with me, *oh scaley one*! I wasn't insulting you. I was simply asking for clarification."

Anger, fear, and revulsion hit me, one after another, each crashing harder than the first.

My head starts to pound at the onslaught. I release her to rub my temples. "You've said your thanks. You can leave now."

She chokes, struggling to regain her breath, then shrieks at me. "Don't do that!"

"You come on too strong. You've tasted a piece of my ire. Be very careful what you say." I reply as indignant as she is.

"What do you want from us?" Lucas speaks through tight lips, breaking up our bickering.

I shiver at the raw emotions coming from both of them. I try to shut my mind to them, but they bombard me like a hammer in my head. There's more the girl desires from me.

Losing my patience, I take a step closer. "You want something from us. Spit it out and be done with it. But be aware, I make no agreements with anyone."

She hisses and now I understand. The sound I heard. It was her. "You're no better than the eldrin, silver mage, and they have the blood of all fishdom on their hands. I should've known. You're *all* the same. Unhelpful. Uncaring. I'll make you help me. Help all of us." Spit flies out of her mouth as she rushes toward us. Though we stand close together, her eyes are on Lucas.

I would die before one more hair on Lucas's head is hurt.

"Get back!" I shove my hands out to stop her and knock Lucas to the side. My eyes heat and my skin is no longer glowing blue but tinged with an angry red haze. Something whispers in my mind. *"Protect him. Touch her. Burn her down, end her."* For a moment I agree. My fire responds, building, getting hotter.

And then my hands are on her. Her skin is cold and damp, my hands orange flames, burning, burning.

Her scream is high-pitched, startling the birds around us into flight. She stumbles back into the water, dipping her hand in and dribbling the cold liquid over the red marks on her chest and arm where I'd touched her. Tears stream down her sickly-green-stained cheeks.

The water responds with murmurs and words I can't fully hear or understand.

"Tambrynn?" Lucas's face is creased with worry.

Horror at what I've done mixes with anger for having had

to do it. I fist my hands and jerk them to my sides. I take a breath and stifle the voice in my head urging me on. "I told you to be careful." I enunciate carefully to maintain control of my anger. "I don't want to hurt you, but if you come at us once more, you may not survive."

Especially if she tries to get to Lucas again.

Shellsea stops crying. "All I ask is for some help. Is that too much? Aren't you here to fulfill the prophecy? Make us all equal?"

"You weren't asking for anything. You were demanding and then you rushed us." Lucas points a finger at her. "And what do you know of a prophecy?"

She sniffles wetly. The voices from the water die off. All of the birds chitter cease. It's silent as if nature itself is listening. She recites: "Silvery moon and Maker's mark. There's one who will bring light from the dark. They'll restore the balance to each and all. Bringing even the lowest back to equal."

Birds call out and the water laps at the banks once more.

I touch my head, willing the pressure to go away. "What if I'm not who you think I am? I can swim, yes. But even as a firebird, I can't go to the depths of the ocean. I barely managed to survive when Siltworth dragged me to his castle. You'll have to find help from somewhere else." I step back, preparing to leave.

"Lies! You're lying!" Shellsea explodes.

"Now, hold on there—" Lucas starts.

Her big eyes glisten and she wails. Giant tears wash down her face. "I'm desperate. It has been a turtle's age since the merfolk have inhabited the seas in our true form. I wish only to regain that which was mine, ours, and reestablish my kin." Her shoulders rise and fall with her sobs.

Sadness and pain echo in the onslaught of emotions

seeping out of her. Guilt nags at my gut, and I'm wavering. Everyone deserves to be helped when in need.

"We cannot help you." Lucas is firm, startling me out of my thoughts.

Anger replaces her anguish. She swipes at her face with a webbed hand. "It was the djinn who first started this with a mage's help. Your kin. Your curse. And we suffer for it." She points a finger at me. "You recklessly broke our curse. It's your fault we can't swim back to our homes. If you don't help us, you're no better than your despicable father."

The confusion that had wrapped itself around my mind is gone as if it hadn't happened. Is it some sort of power the girl has? I'd heard the tales of sultry mermaids with their beguiling voices. And how they lure the unsuspecting with their powers.

My body is humming now. A knowing passes over me. *"Take hold and see the truth,"* it states. I take three steps forward and grasp her hand in mine. They're webbed, and cold, with blue tips and jagged fingernails. My blood rushes in my veins and blue flames erupt from my arms, engulfing both of us.

No sound comes forth as she tenses and jerks.

I see into her mind. There's water, fish creatures, and seagrass meadows. Endless songs lift on low and high tides, the voices singing in a strange underwater harmony. Then I see a man with a leering face. He tried to capture her. Shellsea turns away from the ancient choruses to her own path after the assault. Next are moonlit bays, her rhapsodic ballads, handsome sailors making promises they won't be able to keep before she gets her revenge and steals their breath forevermore —once, twice, a dozen times. More. Their life force fills her up, a tantalizing sensation—energetic and delicious—but it doesn't last. So, she lusts after it again. And again. Ceaselessly again, until there are too many corpses to count.

Next, I spy her captor sitting astride a massive seahorse

among a group of a dozen other froggen behind him that ride atop a stormy tide. They attack her small underwater village, carrying numerous merfolk off with them. A blink and then there's pain at a forced transformation when a younger Siltworth pries her crown off her head and tosses it in a chest full of other crowns, crests, and mantles still bloody from their owner's flesh.

All along I hear the events as if she sings them to me. Her dulcet tone reflects the events in its highs and lows, soft notes, and crashing crescendos.

My stomach revolts and my eyes are tearless though I want to pull back and cry. But I can't let go.

Finally, the memories of what Siltworth made her do come in dizzying clarity in a haunting aria. Turning dozens of innocent fishkin and not-so-innocent finfolk into the monsters he required. Others she devoured to ease the cravings of killing and soaking in their life's energy. Like she craves mine now. My light tantalizes her senses on so many levels. She lusts for my soul's power. The only thing holding her back is the knowledge that I'm the best chance at the help she desires more. There's no other that gives her hope. But it's truly a struggle in her mind, her heart, her soul. Which side will she take?

I'm disgusted and mournful all at once. The depravity I'd experienced as the mergirl churns like acid in my gut. Though my grandfather had warned me that this kingdom was no better than Tenebris, I'm still shocked at the atrocious vision. I've witnessed enough.

In a flash my fire winks out, leaving Shellsea panting on the ground, cradling her arm to her chest. She's so small and yet all I see is her vast appetite. It's large—insatiable.

I don't flinch from the fury on her face, I'm not afraid of it. Or of her. I've faced wickedness before. First on Tenebris and then on Anavrin. All of it leaves a vile taste in my mouth. I spit to get rid of it.

My path is clear, but she may not like my offer. "Equality may not be what you think, mergirl. I will help you if I can and only if I can. You come as a spokesperson for your kin. So, you and your ilk, in turn, will not harm me or any of my allies, even if we fail to retrieve your crowns and scepter. Your underwater world may not be able to be restored due to its wickedness. You may have to come to terms with living as you are currently."

Hatred shines brightly from her large eyes.

I step back. I'm not done yet. "And you will promise not to follow us or try to snoop into our affairs. You won't rally your kin against any of our kind. You will not speak of us at all or you forfeit your life. Agreed?" I'd tasted the greed in her desire to live. I knew ultimately what her choice would be.

She's still panting, her grimace revealing sharp, needle-like teeth. I can sense the inner turmoil within her soul. "Agreed," she snarls.

A flash of magic quickens in my gut. She flinches and shifts away from me as if regretting having approached me.

"Then leave. If I catch you searching for me again, I'll unleash my true fire on you and all of your deceitful kin will be no more." I turn to go.

She laughs bitterly. "You aren't safe, silver mage. Siltworth won't take losing his empire without striking back. At this moment alliances are being made. Dark deals are done. He has a secret that will put an end to all of this." She waves her hands around at the meadow as if that makes any sense. "He won't stop until he drowns you, guts you, then feasts upon your flaming entrails."

3

I stare at the rippling water Shellsea leaves behind.

"Tambrynn, what was that? What just happened?" Lucas asks over my shoulder.

I take a deep breath and ignore the threats the mergirl left behind. "I don't know. I had an impulse to take her hand. Then I saw into her memories. I think she relived it as I watched." I don't tell him about her desire to kill me and feast on my power.

Chilled, I rub my arms. "She wouldn't have been so agreeable otherwise. She and some of her merfolk were unrestrained until Siltworth stopped them. But he was savage in his rule. Neither one is better than the other."

"Maybe you're maturing into your firebird abilities?" He reaches for me.

I lean into his warm body, drinking it in like a sponge. His solid form eases my jittery nerves. "Do you think she's telling the truth about Siltworth?" A shudder slides down my spine. Anavrin is brighter and more beautiful than Tenebris, but the danger here is more intense as well.

"I don't know. And half of what she said is no easier to figure out than a befuddled riddle. She could be infirm, you know." He moves me an arm's length away so he can look at me directly. "But you're growing stronger every day. And we have your grandfather to help us. Whatever happens, we're going to be okay."

I'm sure my half-smile isn't as convincing as I wish it were. I want to believe him. If only danger didn't lurk behind every corner, every branch, every stream we come upon. "Let's go back to the campsite."

He kisses me softly at first, and then deeper. I run my fingers through his silky hair, relishing it. My heartbeat races harder than when Shellsea startled me. I lean into him, my arms around his waist. His heartbeat is as errant as mine.

Memories of him shirtless in the passageway have teased my dreams and chased away nightmares that have tried to steal what little rest we've managed to get. He tastes like wind and the mint we chewed before we left camp this morning. My roving hand accidentally slips inside the back of his shirt, and I'm startled enough to pull away. We both laugh shyly, breathlessly.

I squeeze him and step back, knowing the heated moment is over. "I've wanted to do that since I broke your spell," I admit.

A blush colors Lucas's pale face. "Kind of hard with your grandfather inches away from us for days on end." His smile is impish. "And propriety, of course."

My hand covers the snicker that leaks from me. "Of course."

He glances at the sky. "It is getting late. We probably should head back. But, maybe not so terribly quickly?"

I giggle. "Fine with me."

A last, lonely cloud moves across the sun, covering us in a

shadow, and chilling me. My necklace, which lays against my chest warms again. I grab Lucas's arm and stop. Blue energy wavers over my hands.

"What is it?" he whispers.

A shriek blasts in the sky. I slap my hands to my ears.

A squirrel darts away, with its tail nervously bobbing. It chitters loudly as it jumps from limb to limb in the opposite direction from the noise.

A shadow, possibly a cloud blocking the sun, passes over us. I glance upwards.

The only clouds in the sky are spread out thin and nowhere near the sun. There's no reason for the shadow.

Lucas and I stand back-to-back, scanning the area. My ability thrums beneath my skin in time to my furious heartbeat and I'm ready to change back and take flight. "What do you think that was?"

"Whatever it is, it's big." Lucas's voice quivers.

My necklace agrees as it lies heated against my chest.

Shuffling noises sound in the trees to my left. Usually, my father's beasts announce themselves with howls, not shrieks. And they don't darken the skies.

I'm tense, waiting. An instant before I would change, Arrin, the nomad woman, trudges out of the thick undergrowth of the timber that runs along the swollen stream.

She's soaked up to her flowered dress's chest. "Heh, Tambrynn! Thought that noise was ye. I see ye are none the worse for wear. Belated thanks, by the way, for freeing me from them abominations." When she steps out of the tree's shade, I see her face is bruised, but her stick is held firm in her hand. Bandages are wrapped around both feet and I have to wonder at her trek home from the froggen castle.

I'm relieved it's her and not some other creature. But surely my tingling-warm necklace wasn't sensing Arrin as a threat? I glance upwards again. Nothing there except a mostly blue sky. "It's good to see you. But that wasn't me shrieking." Did I really sound that loud?

More shuffling noises. Nobbert steps out of the bushes, followed by several other nomads. He wears his usual puckered look. "Ugh. It's you. Should've known. Wherever there's trouble ..." His voice drifts as he glances over my shoulder. "And I see you have your beau with you. Oi, and in his djinn form, too. Must be my lucky day. *Again*."

I ignore his less-than-friendly greeting and focus on Arrin. "So, this is where you all are. What are you doing here so far away from your mountain fortress?"

Before Arrin can speak, Nobbert steps menacingly toward me. "Trying to find Colly and a group of others that self-appointed nincompoop of an eldrin took this morning." He hammers his finger in my direction as if it were my fault they were missing.

Well, Colly was partly my fault. But the others weren't. "If you recall, I left so you'd be safe. I can't help it if the eldrin came back. How many did Nyle take this time?"

"Ten women. It might not have happened had I been there. The rain and my injured feet held me up. I returned shortly after the Councilmaster took them. Someone needs to take those blasted necklaces away from them. Things were more peaceful before." Arrin swipes a hand across her nose and swallows hard.

She continues after composing herself. "They were doing the wash. As ye recall, the wash area is outside the perimeter of the kinstone. One of the men tasked with guarding our entry saw one of the women, Aella, run from the trees in a panic. He wasn't fast enough to stop the enforcer before they vanished with her. When he checked, they were all gone."

"At this rate, we'll all get picked off within a week, or we'll starve hiding in the mountains. Them eldrin need to be stopped!" Nobbert stomps past me, his boots sucking into the soggy ground. The nomad men with him don't so much as glance my way.

A flash of my life on Tenebris crosses my mind's eye. I know what it is like to invite the wrath of those in charge. Tears prick behind my eyes, but I hold them back. Nobbert wouldn't thank me for being weepy.

"And how are you going to stop them?" Lucas asks quietly.

I sense his unease, but I also know how unreasonable the male nomad is.

Nobbert hustles back straight for Lucas, the other nomads splitting to let him pass.

I step in his path. "What he's asking is, do you have more of your shackles? Is there some weapon you have that will disable them? Surely, you're not thinking of confronting them without a plan?"

Red-faced, Nobbert turns to glower at me. "It's all your fault. If you hadn't returned here, this wouldn't be happening."

Lucas pushes me aside, anger stiffening his stance. "So, the eldrin weren't taking your kin before we got here? You were best friends with the Councilmaster? Is that what you're saying? I might not remember everything, but I do remember you saying Colly wasn't the first. Blaming Tambrynn might be an easy way to focus your anger, but let's be honest. Magic aside, your inability to keep your clan safe is not our fault."

I'm glad for Lucas's quick ability to reason out a situation. However, guilt gnaws at my gut. "I take some responsibility for Colly's abduction. I also offered to help look for her. You said you knew where she was and that you'd go get her later. Besides having more women taken, what's changed?"

Arrin tsks. "No one's left to cook for them. They *can't eat* my cooking. Said it's like eating charred wood."

I would've laughed at Arrin's animated mocking of the men's taste in her cooking had I not been so dumbfounded at the incredible folly of their situation. "That's it? You can't cook for yourselves? Not even a little?"

Nobbert's face turns so red that I think it might melt off his broad shoulders. "We have a system and a way things work that you wouldn't understand. You and your woo-hoo magic." He flings his sausage-thick fingers around. "Not everyone can change to a bird and feast on worms to get by."

"We don't eat worms to survive," I snap back at him.

I glance at Arrin, who purses her lips, no doubt recalling when Lucas ate a bug after one of my father's hexes hit him. He'd been a bit dazed and lost to his bird self. I'm thankful for her silence.

Lucas puffs out his chest in a magpie manner. "And truly, what's to understand about a system where only one or two of you know how to do something, but no one else has a clue? Wouldn't it make more sense to share responsibilities so you don't starve? Or is that beyond your comprehension?" His words, though sensible, are not received well.

Indignant at being corrected in any manner, the nomad men shout and spit, cursing Lucas and all of *his* kind. I'm thankful I don't understand half of what they're saying. It seems, however, Lucas does as he turns still and stony-faced.

My head hurts. "Stop!" I demand, infusing my words with my ability. Fire creeps over my fingers, and I sense its desire to be used. *"Touch them. Set fire to them all."* I close my eyes tight to hold back the foreign longing. It's too much like the mergirl's cravings, and I reject it. The voice disappears, replaced by a cool calmness. I breathe out my relief and open my eyes.

Everyone is frozen in place, except Lucas, who I hadn't focused my energy on.

He leans into my ear. "Are you okay, my lady?"

"I will be." I step toward Nobbert, asserting as much control as I can. "What Lucas is saying is practical. However, that doesn't change what is happening to you at the moment. I can help you if you're willing to aid us." I let go of my ability, leaving the bunch heaving and sputtering.

"I don't like it when you do that," Hard consonants grind out of Nobbert's mouth.

"Then don't require it." I shrug, tired of his theatrics. "We need to find a certain ring and the bag with the maps Arrin gave me before I left your mountain. Help us, and I can take you somewhere safe for the night with someone who knows how to cook," I add pointedly. "You can trust us."

Nobbert grunts. "Lost something else besides the Eye of Fate, have you?" His chuckle is grating. "I haven't seen anything of yours." The men behind him say nothing.

I eye him skeptically. He's holding something back. Maybe if he stayed with us long enough, we'd be able to wheedle it out of him.

Arrin steps forward. "Oh, ye old coot! We found yer bag, Tambrynn, along the bank upstream. It was empty. And, thank ye. We'll take ye up on yer offer." She glares at the men. "We can help look for the rest of yer things."

"Now hold on, old woman." Nobbert gets nose-to-nose with Arrin. "You don't answer for us."

I bite back a laugh as both of their bulbous snouts bump.

The group behind him mutters in agreement.

"You're not the oracle you think you are." A vein on the male nomad's neck bulges and thrums.

Arrin's hand on her walking stick turns white, her fingers rasping against the smoothed wood. "And ye are? Who was the one that found our mountain and the kinstone? Was it ye—"

A shadow snakes over us. I ignore their heated exchange and look up, scouring the skies. And then I see it.

A dragon. Black as the deepest part of the night.

And it's coming straight down. Crackling energy flashes, zigging toward us.

No, toward me.

4

I n a blink Lucas and I are airborne. Blue fire tickles my wings as it rushes through my veins.

Lightning? How is that possible?

Arrin, Nobbert, and the other nomads scream in terror and dart for the trees. I lose sight of them.

The dragon's firebolt hits a tree where we stood seconds before. It cracks apart and drops. Wood crashes to the ground, splintering. Water gushes where it lands against the wet meadow. Four of the other male nomads, who hid behind nearby trees, race off in different directions.

More lightning streaks through the damp air, grazing my tail.

The fire inside me kindles hotter and I screech out a warning. I lean back and swing my wings wide, sending a wave of blue flames at the dragon. It darts out of the way, disappearing from my sight behind a grove of larger, thicker trees.

"Who are you?" I speak in my mind, hoping that since I was

able to communicate with the fire dragon Audhild, I might be able to communicate with this dragon as well.

I receive no answer.

The creature hovers nearby, weaving its body through the trees. I glide my way closer to get a better look.

"My lady! What are you doing?" Anxiety permeates Lucas's words. *"Even though Audhild was friendly, it doesn't mean this one is."*

"I wouldn't call Audhild friendly, exactly." The buzz in my gut heightens the closer I get to the black creature. The aura surrounding its midnight body is murky, more clear than dark, but not malevolent like my father and his beasts. Each time I get close to attacking it, it zags behind another tree.

I'm confused. Why'd it attack us if it didn't want to fight?

Audhild's voice echoes in my mind. *"Tambrynn?"* I'm jolted by the force of her calling my name and I land in a treetop. I tumble down, unable to stop my descent until I'm sprawled out on a lower branch. A couple of my feathers are broken from the fall and my body aches from the impact.

The energy surrounding my feathers licks at the foliage. Fortunately, the remnants of the rain keep the wood and leaves from catching fire. I right myself, jump out of the tree, and back to flight.

"I'm here. You don't have to knock me out of the air to get my attention." I can't help the irritation in my voice.

"Forgiveness requested, young firebird, I'm unused to muting my abilities when I sense danger. I am concerned because another dragon's energy entered this kingdom. I've been following it ever since. Then I heard you speak to it."

I don't see her or any flash of her red body. *"It tried to attack us and then it backed off. Where would it have come from? Is there something I should be concerned about?"*

"Any dragon is something to be concerned about." Audhild's

blood-colored tail whips out between several large trees. It is gone as quick as I see it.

"My, lady? Is something wrong?" Lucas asks. He's flying wider arcs above where we'd stood, obviously not privy to Audhild's words this time. He joins me as I hang back.

"It's Audhild. She's worried about the other dragon." Worry and ... anger? Yes. That was definitely anger. *"She's not happy about it being here. What do you think it could mean?"*

A roar splits the air. A different growl answers. Fire flashes followed by a burst of lightning. They clash in a blinding display.

"Tambrynn, it seems to be targeting you. Leave. I will find you when I am done dealing with him." Her words are stilted, even if they're spoken in my mind. Audhild's panicked tone leaves me no doubt of her fear.

Panic sends icy tendrils across my bird body, quenching my inner flame. *"I believe it may be time to leave,"* I tell Lucas.

———

The moon is high when we reach my grandfather's campsite. It's now moved back to where I'd first found him, south of the mountain cave. Guilt niggles my conscience at leaving Audhild alone with the other dragon. I hope the nomads found safety, as well. However, the battle I glanced back at assured me there was nothing I could do to help aid the fire dragon. They'd been well-matched.

I land and teeter on my heels this time, falling over onto my backside. I try to ignore Lucas's perfect landing, but it still pricks my ego.

My grandfather Bennett's dark eyes shine with amusement when I stand up and brush myself off. "If you hold your wings out as you drop down, you'll break your speed and help better balance your landing."

I don't acknowledge his advice. "There's another dragon. A black one." I spew the words, my tongue almost tripping over itself in my haste.

"He had some kind of lightning ability," Lucas adds. His hand is warm against the small of my back. He rubs in soothing circles.

The humor leaves my grandfather's demeanor. "Another dragon? This can't be good." He scratches his claw-like fingers lightly across his brow. The skin on his face is taut, but it wrinkles in grim consideration. "Dragons are quite predatory unless they are part of a hoard. Audhild has been the only dragon on Anavrin since your father killed her mate almost twenty years ago. She won't take kindly to anyone infringing on her territory."

"What do we do?" I ask, suddenly frightened for Audhild. She may not be overly friendly, but she isn't threatening to me. She's saved me twice—three times if I counted the black dragon.

"We do nothing for now. We can't move safely in the dark. We rest, then leave for my haven at first light."

———

I wake to find my beak tucked beneath my wing. The grass beneath me is wilted and charred at the ends. Though it is unnerving to wake as a bird, it is quite comfortable with my feathers as a covering. And the fire sizzling from my tail feathers to my crowned head is much cozier than any blanket.

Each night since Audhild had awakened my firebird, I'd returned to this form while sleeping, flames and all. At first I'd welcomed the heat until I'd accidentally singed Grandfather's tent. Now, I sleep under the rock shelf where Bennett cooks meals.

The sky is starting to lighten and I hear someone stirring. With a thought, I'm back to my girl form. My fire recedes to a purr in my gut. I hug my arms across my chest to ward off the air's sudden sharpness. My clothes, which Arrin had given me days ago, are fine and work well when traveling by day when it's warm. They do nothing, however, to keep me warm in the cool of the night or morning. I think back longingly to the cloak little Nellie had given me on Tenebris.

Worrying about her fate, I say a quick prayer for the young maid. Perhaps the Kinsman will look kindly upon her future. A free future, I hope.

It is Grandfather who has awakened and is stirring the ashes to build a new fire. Lucas's feet stick out of the charred tent he and Grandfather share.

"Come, warm yourself by the fire." Already the flames catch the kindling, creating a welcoming glow against the darkness around us. "Tell me what happened yesterday. I fear I was too tired to inquire last night."

My heart swells with delight at his interest, though I'm concerned to hear him admit to being tired when he'd been resting for several days. With the relationship being so new, I'm unsure how to ask him about it.

Instead, I fill him in on the mergirl, the nomads, and end by describing the dragon. Embarrassment holds me back from confessing my temptation to burn the mergirl and the fleeting desire to do the same to Nobbert.

Bennett's eyebrows are raised by the end of my story. "You were busy! No wonder you fell asleep so quickly. It sounds like your firebird abilities are maturing if your intuition is taking over. I can't tell you how many times Audhild knew things before I'd tell her. I made the mistake only once of allowing her to take my hand." His chuckle is deep and throaty. "She'll never let me live down what she saw in my past."

"So, that's a fire creature thing?" Something akin to pride settles over me. Am I for once mastering something before making a mess of it all?

"It is a dragonkin thing. I would be mindful, however, of all water bodies in the future." He clasps his hands in his lap. "The water folk are hard to trust in the best of times. If what she's saying is right, and it sounds like it to me, then Siltworth will be out for revenge. One of their favorite things to do is drown their victims. And don't trust Shellsea to hold up her end of the bargain, either. We'll need to be careful *and* prepared."

I'm quiet as I contemplate his words. The fire pops and a bird chatters in some nearby bushes. Purple light blooms across the horizon as morning breaks. The peace of the moment does not reflect my disturbing experiences in Anavrin so far.

Grandfather places a comforting hand on my shoulder. "Now, tell me more about this other dragon. Were you able to communicate with it?"

I take a seat on the rocks beside the log Grandfather sits on. "I did try, but it didn't answer me. Its aura wasn't dark, but cloudy. I was trying for a closer look when Audhild came. You were right. She wasn't happy about the other dragon."

"Yes, that's not surprising." He rubs the sleep from his eyes, their black depths reflecting the orange light from the fire. "If that dragon finds our mountain haven we're in serious trouble. Not to mention, what is the dragon doing here?" Sparks fly as he pokes at the flames. "There are only a few other kingdoms where dragons remain. Far Starl is one of them. I visited there during my trials."

"What kind of trials?" I ask, alarmed. Images of stocks and

gallows with the nooses ready for the next unfortunate soul come to mind.

He holds a hand up. "It's nothing bad. It's a challenge. All eldrin who wish to be on the council are required to travel to another kingdom, find a holy relic, and return to Anavrin. Officially, it's to study other cultures and kingdoms to further our science and knowledge. Too late in life, I realized it was to strengthen the eldrin's coffers and allow them a less impeded rule over the other races."

He takes a deep breath. "Anyway, when it came time to draw kingdoms, I drew Far Starl." His grimace belies the calmness of his words.

"I am one of only two who have ever drawn this kingdom. The other was my friend, Jarmon, who accompanied me on the journey. We thought ourselves the luckiest of eldrin to receive this assignment. You see, Far Starl is a kingdom full of dragons, dragon riders, and a noble race of guardians. Our dragons by that time were facing extinction, there was only a handful of them left, so I longed to study them and possibly bring back an egg or two."

He shifts on the log. "Only we found that the guardians weren't so noble and the eggs were guarded more than the Kinsman's secret treasures. The dragons were treated like badly raised farm animals. They were overbred, treated harshly, and slaughtered if they didn't live up to their owner's expectations. It was quite legal, I'm afraid. Jarmon and I found fields full of dragon bones and rotting corpses. It was despicable."

He bows his head. I stare at his misshapen ears, a cross between pointed eldrin ears and the wolf-like ears of the undead sluaghs, my father's beasts. My heart aches for him, having had to witness something so cruel.

"What'd you do?"

"There's nothing I could do. They're more advanced in weaponry. Their whips are like lightning, and they have rods that shoot metal fire bullets. Even if I wanted to do something, they were too many. I was outnumbered and in over my head. I'd never been so useless in my whole life before or since."

He sighs. "Where I was disgusted at the whole practice, Jarmon was fascinated. Where I saw death, he saw opportunity. We parted ways after a particularly heated row." He studies his hands, then rubs them back and forth. "So, I found what I needed and hightailed it out of the kingdom as fast as I could, leaving Jarmon behind. I—I couldn't stand to see such unnecessary destruction."

"That's terrible." I think of how Thoron had used the dragon bones and blood to perform his dark magic spells. "But you said dragons are holy messengers from the Kinsman. Why would they treat something so special like that?"

"They don't change forms there. I never figured out why. Maybe the kingdom is like Tenebris and suppresses different types of magical abilities? There's no regard for a higher power, or any moral compass there to follow. Charity was an unheard-of action and thought to be a weakness. It's such a shame." He reaches over and squeezes my hand. "Your grandmother was the most charitable soul. She did so much good before she died. I can see her generosity in you."

A rush of joy fills my heart to think that I, despite my flaws, could live up to such a revered person. It's the biggest compliment I've had, and I can't speak past the emotions clogging my throat.

Lucas rouses behind us before crawling out of the tent. The violet sky brightens to a stunning yellow and orange. It's almost time to leave, and I can tell Grandfather is done speaking when he starts to unload items from his pack.

Grandfather shares some of his dried meat, nuts, and water

from his canteens. Lucas's sleek hair is handsomely ruffled from sleep though he has the start of dark rings under his eyes.

Worried, I kiss his bristly cheek. "You need a shave."

His eyebrows raise. "Ah, good. It's only taken a couple of days for it to grow this time." He yawns wide and scrubs a hand across his face.

"You don't normally grow a beard?" I ask, confused.

"Not only do I not age, but my hair doesn't grow when I'm a bird." He lets out another strangled yawn.

"Tired?" Grandfather laughs at him.

"I kept having dreams of fish folk and dragons coming after us. Attacking us everywhere we went."

"I'm so sorry." I give him a sideways hug and place my head on his shoulder. He's suffered so much since we reunited in that cottage, I hate that it's affecting his sleep, too.

He slips his arm around me and I revel in the warmth and comfort.

"Audhild will keep us safe, I'm sure," I say hopefully. However, she hasn't shown up yet.

He rubs the chill off his arms and squints. "You're a terrible liar."

I slap his arm playfully. "Hey! I can lie. I got out of the deal with the froggen, didn't I?"

Lucas frowns.

Grandfather grunts. "That, granddaughter, was pure luck. And we'll need more than that to get us to our destination today. Pack up. We've got a long road ahead of us."

5

Grandfather and Lucas have the tent broken down and packed quickly. I take care of the fire, ash, and debris from our campsite. We're ready to go before the sun has fully risen.

"How are we going to travel without being recognized?" I ask. Not only am I strange-looking, with my silver-spun hair and star-shaped pupils, but so is Grandfather, thanks to my father's failed spell. His nose is elongated, more snout-like. His teeth are larger and sharp, his cheeks accentuated by deep lines as if the skin were stretched and then sprung back out of shape. Hair covers his curved, wolfish ears and runs down into thick sideburns which disappear behind his neck.

Everyone had thought him dead, but he'd survived somehow. Even Grandfather couldn't explain it except to say Thoron's spell was faulty at first.

"I have a disguise. It has helped me hide in front of everyone all these years." He digs into his bag and produces a small hoodless, gray mantle. It's not cloth but more like untanned leather.

I'm shocked to see it's similar to some of the skins from Siltworth's chest in the mergirl's memories. Like them, it's thick and pliable, almost lush-looking. I swallow hard. Surely, Grandfather hadn't done the same things as Siltworth. "Wha —what is that?"

Grandfather swings it over his shoulders and is instantly transformed. His dark graying hair is now blond. His face is polished-stone smooth. There's no sign of Bennett beneath the image even when I squint. He resembles Nyle in the Councilmaster's shallow beauty and rigid stature.

"It's selkie skin sewn into a rutch." His smile is sad as he rubs the material. "It was a death gift from a dear friend. He was wise but had become sick from something that tainted the water." He glances up at us. "A poison Siltworth used to intimidate the water creatures into submission."

"That's incredible!" Lucas steps over to touch it. "Not that your friend died, of course."

Grandfather bends his head in understanding.

Lucas caresses the mantle. "I've heard tales of selkies. Having lived so far inland, I didn't know if they existed. Does it use your magical energy or is it magical itself? My illusions are always exhausting."

Surprised, I whirl on him. "You never told me that."

His face flushes, but his dark eyes remain intent on the rutch.

"You always seem so capable, even during the Masquerade Ball." Probably especially then. Guilt nags at me. "Is that why Thoron's spell hit you so hard in the Passageway? You'd used most of your energy up at the Spaw?"

He relaxes his posture. "No. His magic *is* that powerful. And though your abilities are remarkable, on my own I am not strong enough to withstand his spells."

Grandfather scratches his now perfectly coifed blond head.

His dark, beastly eyes have changed to a sparkling green. "Nor was I. It was only due to Cadence's help, and my eldrin charms, that I managed to escape becoming Thoron's first monster." He glances away and rubs at the smooth material. It's seamless against his sleek tunic. I wouldn't know it was there had I not seen him put it on.

However, I sense there's something he's not saying. Birds gather on the ground around us searching for their morning meal, distracting me from our discussion. I grow antsy, wanting to leave. However, I don't know where we're headed and I do love hearing Grandfather's stories.

"Unfortunately, I only have one since they are incredibly rare, not normally gifted like mine was. And selkies, like the merfolk, used to roam free until the froggen took over the waterways. Since then, many finfolk have been murdered, snatched, or enslaved by the fishkin."

"What is a selkie?" I try to pronounce the strange word correctly, unsurprised by my grandfather's words. Shellsea's vision flits across my mind and I cringe. "How are they enslaved?"

"During a springtide, a seal can shed their mantle and become human when they're on land. Humans are similar to eldrin in many ways except for their rounder features and webbed appendages." Grandfather wiggles his fingers.

He continues explaining. "Seals are large, air-breathing sea mammals that survive off the sea, but live mainly on land. They have flippered feet and arms which they use to move around, called pinniped, which means fin foot. That's why they're called finfolk. They're more tribal or communal than the independent fishkin and less prone to the destructive, addictive behavior of the merpeople." He resettles the pack on his back. "Are you versed on the history of the froggen?"

"Lucas told me the story of a noblewoman, a mage, and a djinn, yes," I answer.

"Then you're aware the froggen are a cursed race. They were created by dark magic. Muriel, the noblewoman turned froggen, grew restless and bitter. While the fishkin weren't opposing or approving of her actions, the finfolk were horrified that she murdered the frog-djinn and the mage. She was ostracized, chased, and abandoned near an uninhabitable island in the North Ocean."

I rub my arms, soothing the gooseflesh that rises. It wasn't her fault that she was changed into something without her consent, something I sympathized with.

Grandfather picks up several palm-sized rocks which had been placed in a circle around our campsite. Each has strange markings. "A displacement spell," he explains. "Much like the djinn's illusions, it keeps anyone from seeing, hearing, or sensing us." Smiling, he tosses one in the air and catches it neatly.

"Kind of like the passageway?" I ask, curious. It explains how no one had found our camp at the base of the mountain. And possibly why I hadn't sensed them.

He puts the stones into a side pocket of his bag. "Similar, but not the same. The passage takes a whole lot of energy to stay viable. It connects each kingdom through the Zoe Trees, a lifeline of sorts. That is old magic, the kind that sustains life. This spell only needs intentions, the right words, and manipulation of the elements to work."

We follow him down a rocky incline. Trees, some with limbs broken from the storms, were sporadic, the space quite open around us as we leave.

"Anyway, back to Muriel," Grandfather continues. "Without anyone to share her life with, she came up with a wicked plan as retribution. She befriended an unhappy female selkie named Eilith. After she'd lured the seal onto her island during a springtide, she stole the selkie's skin, which holds their ability to change shapes, trapping the girl in her changed form. Then, Muriel used the frog-djinn's spell to turn the selkie girl into a froggen."

The food in my stomach sours. How could someone, who knew the downsides of such a curse, do something so evil? My empathy for Muriel disappears.

Lucas takes my hand and squeezes it. "That's horrid! What happened to Eilith?"

We've made almost a full circle around the camp. Grandfather picks up a last carved stone and straightens, tucking it into his pack. Air rushes at us like something had been holding it back. "Legend says she's buried in the Sunken Graveyard along with many others. It's hard to know since she'd be reduced to bones by now. It has been several generations since then." Bennett's green eyes turn serious.

I grimace, recalling the dreaded waters I'd tried to navigate when Lucas and I first arrived on Anavrin. *And the arm.* I shudder. "Is that how the froggen got so numerous?" A terrible thought caught the air in my chest. "They're like Thoron's beasts, then? Turned into something they weren't originally and stuck in that form?"

"Yes. The spell is similar, though different in many ways." Grandfather acknowledges.

I turn towards Lucas. "But, hadn't Siltworth called Thoron's spell an abomination?"

Lucas's gaze is solemn. "He did."

My huff ends in a snort. "Isn't that hypocritical? I mean, how can you resent something someone else does that you yourself do?"

Grandfather clears his throat and resettles his pack on his shoulders. "You'll find that evil people at their core are duplicitous. Some justify their own actions by comparing them to something worse. Good people fall into this trap as well. Never forget that, granddaughter. And never trust a froggen."

Once again, the warning about Siltworth and his kind sends an unbidden prickle of warning up my body. I'm thankful I hadn't agreed to Siltworth's pact. Especially now with the mergirl's warnings.

"Now, we must do something with your appearance before we leave." He touches my long silver hair. "How did you hide on Tenebris?"

My heart pinches at the memories. "I used a cloak to hide my whole head when I could. When I couldn't, I used coal dust to hide my hair and avoided eye contact whenever around others."

His smooth brow wrinkles. "Yet, you changed somehow. Something I cannot do. Dragons and their kin have the ability to shift their appearance. Is that how you were able to become the silver bird?"

I glance at Lucas and shrug. "I don't know. Lucas helped me when Thoron found me. I simply took his hand."

My grandfather stares at me, seeing something beyond who I am. "It could be that Lucas unknowingly used some of your innate ability when you joined hands. It would explain how you became a bird so easily since that is your true gifted form."

My mind whirls. Lucas had stated before that he'd tried to change me years ago when I'd been asleep. I had assumed it was all Lucas's magic that changed me. Could it have been because I couldn't join my ability with his? I shrug the thoughts off for now, wanting to revisit them later.

Grandfather touches my arm. "Try this. Close your eyes, picture someone else, and then step into that person in your mind."

"Okay." I shut my eyes. Who? Adelia? She was about my age. But, no, she was too sneaky. What about that eldrin who stole the nomad girl? I couldn't bring myself to look like a child stealer. Maybe I'm overthinking it?

"Who won't draw any attention?" I ask, my hands twitching. "An eldrin? A nomad? A child? I don't know any other djinn besides you. Surely you don't want me looking like the mergirl."

A hand on my shoulder jolts me. Lucas gives me a reassuring smile. "It might help not to try to look exactly like someone else, but to add some of their physical attributes at first. It's easier to keep hold if you don't completely change but switch some things like your eyes and hair color. That way you're not easily detected."

I take a deep breath and let it out. How had I done it so easily on Tenebris without even trying? "Okay." I close my eyes and concentrate once more, beckoning my ability. It hums in my gut, answering my call. I envision my mother's dark brown hair and eyes. Her comforting voice. Her grace. I open my eyes and glance down at myself. I'm disheartened to see I'm wearing the same green eldrin clothes.

Bennett steps back. "Madrigal?" His words come out strangled like I'd punched him in the gut.

I jerk my head up. "What? No, I pictured my mother."

Lucas's crooked grin is sad. "You're the image of your grandmother."

Shock steals across my body and I grow cold as if chilled. "How? I've never even seen her?"

"I don't know." His hand on my shoulder is comforting. "Not even djinn can get a disguise so close—" He stops speaking and shrugs.

My grandfather visibly shakes, pain pinching at his perfect

eldrin façade. "I hadn't expected—" He rubs his face with a trembling hand.

"I'm so sorry. I didn't mean to upset you." I reach out to him, but he pulls away, though not unkindly. I have to wonder about what Lucas mentioned of eldrin marriages being loveless. This is not the reaction of a man who didn't love his wife.

His chest heaves as he drinks in the air. "You took me by surprise is all. And I miss my wife." He grasps my rejected hand and squeezes it briefly before turning to stare at the sky. Though it resembles a normal hand, I do feel the thick, sharp fingernails beneath.

The warmth from his skin is gone instantly. I ignore the choked way he speaks, not wanting to bring attention to it since I'd already distressed him with my illusion. "Will this do? Should I try something else?" I whisper to Lucas.

Bennett sends me a tight smile. "It will do quite well, granddaughter." He inhales and straightens his shoulders. He grasps my necklace, the one he sent Audhild to give me. His smile is genuine as he places it gently back against my collar. "We need to get to my refuge. Will you become your bird, Lucas, or will you go as is? Did anyone see you in your djinn form?"

Lucas winces. "Thoron saw me, and I'd rather not be airborne if something happens on the ground. However, wouldn't a djinn with two eldrin stand out?"

"Are you able to hold an illusion for an extended time?" my grandfather asks.

"I should be. I've recovered from Thoron's spells, and I feel stronger here than when we were on Tenebris." His voice is confident.

However, his admission that his illusions sap his strength

46

makes me reluctant to pressure him. "Are you sure? I don't want to overwhelm you."

A grin quirks one side of his mouth. "I'm supposed to be *your* Watcher, my lady. Not the other way around. And I will be quite fine with you beside me."

The band across my chest eases. "If you're sure?"

"I am." In an instant, he becomes taller, more imposing, as he takes on an eldrin shape. His hair lightens slightly to reflect the mahogany of Mother's tresses. His narrow eyes widen to show glittering green orbs. His pale skin darkens to a tanned guise.

Lucas must indeed be stronger since it's harder to recognize his real image below the illusion. I find the difference less appealing to gaze upon, though.

He winks at me.

I wrinkle my nose at him. "How long did you say it will take to get to your refuge?" I ask Grandfather.

"If we are not disturbed in our travel, it should take two days. Less if I could fly." His grin is full of teasing. "This way." He shifts his pack higher on his shoulders and set off at a quick pace away from the mountains and into the open meadows that stretch out as far as I can see.

It's apparent that he's recovered from being tired.

I follow behind him, Lucas at my side, a careful eye on our surroundings. A bird flutters out of a low branch as we pass by. I flinch and my heart jumps to my throat.

I groan at myself. *This is going to be a long couple of days.*

Grandfather's footsteps rustle in the still-damp grassy pasture beyond the stony edge of the mountain. "Stay alert! You never know who's lurking where."

6

Grassland turns to forest as we trek across Anavrin. We travel over a half day, skirting several small villages to avoid as many people as possible. So far, we'd attracted no attention that I could tell. I stop jerking at every noise or shadow and begin to relax at our current pace.

Relaxing, however, makes the questions in my mind spin one after another. When I finally can't hold them in, I turn to my grandfather. "How is it that the eldrin I'd met can suddenly appear? Arrin said it had to do with the necklaces they wear?"

We walk beneath a thick canopy of trees, the sunlight mottling the lush ground and highlighting the animal trail we follow.

"The ivory apatestone, or lightstone as some call it, moves the person to wherever they envision." Grandfather squints as he scans the area in front of him. "The stone uses the movement of light and space to shift the person from one place to another."

"With only a thought? What stops someone from going anywhere, then?" I consider my life on Tenebris. How easy it would've been to have left the wrecked carriage and travel someplace safe. And yet, that would mean Mrs. Calvin, the housekeeper, could've gotten me back as easily. The possibilities of something like that are staggering to think about.

"I'm told you must already have been somewhere first, or it won't work." His voice is matter-of-fact.

"You don't know, though?" Lucas asks. His stride is almost as strong as Bennett's and I fear I'm the weakest in our group.

Grandfather frowns, though there are no lines or wrinkles in his smooth illusion's face. "The stones were taken after my time in the Council and before the war. Hidden in one of the vaults which held relics and books retrieved from council hopefuls in their trials throughout eldrin history. Only the chief curators were allowed to handle them."

His attention wanders before coming back. "If I recall correctly, they were said to have originated before the One World split. It enabled our ancestors, who were more advanced than we are, the ability to travel across the wide expanse of that world. If you can imagine this kingdom and Tenebris and then add a dozen more kingdoms on top of that. Each kingdom is like a slice of a pie if each piece were a different flavor. Anavrin only hints at the fullness of the whole. It's incredible to consider."

I'm wide-eyed at the thought. "I can't imagine it. Stones that can move you across distances? I had thought many things fantastic, but I'm adding that to the top of my list of impossible things."

My grandfather glances over at me. "If Far Starl is any indication of the advanced abilities of other kingdoms, we are antiquated in our understanding. We're infinitely not as progressive as we'd thought." At Lucas's questioning glance, he explains his trip to the other kingdom where dragons were treated much like cattle.

"So, you see, there are many things even we don't understand. For generations, the eldrin kept a close watch on many of the Kinsman's holy items. But the secrecy they were shrouded in has lessened our knowledge. Without true understanding, we have no power. Not real power, anyway." Grandfather sits down on a log to rest. Leaning his pack against another tree, he takes the canteens out and hands us one to share.

"How many relics are there?" Lucas asks after a deep drink.

Grandfather's gaze is straightforward. "Thousands. And I'm unsure which ones Thoron managed to steal in his raids. Then there's the younger eldrin who raided the inner temples when they realized Elysium, or the sanctuary, was falling. It solidifies my choice to divert the dangerous objects to my mountain keep. I store many of the items there, which may be what has Audhild in such a fiery snit. We both hide objects we don't wish to fall into the wrong hands."

We finish resting and resume our trek. The rocky land is replaced by a meadow with forests edging it on two sides. Bees buzz from flower to flower and birds chitter, filling the air with tranquility I rarely experience. I walk for a while without speaking and ponder what my grandfather said. "If the eldrin have so many wondrous items, why do others live in such squalor? Why hoard everything?"

Bennett frowns. "I was taught from the time I could walk that the eldrin were the chosen race. I started questioning it after my trip to Far Starl. There, I saw how corrupt leadership ruins its citizens. Perverts their understanding. It affects the whole kingdom. I'm sure you saw Tenebris has its share of moral decay?"

Lucas responds first. "I found the cleric's notes about the

kingdom's decline. They noted that Tenebris itself, having rejected magic, warps or depletes anything magical that comes within its borders. I experienced it firsthand."

"How so?" Interest gleams from Grandfather's eyes.

"I got lost in my bird form for years after Cadence died, and I couldn't rescue Tambrynn from her servitude." Lucas's illusionary green eyes, so different from his narrow dark ones, glisten with unspent tears.

Grandfather leads us out of the canopy and across a wide, flower-filled pasture. The outline of a small village lies at the edge of our view. "What woke you up?"

In the distance, voices call out to one another. There's the sound of children playing and the rattling of wagons. I can't help the impulse to shrink back, hide. Then I remember I'm safe. Disguised. I roll my shoulders to ease the tension.

Lucas runs a hand through his hair. "Thoron. I sensed it. His presence. It was like a thousand knives stabbing against my insides. I woke up one day in my boy form and started to remember. But I have to wonder if Thoron hadn't returned when he did, would I have ever come out of it?"

I put my arm around his waist and squeeze him. I hadn't considered that or what he had gone through. It had been overwhelming to learn about magic and my father all in the same shock. I should've been more aware of Lucas's struggles.

Grandfather glances, considering. "I have to wonder at a possible connection. There must be a reason each kingdom seems to collapse in so many similar ways." He shifts his pack. "If we have a chance, we should research it at my keep."

The trees thin, and we step out into a bare grassland akin to the farmlands on Tenebris. The noises of the township we'd passed are replaced with the lowing calls and braying of animals. Sheep and goats roam freely, feeding on the abundant grass and flowers growing wild. One or two look up at us, but none spook or charge. I don't recall ever seeing such docile animals on Tenebris. Here I see no fences penning them in.

"How far do you think we'll get today?" I ask. The sun is high and the air has grown warm.

"We should reach Anatolia before we need to resupply." My grandfather wipes sweat from his brow with an old cloth he pulled from his pack.

We come to a modest bank along a small stream. I stand back, well away from the whispering water. Lucas remains with me while grandfather climbs down the incline to refill the canteens. He is watchful but confident as he steps into a curved nook along the shallow bank. Many streams we'd passed had run muddy from excess rain. Those sullied riverways didn't speak to me as much as this clearer one does. It burbles like the water around the froggen castle. I can't help the fear that twists my insides at the thought of the frog-king.

I take another step away from the brook. Lucas raises his eyebrows, but he says nothing.

"What is Anatolia like?" I say loud enough for Grandfather to hear me over the sound of the water.

He caps the last one and returns to where we stand. "Anatolia is the biggest city in the northern region next to the Sea of Marmara, and one we have to pass through due to the marshlands to the south. It's a large city, having expanded past its initial borders in the past couple of years. Ships from as far as the Northern Reaches come to the port to trade. I wouldn't consider it completely safe, but it's one you can get lost in easily. Which hopefully makes it safe enough for us to pass through undetected."

I jerk my head in his direction. "You doubt that we can make it?"

He attaches the pouches to the bag he'd removed from his back, the mantle still on his shoulders. "I worry if you're both strong enough to hold your illusions. I'm also wary after hearing about the mergirl and the rogue dragon. Even the eldrin stepping up attacks on the nomads is concerning. I'm unsure what it all means. I don't know what our next encounter may be and that makes me nervous."

I understand his hesitation. I try to reassure him in the only way I can. "I'm barely using any energy for my illusion." I peek questioningly at Lucas.

He waves away my concern. "No problems here. And if anything were to happen, I can always change and follow you two discreetly. I have had years of practice trailing a difficult young woman. I'll be able to hide in a crowd easily." The grin across his illusion's face is wide, encouraging.

I smirk at his cockiness. "I don't believe I am the only difficult one here."

Grandfather gives Lucas a serious look. "We must be vigilant. We can't have anyone trailing us to the keep. There's too much at risk. Imagine if Thoron or Siltworth got hold of one of the apatestones or if either had access to the maps and keys to the other kingdoms? They could learn any number of secrets the eldrin has kept since the One World split. It would be devastating."

———

Night creeps across the sky as we reach the outskirts of Anatolia. We're far enough north that we leave the lush fields for coarser grasses and rock-strewn roads. Horses with open carriages and carts clog our way as they hasten to and from the city. Here, there are no more trees, though I see evidence of old forests. Chopped-off trunks and long-dead limbs clutter each side of the wide, worn path.

Grandfather studies the area. "Every time I return there's more signs of destruction, more people than the time before."

Lucas walks to my right and Grandfather to my left. It's far more protection than I'm used to and I find it reassuring. "Is that a good thing?"

My grandfather grunts. "Not in my book. Too many people together mean trouble. Everybody vying for control, or what small control they can manage. Especially now since the eldrin have decided to take over the newer side of the city. Soon, there will be taxes and more laws passed until even breathing the wrong way will become illegal."

Tents dot an area to the left of the road. The makeshift community which includes several different kinds of people continues to a stream that forms Anatolia's border. Some of the canvas huts are similar to the one Grandfather uses. Some are larger, probably used for families, since children dart about, playing and squealing. I watch the young ones fondly, having had such a short childhood. I'd longed to play so carefreely after becoming indentured, but it wasn't to be. When I glance up, the same melancholy pinches Lucas's illusionary face. Some emotions are too hard to hide.

Grandfather clears his throat. "Try to look more nonchalant. Eldrin walk as if they don't have a care in the world. And they don't have a soft spot for children of other races."

I school my face. It's not hard after life as a servant. Old habits, it seems, come easy.

Nomad-looking travelers stare at us as we stride by. I remind myself once more that we're in disguise and squash my instincts to shrink back. I can't help, however, running a hand through my hair. *Not silver. Not silver.* I repeat the mantra in my head.

Lucas catches my fingers in his and tugs me gently. Without looking at him, I squeeze back.

Grandfather was right, there are an incredible amount of people in a small area. I'm unused to so many people, though there was quite a crowd at the Spaw Ball before we left Tenebris. "Do you think anyone here will be hexed by my father?" I whisper.

"It's harder to hex magical individuals, though I'm sure Thoron could put one on a nomad. Usually, they're thought to be less useful than animals due to their stubbornness and strength of will. Be on the watch, just in case. Let me know if you spot anything suspicious." Grandfather murmurs back.

A cluster of dark-haired individuals stops their boisterous conversation to glare at us. Others notice and more heads turn our way. My necklace warms against my chest. I gulp and steady my breathing.

Lucas subtly motions at the last group with his head. *"Djinn,"* he speaks into my mind. *"Troublemakers. Keep your wits about you, my lady."*

"How much farther?" My shoulders pinch tight together. I can't help it. I feel as if I'm back on the Pauper's Block with the house stewards or housekeepers and their piercing gazes.

"I'm hoping we can get across the old bridge and edge the western half of Anatolia without an incident. Once we make it to the newer part of town, we should be safe." Grandfather's body is tense as he scans the crowds. "I do have some tricks up my sleeve, but nothing I want to use to draw too much attention to us."

"How much danger are we walking into?" I scan the crowds but spot no third eyes, no hexes.

He lowers his head, but I catch his frown. "Eldrin aren't exactly welcome in most places anymore. Not since the Council broke apart, and each time I travel it gets worse. And with how they're reacting to us simply walking along? It doesn't bode well."

I glance behind us, pretending to adjust my hair, and see some of the crowd have lost interest in us while others still stand and stare. As calmly as I can manage, I face forward.

After having dealt with Nyle, I can understand why the eldrin would be unpopular. I'm having second thoughts about our disguises. I fist my hands against my sides. "If the Council is no more, why does Nyle go by the title Councilmaster?"

"He, along with his self-title, holds no merit. The only thing I can figure is that Nyle somehow got the Scepter of Fate and because of that power was able to gain some followers. He has committed worse crimes than he charges others with. That, if nothing else, nullifies any claim to a role in eldrin leadership." He speaks low enough for me to hear, but not enough to carry to those gathering along the path on both sides of us.

My fists buzz and my eyes are warming. I pray silently that my disguise holds. "What's happening?" I hurry to keep up with Grandfather, who is taking longer strides.

He sneaks a glimpse at a trio of large, muscled men. They're shaggy and a bit unkempt but imposing enough that I wouldn't want to cross them. He groans. "We need to keep moving. Hurry."

His chopped response raises my unease. I focus more of my energy on my illusion.

The rocky ground turns to smoother cobblestone the closer we get to the bridge. Barely wide enough to fit a large carriage, its massive wood pillars are a sturdy frame against a steady wash of water.

Upstream from the bridge, a mill's wheel splashes water. The wheel is covered halfway by the burgeoning, murky flow and lined by muddied banks. Thankfully, there's no babbling in the stream.

"Don't look back." Grandfather's words are clipped.

I can sense a crowd following us. There's a growing din, voices getting louder. Closer. Fire runs through my veins at the unspoken threat. I fear I'll lose control and burn down the whole tent village.

A man with broad shoulders pokes at a fire in a metal barrel lit beside the stone path ahead of us. There's only a wagon and a half's width left before we enter the shelter of the covered bridge that leads across the winding stream and into Anatolia.

The burly man steps into our path, a scowl on his face. "Who're you?" He wields a torch in one hand. He blocks our passage.

My hands prick with energy, and my gut churns with my anxiety. Boards on the bridge tremble in response. I can't lose control here. *Please, Kinsman, help me hold on!*

My grandfather straightens to his full height. It is more illusion than truth but imposing as I'm sure he meant it to be. Eye to eye their gazes meet and hold. Though Bennett is smaller in bulk, his hostile expression is intimidating.

The other man flexes his arms and pushes me aside to get closer to Grandfather.

I lose my balance. I grab his wrist holding the torch, and his arm lights up with blue fire.

Burn them. Burn them all! shrieks the voice inside my head.

I cringe against the man's high-pitch scream and look on in horror as flames race across his shirt.

7

The man's torso is engulfed. Smoke and the stench of burning flesh sear my nose. Like a spark on kerosene, the fire spreads. He drops to the ground, shrieking. Several others slap at him to put the flames out.

What have I done? I shift uneasily on my feet, unsure of what to do. Instinct tells me to change. Fly away.

Lucas's firm hand on my arm grounds me. His gaze lets me know he understands my turmoil. He eases me to his other side, away from the more vocal in the crowd. Several throw curses around, their arms flung with the same anger. And though most of the throng quietly watch with a strange interest, I'm well aware of how easily this can explode into full-on violence.

A second burly man, his face red and angry, shoves past several people to get to us. A nomad-looking woman douses the first man with sudsy water from a bucket. At last, the fire is gone. The man lies on the ground, whimpering and panting. His clothes are mottled with scorch marks and red, angry burns mar his tanned skin.

The second man turns to face us. "Eldrin scum. Always causing trouble everywhere you go. We don't want your kind here." He punches the air with a calloused finger on a hand already missing the middle digit. He has scars on his face and arms, and he walks as though he's lame.

Bennett stands calmly, staring him down. I don't know how he maintains his composure after these events. "Has Anatolia sunk to hiring wounded treller watchlords? What's next? Nomad magic wielders?"

The man narrows his eyes. His skin is dark and deeply bronzed from the sun. "I am lord to any peccant conjurers who try to cross our side of the Marmara. And whichever of you who did this will be held accountable." Veins on his tense neck bulge and throb. His aura darkens with his violent intent.

Bennett reaches out with his forefinger, and with a blindingly quick movement taps the man's forehead. He barely grazes the other man's skull, but the man's eyes roll and he slips to the ground in a pile of muscle. Gasps and shouts of rage ring out.

My fists ache with the power I hold back. *"Burn them all down."* I stifle the voice by taking a deep breath and focusing on my illusion. My eyes heat and I pray silently they are not glowing.

With careful steps, my grandfather walks toward the most incensed part of the crowd—the burly men. "Would another treller like to test my conjuring skills?" Red-faced with chests cocked out, hostility hovers around them like a shield. Grandfather faces off with them. Furious silence answers him. He then turns to scan the rest of the alarmed crowd. "No? Anyone else? What about my fellow magic brethren, the djinn? Are you not scum conjurers as well? Or have you become entwined in the affairs of the forest dwellers now?" He waits a few moments, his hands clasped in front of him at ease. "Then my companions and I will be moving along, *unimpeded*."

He waves his arm in front of him, his fingers held in a strange crossed position. He whispers garbled consonants. Wind gusts in answer to his beckoning, battering those blocking the front of the bridge. It's disconcerting to watch, though it's not against me.

More shrieks of alarm break out, but the crowd is quick to move aside. Their steady gazes declare their loathing. The hair against my neck lifts in response to the flow of my ability around my body. *Please hold, please hold,* I plea.

There's only room for us to move in a single line past the angry mob. Spit from their enraged shouts flies, but doesn't hit me in the face. I can't see it, but I can sense the protective bubble around me. It lessens some of my anxiety.

I don't hold onto my grandfather or Lucas, though I want to. I know it would be a sign of weakness. And that's not something an eldrin would show. I make each step purposeful, my chin held up, mirroring when I left the Broodmoor estate. I encompass a nonchalance I don't feel.

Inside I'm shaking, wanting to collapse.

When I step up on the wooden planks of the bridge and past the crowd, Lucas moves to my side. He matches my stride. He, too, walks confidently, though I can read concern and fear across our bond. Our footsteps clunk as we trek across.

There are lanterns hung by large, square metal nails from the lattice-patterned framework beneath the roof. White paint is peeling and stained in several areas, belying the age of the structure. The flame light flickers, throwing moving shadows all around us. I squash the sensation of being swallowed alive and continue to follow my grandfather.

Though we are the only ones walking into Anatolia, many

travel in groups leaving the city. Luckily, they are unaware of what had just happened and we are ignored as we cross.

Halfway across the bridge, Lucas rolls his neck. "My skin is prickling. We're being watched."

"I believe it. No one has ever stopped me before. I have to wonder if this has something to do with an eldrin faction taking over the newer part of Anatolia or if there are other issues I don't know," Bennett says over his shoulder. We finally reach the edge of the bridge and wait for a carriage to enter before moving forward.

I let out a groan of relief once we leave the bridge and Bennett leads us to the side of the road into a grove of fruit trees. Blossoms sweetly perfume the air.

My hands are shaking when Lucas grabs them. "You did a fine job, my lady."

I sway to the side and catch myself before I topple over. "I set a man on fire." My nose tingles with the need to cry. I scratch it and blink. "I could've killed him." My throat closes painfully and I lose the ability to speak.

Bennett scoffs and sets his pack down on the ground to stretch his back. "Trellers are brawlers. And drunkards. He'd be taken to the work fields if you were a true eldrin, which is a fate worse than what he received."

Though he makes light of it, guilt nags me that my fire is so unpredictable that it makes this trip more dangerous than it was to begin with. "How much farther do we have to go to get out of here?" My voice clogs and I clear my throat.

Grandfather places a hand on mine. His gaze examines the merchants with their canvas and wooden stalls. One or two people cross the bridge from the direction we'd come from, their eyes searching. He guides us farther back into the small orchard, carrying the pack beside him. "We get out of here by keeping our wits. We'll have to be careful not to be followed.

And we certainly don't want anyone else touching you accidentally."

His words are harsh, yet spoken with understanding. I shake my hands out, willing the power within me to recede. It doesn't, though. It still buzzes heartily inside me.

Lucas scratches his head. "I can change my appearance. Surely Tambrynn can, too. Are you able to change with your rutch? Maybe look like a djinn? They aren't normally accosted because of the fear of retaliation."

"I've never tried another form. However, now that we're on this side I wonder if we shouldn't stay eldrin. Surely with them in charge here, we'll be safer. Let me try to alter my appearance, though." He shifts the mantle, his back to the crowds.

We're hidden among the shadowed cover of the trees. Though it's now evening, the festive lights along the streets are bright enough to see inside the shade of the limbs. Lucas nudges me in the arm to turn and we all have our backs to the market.

I close my eyes and concentrate. Instead of brown hair, I envision blonde locks and light blue eyes much like Amira, the eldrin who stole Colly. Deep breath in and out and then I open my eyes.

Lucas smiles down at me. He is different as well, with darker blonde hair and sparkling light-blue eyes. His clothes have switched to a deep blue. I glance down and sigh when I realize my clothes weren't altered.

"I'll never get the hang of this." I run a hand across my green sleeve.

"Nonsense. You're doing extraordinarily well considering you've had no formal training." Grandfather blinks as if waking. He is an older version of Nyle the Councilmaster. "Did it work?" he asks.

I nod while Lucas says, "yes."

He grabs the pack and it disappears into his illusion as he settles it on his back. "Let's move."

As one, we leave the cover of the trees trying not to look suspicious. Spices, flowers, and the smoky scent of cooking meats flavor the night air. My stomach growls, something I can't disguise. My cheeks heat.

A stout-looking nomad woman stands on a crate dangling a sparkling necklace lined with red gems yelling, "a pretty for the pretties, best deal around." A nomad man with her, the first I'd seen without a brushy beard, sits inside their canvas shop with an instrument against his eye as he peers at other rough-cut stones.

Though there's nowhere to truly hide, we try our best to blend into the passing crowds while avoiding the more aggressive hawkers—one gets close enough that his garlic and onion-soaked breath washes across my face. I gag and step away.

Bennett grabs the flowered blue shawl in his hands and tosses two coins at the grinning merchant. In a swift motion, he swings it over my head, tying two ends about my chest. I'm startled, but grab hold of the soft fabric. Thankfully, it doesn't smell like its seller.

Grandfather urges me with his arm, directing me away. "Come along."

The main buildings are wooden and red brick with bright signs. They're mainly shut down for the day's trade except for a few pubs. Light from their windows creates yellow haloes on the smooth, gray cobblestone streets. Raucous voices spill out like water gushing from a leak. Bennett steers us down a row of businesses and away from the livelier section of the town.

We are not alone traveling in this quieter direction, but Lucas's hold on my arm relaxes as we continue. More tents pop up when we leave the closed buildings behind. Women here wear head coverings much like the one Bennett placed on me. The tents are scattered, without order. There are several laundry lines with clothes hanging from end to end. Bennett leads us through the makeshift village using the least obstructed paths.

We're at the edge of the tent village beyond the shelters when my necklace warms once more, warning me of danger. Blue energy lights up my hands. I clutch the shawl tighter.

"We may need to scout, my boy." Grandfather's calm voice belies his tense jaw.

Lucas drops behind me, stepping around the side of the next tarp, and is gone from sight.

A shriek pierces the air.

I know that call. It's the black dragon.

8

My heartbeat thunders in my chest. *"Lucas?"*

"I'm here, my lady," he replies. It's too dark to see him.

Grandfather takes my arm, leading me out of the tents and into a bare area. The ground is trampled down to mostly bald spots and grass struggles to survive along the edges. More tree trunks dot the area. Without the lights from the buildings, we'll be stumbling around. "Was that a dragon I heard?" he asks.

"Yes. Should I do something?" My words are shaky, unsure. I don't want to confront the beast. Audhild had insinuated I shouldn't try to fight it. "What if it attacks?" The thought of going up against the creature pokes needles of fear across my body.

"We must trust Audhild." Grandfather's words are filled with conviction. "If it were a true danger, she would've killed it."

Lucas lands beside me. "It's the black dragon. I can hear it, though I can't see it this time. Its scream was coming from the direction of the docks."

"Good, that's away from our path. But be watchful." Grandfather rubs his chin. "If it starts to attack, don't panic. We *need* to stay together. If we end up parted, head northeast toward the mountains." He points ahead and to our right. "We'll regroup there. Now, come, this way."

We skirt around the outside edge of the newer-built side of Anatolia. It's cleaner, the roads straighter, and the buildings different in construction. Massive metal and stone structures multiple stories high spill light onto the paved streets below them. It's almost as if the city is more alive at night than it is during the daytime.

"Do they not sleep?" I ask.

Grandfather's steps have slowed, the first indication he might be tiring. "The last time I went through, they were building a gambling den along the riverbank. I was told it would run during the evening as well as the day. I'm sure the sailors docked for a night or two are glad for the diversion."

"Happy enough to lose their wages before their ship sets sail again?" Lucas chuckles. "What of the eldrin? Don't they normally put a stop to such nefarious activities?"

"Normally, yes. But, the newly elected Council has sent one of their own, a Domicus, to rule over Anatolia and keep order." Bennett spits the words out. "If what I recall of him is true, I'm sure he's keeping part of the profits."

We wait while a small two-seat buggy driven by a single horse rumbles past before crossing a newly built street. It's smooth and seamless, made with pebbles instead of large stones. The difference between this side and the other side of Anatolia is obvious. There's no mud caking the roads, or stones sticking out of place. Walkways resembling cut marble line the streets where people stroll casually as if it were the middle of a grand spring day. I do glimpse men and women idling around. They resemble eldrin—tall and lithe with smooth complexions. They all wear similar dark blue outfits, like a uniform.

I adjust my long hair across my sweating nape and look away from anyone when they glance our way. I wish I'd been able to change my clothes to blue to fit in.

Lucas bumps into me gently. "Don't act guilty or they'll think something is wrong."

"It's a hard habit to break." My nerves are snapping again. It reminds me too much of the high-ranking villages where the hawkers would lead us all in a line, our hands bound by ropes, to be sold to the highest bidders. If rejected there, we'd be shackled to the poles in the market squares. I fight off the deep-set terror that wants to climb up my chest.

"A few more blocks and then we'll arrive at the road we need to take." Grandfather's words are spoken lightly. He pats my hand that's clutching his arm.

"Hey, you there." One of the uniform-wearing eldrin stops us.

"Yes, how can we help you?" Grandfather grins at the man and his female companion.

"You look familiar. Do I know you?" The man holds out his hand.

Oh no! Does he know Nyle? This could be a disaster.

Grandfather doesn't show any sign of distress, though. "I'm Bernard. We live in Elysium. My daughter Anelle, son Jardon, and I are passing through on our travels. We'd heard about the grand expansion happening and were curious. Much better than the ruins, I have to say." Grandfather drops my hand and grasps the other man's arm in some sort of strange greeting.

The man puts his hand out to Lucas, who repeats

Grandfather's embrace. The woman searches my face as if seeing past my disguise. The shawl Grandfather forced on me slips to my shoulders. My hands grow twitchy, so I interlock them in front of me, hoping for a casual pose. I force myself not to jerk the shawl back over my head.

"Your daughter, eh?" The man smiles a bit too friendly at me. "Doesn't look anything like you."

Bennett laughs. "She takes after her mother, Alivia. Kinsman rest her soul. We lost her in the first battle. Sorry, but Anelle hasn't been the same since. Doesn't like to touch anyone. Doesn't talk."

His last words are a warning. He needn't worry. I'm too unnerved to speak intelligently at the moment.

My eyes are too warm. I glance down and away from both of their inquisitive stares. I keep my hands fisted tight to my stomach and take deep, measured breaths to ease the buzzing in my gut.

"Yes, we lost a great many to the upheaval. Where are you traveling?" The man's friendliness is edged with suspicion.

"We were hoping to see the Olivine Falls. It's where her mother and I met while I was on campaign with the Council Corps. It's been a dream of ours since we lost Alivia to go and see them and maybe set up a new home in the Gray Mountains." His smile is wide and congenial, though I can tell there's a double meaning to his words.

"Gray Mountains, eh? We wish you well on your way, then." The man steps back, allowing us room to pass by him.

The woman's gaze never leaves me.

Lucas takes my elbow gently. I keep my head low, playing timid the best I know how. The lights shining down from the giant stone buildings illuminate me like a beacon. Sweat dribbles across my collar, making a path down my spine. I don't look up until we're at the end of the walkway.

"Do you think they believed you?" I whisper.

"They aren't following us. I wasn't stopped before so maybe this is a new eldrin recruitment tactic. He wasn't as interested once I mentioned the Gray Mountains." We cross the road to another road where a small open buggy passes by.

I'm awed by the texture and evenness of the village paths. It must be some new method of fashioning stones, or is it sand?—into a flat surface. Like the metal and stone buildings, it sets Anatolia apart from the rest of the countryside, but it exudes a sterileness with which I'm unaccustomed. I wouldn't care to live here, nice as it seems.

I suppress the need to rush away, forcing my feet to take measured steps. "What's wrong with the Gray Mountains?" Anything would be a welcomed change from the refined unnaturalness of Anatolia. It's stifling. I move over to allow a bit more space between the three of us so I can breathe easier.

"It's where the misfits, or those who are dying, go to spend their last days. Many djinn go there before madness takes them. They must've assumed you were dying." Lucas helps me over the edge of the walkway. The buildings aren't as tall or crowded here.

"I'm hoping he took the hint about Anelle. Good acting, by the way, Tambrynn. You were shy enough to pull off being traumatized. It happened to many eldrin after the battles. The Council, though they rule, aren't used to war, nor are we trained in fighting. After seeing Thoron change some of their kin to his monsters, a few snapped. They became lame in the head. Their families journeyed to the Gray Mountains to hospitalize them there."

A far-off look crosses grandfather's face and he puffs out a breath. "I considered it once, after Thoron—" his voice dies down, his meaning clear. "I figured they wouldn't question it and they didn't. Besides, I didn't want them to know our true destination."

———

The noise and the glow of lights surrounding Anatolia are far behind us when Bennett deems it safe enough to set up camp. The night air is crisp and clean and the terrain has turned rockier as we make our way closer to the Meridian Peaks.

I can see the dark outline of the peaks against the twilight blue sky. There are boulders scattered among the trees. The grasses have curved, shaper blades and grow in bigger tufts as if they're villages of greenery unto themselves. Flowers grow sporadically as well, their heads brown and dying. It reminds me of Tenebris. Had the rain missed this mountainous area?

"Is it my imagination or are the trees taller here?" I ask as Grandfather lowers his backpack with an 'oof.'

"It's not your imagination. The Bloodthorn Forests are not far from here. The trees there are giant, brushing the clouds with their height. Their sap is blood red and useful for many ailments."

He takes the rolled canvas and some flexible poles and, with Lucas's help, begins to put up their tent.

This whole kingdom baffles me, and I fight the revulsion at the thought of bleeding sap—especially after seeing the forest that had been cut down around Anatolia. Had it been those trees, it would've looked like a slaughterhouse. I glance around, curious where I will sleep for the evening. There's no cleft or shelf to lay under, though the ground is harder and less prone to catch fire in my sleep. The spots of foliage are too spaced apart for any real damage.

"Should I turn to a bird and nest up in a tree?" I turn a full circle and come to a stop.

My grandfather grunts. "Do you wish to burn it down?"

"Of course not." I let my illusion go, glad to be rid of it, though it used little of my ability. The effort of holding it had become wearing, like trying to remember not to bump a cut finger. I find a smooth spot and sit on the ground.

"There's a dug-out boulder I use as a marker nearby that should work for a nesting place, Tambrynn," Grandfather says as he prepares the area for our campsite.

They pull the last rod taut and tap it into the ground. It's hard work, and more rock than dirt, but they finally get the job done.

Lucas hugs me. His essence of meadow grass sweeps over me, easing my discomfort. He has also removed his disguise, and I am grateful to see his true, handsome face. "You seem to be wound pretty tight tonight."

"I can't help it. Anatolia reminds me of the Pauper's Squares." *And the shackles and the beatings.*

"I'll help make you as comfortable as I can. I promise." Lucas kisses my brow.

Grandfather clears his throat. "Who wants to search for firewood and stones?" He removes a basket he uses to stow the remains of his food supplies.

"I will." Lucas gives my arm one last squeeze before he heads away toward trees with broken limbs piled around their base. The moon is bright in the sky. It's much clearer in the open expanse than inside Anatolia.

"I'm sorry that was so hard for you, Tambrynn." Grandfather removes his pan and the last pouch of water. He cleans the inside of the metal that's dusty from our travels. "We have one more day of travel and we'll be safe inside my mountain keep."

I help him sort out his supplies and food items. "I'm sorry to be so dour. This kingdom is so different than Tenebris. I knew what to expect there. Here?" I shrug. "Every minute seems to uncover another strange creature or odd custom."

He removes the rutch from his shoulders and his stretched face is once more revealed. It doesn't bother me any longer. It's more familiar than the illusion's perfectly smooth one, even if I've only known him a short time.

He folds the worn skin and places it carefully inside his bag. "I can imagine what it seems like to an outsider. This kingdom is changing fast. If you would have asked me when I was a child if I could imagine a mage changing me into a half-monster or if the eldrin would war against themselves, I would've called you crazy."

He dumps the dirty water, adds the last of the clean water to the pan, and sets it aside.

Lucas returns with an armful of sticks and larger branches which he sets in a neat pile. "I found a nest with some eggs. I took three of the ten." He gives them to Grandfather, who shakes them before setting them in the water. White and oval, they resemble chicken eggs from Tenebris, only a bit larger. They all sink on their sides to the bottom.

"Good and fresh. That'll be a nice treat, my boy. Well done."

While Lucas searches for stones to place in a circle for the fire, Grandfather takes me to a large, triangular boulder that leans crookedly into the ground. Beneath it are several chunks of rubble and when I look closer, I notice mushrooms that glow a brownish color.

"Try to pick a rock up," he tells me.

They don't look that big and so I'm confused by his request. I try, however. Though I can get my fingers around the stone, I am unable to move it. I dig around it, but it makes no difference. "I can't."

He plucks the mushrooms from the ground. They cease

glowing, looking quite like typical fungi, and the earth opens to reveal several items wrapped in cloth.

"These are spelled to make the rocks impossible to pick up. I keep some important items hidden here." He gestures to the stone I had tried to move.

It's easily removed now. I chuckle. "Handy, to be sure."

"Yes, well. I can't take everything with me, nor would I want to in case I'm stopped or robbed. This way I can keep certain items safe for long periods." He shakes the mushrooms at me. "I'll teach you this and many other things."

"This is my stash." He unwraps the articles. Inside is a jade-bladed dagger, a carved, wooden star, a small jar with dark liquid, a scroll, and several jewels. He reaches once more and produces a dirt-crusted metal staff which he brushes off. The metal is several rods braided into an intricate pattern. When it is free of most of the debris, he places the different-sized, peach-hued gems into matching holes in the staff.

He holds the last one up. "Sunstones. Very rare. They need little sunlight to charge and they stay bright for long periods." When the stone is in place, a metallic scratching noise is followed by a white-hot light. I close my eyes against the radiance, but it dies down almost as quickly as it flared. "Sacratus, my scepter. It is a light in the darkest of places."

He lifts the jar with liquid. "This is a netherlight. Shake it and it stays lit for hours." He slips the tiny bottle into his pants pocket. He hands me the blade. "The Mortifer Blade. Keep it with you at all times. It's sharp enough to split air if your intentions are clear."

I'm about to ask him what splitting air does when he bends over, grunting loudly. His face reddens and he starts panting, pain pinching his face.

I reach out to him. "Grandfather? What's wrong?" My

necklace heats against my chest. I jerk my head around but see nothing.

Grandfather moans, his arms crossed over his stomach, a grimace on his face. "We need to—"

A howl pierces the air. It's far away and barely audible, but birds break out into the sky in a mad dash and there's rustling in all directions as critters scurry away from danger.

My aching shoulders droop at the sound. Fear and anger clash inside my mind. I glance at Grandfather to see what we should do.

His eyes are open wide, true terror shining from the dark depths. "It's the ... sluaghs. Get ... my ... sh—shifting ... stones."

9

I snatch his backpack and return. He digs in a pocket. His hands are so clumsy, he drops a few of the rocks. They're the rune stones he'd gathered from our last campsite.

"Put them ... in a circle." He puffs.

"Can I help?" Lucas rushes to our sides.

Grandfather jerks his head 'no.' He doubles over again, growling and shaking his head. His snout lengthens and he snorts.

Is he changing?

Lucas stands behind me, watchful. I move to the boulder and take two steps beyond it. My hands shake, even with Lucas's warm hand on my back to reassure me.

"Ebargofiant!" he shouts, his eyes scrunched, his body bent over. A breath and then he growls, "repeat it." Another breath. "Nineno arodente, ebargofiant." His words are uttered through his bared teeth.

I recite them a couple of times. My arms tingle when I get the words correct. I rush a few paces until Grandfather snarls at me to stop. I do, placing the stone and repeating his words. My necklace hums on my chest.

"Lucas. Water." Grandfather points. "Stream," his words are pushed through gritted, beastly teeth.

More howls echo across the rock-strewn valley.

Lucas rushes to grab the pouches and dunks the first one in the stream.

My hands shake so badly that I drop several stones and waste time bending over to pick them up. The seconds seem like an eternity as I circle an area large enough for all of us. My heart pounds out of my chest. I run to the next spot, trying to make sure there's enough room for us to make camp though I'm hurrying. "Lucas, come on!" I yell at him. He's beyond Grandfather's stones and too far away from my safe boundary.

Lucas dunks the last pouch and runs back past me, water dripping from his arms.

"Ebargofiant," I spit out, nervousness making me jittery. "Nineno arodente, ebargofiant." I don't even know for sure if I'm saying it correctly now, but when I place the last stone not far from where I started, all noise muffles. I glance around, my chest heaving. "Is it safe?"

The area isn't large, only about the span of a small barn, but it's plenty of room for all of us to move around comfortably.

Grandfather straightens up, his features smoothing out. "It's sealed, thankfully. Not as wide as I'd like, but you did well, Granddaughter," he replies breathlessly. His shoulders are still hunched and his face has a gray pallor. As if some of his life had been drained from him.

Moments later, dark shapes crawl out of the trees close to our camp. My father's undead beasts. They wander around, hunched and sniffing. I collapse next to the water canisters and where Lucas piled sticks and wood.

"That was close." I wipe my jittery, chilled hands across my heated face.

Grandfather topples to the ground across from us with a loud, wheezing groan. "Far too close." He slumps over, panting. "For clarification," he wheezes, "the chant means 'here but," he takes a deeper breath, "separate, apart, untouchable.'"

"Good to know." I watch him. His face is stretched more than ever, eyes sunken and dark-ringed.

Lucas eyes Grandfather, handing him a pouch. "Are you all right?"

"Thank you. Yes, I'll be fine. I'm not as young as I used to be." He drinks, but doesn't meet our eyes.

"What's going on?" I glare, willing him to tell me the truth this time.

He watches the wolf-like creatures circle, on the hunt. They knock branches down, scratch up spots of grass, and damage all they cross.

"I haven't been wholly truthful." He closes his eyes and cranes his neck back and forth. When he opens his eyes again, sadness and regret shine along with some unshed tears. The warmth, however, is back. "I've managed to avoid your father's beasts for years, but they still affect me."

"The beasts?" Lucas hands me some dried meat.

Grandfather drops his head. "Yes. Thoron as well, though I've only been near him once or twice since—" He is silent for several moments before he takes a deep breath and peers back up at us. "Since he tried to change me. But you don't have to be afraid."

"What is it you're not telling us?" I place my hand on his arm, but he jerks away.

"I'm sorry. It's—" He struggles. "This hasn't happened for such a long time. I almost thought I was beyond it." He exhales deeply. "I didn't fully change, but I'm not fully myself, either. Thoron's spell still affects me. Whenever his undead creatures get near I can feel the remnants of the spell, like a dying ember burning my bones. It rips at my soul." His fist is tight against his chest.

I slip my arm around his shoulders and share a worried glance with Lucas. "I'm so sorry. Is there something we can do to help?"

"Thank you, Granddaughter. You did it. You put the shield up, protecting me from them and myself." His voice cracks. "We're safe as long as I stay in the shelter of the runes spell."

"It's growing cold. Let me get a fire going." Lucas takes the sticks and some stones and begins to build a fire.

Grandfather pats my hand. "It's okay now. I'm okay."

The breath in my chest hitches and I decide to change the subject. "Tell me about the stones. How do they work."

"It's an obfuscation spell. Like I said, here, separate, apart, untouchable. We are here but not here. If you were to step outside of the boundary of the stones I placed, they'd be able to see you. Inside, they don't see us, hear us, or smell us. It's as if we exist outside of their reality."

Lucas hands him some dried meat. "Here, this might help settle your nerves."

Grandfather takes it and chews thoughtfully. "What they're doing now is sniffing where we were, not where we are. I found out about them on Far Starl. A crippled dragon rider showed me how to make and use them. He'd hidden from others who would have him killed for his disability. He and a few other outcasts. I've used them for years to remain undetected, safe."

"So, you put them around the area you want to be in? How long does it last?" I frown at the dangerous half-animals roaming outside of our sphere of protection. It's unnerving how accurate the sluaghs are. But, since our trail leads to where they cannot sense, they meander around, confused.

Grandfather rubs his ear thoughtfully. "The dragon rider had been using the same ones for over seventeen years. So, indefinitely as far as I know."

I take a stick and toss it into the flames. One of the creatures comes closer, standing almost on top of one of the stones I placed. It—he—looks familiar. Garrett. His dark eyes stare in our direction as if he catches a glimpse of us. Can he smell the smoke from the fire? He moves on, completing a half circle around our perimeter before snorting loudly and stomping off.

His behavior has me curious. "Notice that one. Could it be his soul is still within the beast and not gone completely?"

Grandfather studies me for a long moment. "If you're asking could they be redeemed or returned to their original form? I was an exception as I told you. Without some magical protections such as your mother or charms like I had to ward off the evil, I'm not sure. Why do you ask?"

"When Thoron and those beasts chased us to the nomad's mountain, they changed back to look like real people when they crossed over the kinstone's border. I've seen some hesitate to do Thoron's bidding. Even more of them have cringed at him. And now Garrett acts as if he's thinking, not blindly following an order. If they are mindless creatures, only doing his will, would they show emotions?"

My grandfather rubs his cheek, now rough from a day's growth of beard. The scritch-scratch of his hands against the stubble is the only sound except for the snuffling of the beasts. "It's a fair question. As you know, I didn't fully turn. And as you witnessed moments ago, I still suffer from the effects. But I recall the malevolence that tried to take hold of me. It's a strong urge, a voice really, that takes over your mind until you can't help but give in to it. It changes your will to something else entirely."

My heart squeezes painfully. Could that be what the voice urging me to burn everything is? Am I turning into my father? It's too horrifying to believe.

One of the beasts lets out a piercing howl, and as one, they all turn and head in a different direction. Last, however, is Garrett. He glances back our way before grunting and swatting the air. He shakes his head and then skulks off behind his companions.

"They're quite organized." Lucas pokes at the fire with a limb. "Almost as if they have one mind."

"Yes. They're linked through Thoron's dark magic. So, it's similar to your and Tambrynn's ability to communicate, but it's one-sided only. Thoron can speak to them, manipulate them."

I wrap my arms around myself. "Did he speak to you?"

He stills, his head lowered. "Maybe? I don't remember much about the time shortly after he cursed me. The first thing I fully remember is waking up in a field. I couldn't remember getting there. At first, I didn't recall what happened to me. I slowly pieced things back in place, but months passed before it all came back to me. By that time, I realized what I looked like and how others reacted to me. I never knew how vain I was until I became what I'd despised before. It was eye-opening."

My heart aches for him. I'd been judged by my appearance my whole life, and so had grown used to it. It had to have been distressing to suddenly have it thrust on you. "I'm sure it was. Did you ever go back to Madrigal and explain what happened?"

His smile is sad. "I tried once and was turned away by the Elysium guard. Quite brutally, actually." He rubs his head absently, his eyes glazed, remembering. "So, I used my knowledge of the Sanctuary and took the back way into the city. There are hidden doors in and out of the mountain. Not easy to get through. But if you know what you're doing, it isn't impossible."

"I managed to gather many items from the eldrin by using those entrances, including my mantle that had been hidden in my residence. After retrieving it, I was able to come and go freely. Nobody suspected a thing." He digs into his bag and removes a rolled cloth. Inside are three brown eggs. "I've been saving these," he says as he cracks the eggs into the hot pan and then adding Lucas's white eggs.

He continues. "I couldn't take things out Elysium's front door, that would be too suspicious. So, I would stack the relics and books and come for them through the back entrance. It took years to gather what I did. And I wasn't able to find Madrigal before Thoron attacked. She stayed in the villages helping the outcasts after I supposedly died in Thoron's attack. They were always moving, trying to find the banished, saving anyone in need, and growing the villages. It's a tragedy they were all destroyed, the people she tried to save, scattered to the wind."

After a moment of silence, he carries on, "I was so focused on stocking away the most important items from the increasingly destabilized Council, I never managed to find her." He shakes his head. "I will regret not trying harder, being so focused on items and not her for the rest of my life."

The remorse in his voice brings tears to my eyes. "That's so sad."

He shrugs one bent shoulder. "It was my fault for thinking I was strong enough to face off with a dark mage. I was too cocky, believing myself indestructible." He leans forward again, tears in his eyes reflecting the flames. "And the worst part is that I took Cadence with me. She could've died. *You* could've died." He sniffs. "It was a huge time of reckoning for me. I realized the way I and we, the eldrin, viewed ourselves and others was wrong. I began to see the folly in our ways and saw how they would lead to our destruction."

He flings one arm out, his hand raised to the sky. "You see it in the younger eldrin's arrogance. They set themselves on false thrones and believe themselves immune to their own laws. We've fallen so far from what the Kinsman had intended. Being educated from birth doesn't make us chosen, or better than anyone else. We are not gods."

I shrink back from his impassioned words and the fists he's formed in his anger.

Seeing my distress, he relaxes and gently pats my knee. "Forgive me. I've learned some hard lessons. When I look back, I was as awful and self-centered as the others are now. All I can do is hope to make a difference going forward. And that starts with helping you, Tambrynn."

———

The next morning, I wake beneath the boulder my grandfather and I dug out the last eve. I open one eye, not wishing to rise from my warm shelter. I see flames and I squawk, darting out of the indentation, my heart racing in my chest.

"What's wrong?" Lucas rushes over to me from the firepit. He stops several paces away, staring. Humor spreads across his face, crinkling his eyes.

Grandfather walks up from behind him. "Ah, good morning, Tambrynn. Did you sleep well?" He puts his hand on Lucas's shoulder and grips it tightly.

I try to speak again, but it all comes out in bird gibberish, and not at all like the melodious sound I had before I became a firebird. I stop fretting and settle down. With a thought, I'm back in my girl form.

"Good grief! I thought I was on fire." I rub a hand over my face. I'd been so tired the night before that it had taken no time for me to fall asleep after we'd bade each other good night. And I had no nightmares, which was a change from usual.

Grandfather laughs. "You were. You *are* a firebird, granddaughter. Though I have to say, your flames were brighter than before."

Lucas's lips tremble, but he manages not to laugh.

I frown at their amusement. "Am I always going to wake up this way from now on?" Panic spreads like icy water from my head to my toes, chilling me. "Is it going to get worse and worse?"

Grandfather squeezes my shoulder. "It will remain until we find out how to control it. It's not like the djinn who choose when to change. We'll ask Audhild when we see her again, and I'll check the records in my keep's library. There must be some account of firebirds from one of the kingdoms somewhere. I'm confident we'll find some answers and solutions there." Grandfather leaves us and heads back toward the fire where he is cooking something.

Lucas beckons me over to sit with him. "I went scouting this morning before you woke and captured two rabbits to eat." He points to the pan. Flakes of green and browned spices fleck the sizzling food. The delicious scent of a meal wafts around us, though I know something had to die to provide it.

I hold back a wave of revulsion, though my stomach grumbles. "Ever since I've become a bird, eating meat isn't quite as satisfying as it once was."

Grandfather grunts. "Maybe not, but you need the protein to keep up your strength. We have a long way to go today to reach the keep by nightfall."

The sun is already well on the rise, casting the area in a golden light. "I feel like a lollabout. I don't normally sleep so late." I yawn and take the canister of water Lucas offers me.

"It's not unusual for those with abilities to become tired when they mature. I'm surprised you're both as active as you are considering how far you've come in such a short time." Grandfather divides the meat and some sauteed mushrooms equally on three plates.

My stomach gurgles. I take my portion. "These aren't the mushrooms from last eve?" I poke at one with a stick.

He chuckles. "No, no. I found them by the stream."

Everything's seasoned perfectly. There's a touch of salt and whatever the other herbs are. Though the thought of eating meat isn't wholly appealing, the image of the nomads starving because none of them can cook pops into my mind. I hungrily finish before the men do.

"Time to clean up before we pack and leave. It'll be a long day." Grandfather holds out the jade dagger, packed in a leather pouch and sewn with a long string. "I don't sense anything dangerous, but take this to be safe."

I accept the weapon and tie it about my waist. Lucas banks the fire and Grandfather heads to the tent. I grab the canteens and make for the stream.

A shadow passes over me and I freeze. I've gone beyond the stone's protection. However, my hands aren't blue. My necklace remains cool at my collar. I glance up and around but see nothing. There aren't even any trees nearby that would cast any kind of shade.

"*Audhild?*" I ask in my mind.

Silence.

"*Other dragon?*" It's ridiculous, I know. But I have no name. No way of identifying it.

More silence.

Maybe I am mistaken and only think I saw something. I continue my tasks.

After taking care of my morning needs and filling the containers, I rejoin the men and distribute the canteens. Grandfather removes the carved stones and puts them in the backpack, then hands me the staff.

My arm drops with the weight.

He depresses a couple of the stones. Magic vibrates from the top to the bottom and the staff lightens. "Gravational spell. It'll help you keep your balance on the way up the steep inclines. Inside, when it gets dark, it'll glow so you can see." He leads us away from the rocky valley and toward the Meridian Peaks. They don't line the horizon like the nomad's low mountains, nor do they form such a sharp silhouette as the eldrin's mounts. It's more clustered peaks with spaces between each set.

As I trail after Grandfather, I'm certain I'm not mistaken. The hair rising on my arms confirms it.

I grab his arm and stop him. "We're being followed."

10

His dark eyes are serious as he searches mine. He scowls, showing his sharp, beast-like teeth. "What do you see?"

"Something large in the sky. But I can only catch a glimpse in my side vision." I try to locate anything as I scan the air, but whatever it is must be gone. Or hiding.

"I see." He glances above and turns a full circle. "I sense nothing. No danger. Audhild, old friend?" There's no answer. "We don't have time to waste. We'll have to address it if it presents itself. Be on guard."

We resume walking, all of us peering around from time to time to reassure ourselves it's safe.

Unlike yesterday's travel, there are no settlements this far up. Skittering animals in the brush and birds chirping in the trees are our only witnesses. It grows craggier as we continue.

"Is it getting harder to breathe?" I ask, puffing.

Lucas turns toward me. "It's the altitude. The higher we get, the thinner the air becomes."

I can't help but notice it doesn't seem to affect him.

Grandfather slows down for us. "We'll stop once to eat and rest. We can't afford to dawdle."

After rolling an ankle and almost stabbing myself with the dagger at my waist, I stop trying to keep a constant eye on the sky. Wind rustles through the treetops, distracting me from other sounds I'm listening for. It sets my teeth on edge.

A couple of hours past midday we stop. I sit on a fallen log, pine needles at my feet. We'd already passed one large mountain and are headed to the next. I'm twitchy and want to think about things other than possible hidden forms of danger. "Can you tell us some about the other kingdoms?"

Grandfather finishes a bite of dried meat before answering. "That's an awfully wide topic. Each kingdom is different, as you've probably gathered."

He's correct, and I consider before speaking again. "Besides Tenebris having no magic, it's plainer, if that's the right word. Darker maybe? They believe in old wives' tales and superstitions. When Lucas would describe how wonderous Anavrin was, I didn't know what to think. Seeing it now, I understand. Even these woods are more breathtaking than anything there except the Narrow Cliffs and the Spaw."

"Spaw?" he asks.

Lucas answers back. "It's a hot water reservoir beside the sea. They use the minerals in healing lotions and the hot water to relax and soak in. It's supposed to heal, but I never saw anything too miraculous. We went to a masquerade ball there the night we escaped into the Zoe Tree."

"Ah. We call them thermal springs. There's one near my keep." He grins. "I haven't had a hot bath since the last time I was here. I'm quite looking forward to it."

I catch the moving shape out of the corner of my eye again. "Whatever is following us has returned."

The animation on Grandfather's face drops. "Well, we

must keep up the pace. We'll talk about the other kingdoms when we get to where we're going. Somehow, I have to believe if it meant us harm, it would've come for us before now. And hopefully, my shielded keep stops trouble from visiting our door." He stands and gathers his pack again.

With a deep breath, I follow behind him with Lucas at my back.

———

Though I'd kept one eye skyward and one eye on the ground, I don't see or sense anything else as we continue. We are across to the end of the second mountain when the skyline turns from a dazzling blue to a pinkish-orange.

"We'll stop there at that wizened old tree." Bennett removes the pack from his back. He digs inside it and finding the stones, takes them out. "Lucas, if you would carry this for me?"

"Sure." He takes the pack.

My legs and back ache and my feet burn. I scrutinize the area, searching for anything unusual or something tracking our moves. At the base of the mountain, wavering at the corner of my sight is a large rock balancing precariously atop two other boulders. Much like a table, it's big enough I could walk beneath. "An illusion?" I ask.

"Good eye! Most people don't spot it. Here's the tree." Grandfather grins at me and pats the thick gray bark.

The trunk is crooked and knotted like arthritic hands. Despite its age, long, thin leaves and round, black fruit hang from the limbs. The breeze carries the tree's fruity scent. My mouth waters in response.

"It's the Wehyah Tree. It and the Zoe Tree are the oldest trees in this kingdom." He takes the stones and strides five steps from the tree, placing them equal distance apart in a semi-circle. Again, I catch a glimpse of the table rock, but it's gone when I look at it directly. Grandfather chants the same words as before as he places the stones.

When he finishes, he exclaims, "Ebargofiant!"

Immediately, it's as if time itself stops. There's no whispering of the wind outside, no hint of birds calling. It's complete and utter silence.

"What happened?" I spin in a circle. I can still see the sun setting, the trees waving in the breeze, and, surprisingly, the table rock is behind the tree where I'd almost spotted it before.

"I already have other protective measures in place. So, when the stones are set, it becomes a double seal." He stands tall, his chest puffed out. It's the most relaxed I've seen him yet. "Welcome to my mountain. Come."

His steps are a bit jauntier as he leads Lucas and me through a rough cave opening where I could've sworn there was nothing but mountainside before.

"I've kept my entry hidden for years. Not many pass by who would tamper with it. But you never know when you've been followed." He claps his hands and then takes his pack back from Lucas.

As we step inside the dimmer interior, the staff I've been using to ascend the steep inclines lights up. Though the stones are a peachy color, the light glows white. Clear enough to see but not be blinded as I hold it in front of me.

Grandfather swipes away some dusty cobwebs as we enter. The walls are jagged and pocked as if a giant took a shovel and dug it open. The stone is gray-mottled with rust and dark-colored veins that zag across it like rivers. It sparkles and reflects our light.

It's dry, but water drips from somewhere, echoing across the barren walls. Though there's a light mildew odor, I catch no stench of standing water, which is a relief. I'd spent too many nights forced to sleep in dank places.

We cross the wide expanse to an enclosed stairway that leads upward beyond where my light can reach. "Watch your step. Audhild and I built the barrier so we wouldn't fall over the side, but it can be steep in places." He takes the small jar from his pocket, shakes it, and it lights up as bright as day.

My staff's light goes out with the Netherlight's stunning glimmer.

"How can a dragon as big as she is build such a stairway?" Lucas asks.

Grandfather's eyes crinkle as he grins. "Like you, dragons can transform into different forms."

Lucas and I share a stunned expression.

I shouldn't be surprised, but I am. I consider changing to a dragon. It's unfathomable. Soon, I'm winded due to the steep climb. Part of the way we have to duck through gritty openings before finding more open stairs. When I look over the barrier, I'm amazed at how far up we've traveled. My stomach drops dizzyingly and I turn away to ease the sensation. My feet grind as I turn to step through another opening carved into the stone. A musty dust smell permeates the air as we climb deeper inside the mountain. I sneeze.

Lucas is beside me, his warm hand on my back. "How much farther inside the mountain is it?" he asks.

I smile gratefully. He must notice how breathless I've become.

"Not far. I'd found this mountain was split, giving way to wind tunnels and expansive cavities. I use the natural formation and carved inward as best I could." He laughs. "I'm no miner, but it gets us to my keep." He smiles back at us as he turns another corner and shadows engulf Lucas and me. My staff glows again, and I'm thankful for it.

Minutes pass and we start to head down, slowly at first. It slopes toward the end, and I'm grateful the pathway is staired instead of smooth, or there's no doubt I would've ended up on my backside and sliding down it.

One more sharp turn and Grandfather's light reflects off a glittering dome. I blink to take it all in. It's stunning.

He swings toward Lucas and me, his arms held open wide. "Welcome to my keep."

A deep guttural growl resounds, bouncing off the walls. I'm unsure where it comes from. My hands light up and my necklace warms. I'm instantly alert, but am unable to see any threat.

"Who's there?" Grandfather steps in front of us, blocking whatever awaits in the depths. Something moves and objects clink and clatter. Grandfather glances around, searching. "Answer me."

There's no response. More rattles and jangles echo, bouncing from every direction. Is there more than one being? My energy shifts and comes to life, tingling in my gut like a leg that's been sat on for too long.

Lucas's arm moves around my waist, comforting, and protective.

"Tambrynn, hand me the dagger, please."

I hand it to him, unsure what to do. I try to slow my panting breaths, but my lungs don't want to cooperate.

I lean into Lucas's side, afraid of what kind of creature is hiding. Our lights only reflect so far and it's not the only room in this large inner chamber.

"Always remember we can change to birds and fly away." Lucas's voice wavers even though he whispers.

A hiss. Golden, gleaming eyes. And then the black dragon steps out of the dimness. It steps on something metal, crunching it.

The hairs on my arms and the back of my neck prick shortly before I can sense the sphere of protection that bubbles up around me. I waver between wanting to run away and standing my ground. Once again bravery seems more like choking fear than actual courage.

My grandfather's eyes reflect the warmth of his netherlight. "Who're you to trespass in my lair?" The dagger glows an ominous green. Grandfather holds it in the air threateningly. "This is a Mortifer Blade. One slash and your life is ended. Do not come any closer." Though his words leave no room to disagree, his voice wavers.

Another hiss, but no response. It creeps forward, knocking several glittering things with its huge feet. There's no doubt now that it's bigger than Audhild. With a roar, its mouth opens and the lightning I recall from before is loosed.

In my stunned state, I'm too slow. The energy hits me, crackling up on the protective bubble that covers me. It sizzles against my barrier. Before I can blink, I'm a firebird. I fly over Grandfather's head and call out a warning in a high-pitched shriek. *"Stop or I'll attack!"*

"Tambrynn! What are you doing? Lucas's concern pours through our bond.

I don't take my eyes off the creature. *"I didn't mean to change. It was instinct."*

"Be careful. I don't think we can trust this dragon!" Lucas flies in a wide arc around the creature, but its eyes never leave me.

"I'm sure that's why I changed so quickly. I sense danger coming from it."

"Tambrynn, don't attack it unless I say to. This is an elemental dragon. They are far more dangerous than you might realize." Grandfather's voice, still wavering, is low and calm.

His unspoken belief that I'm not strong enough to battle it

makes me hesitant, yet angrier. How dare it! It's not welcome here in what's supposed to be a shelter for us. I didn't travel across Anavrin for this to happen.

Lightning crackles across the dragon's body. It streaks through the air in a blinding flash. It's headed straight for my grandfather.

I lean back and send both wingspans of flames at the energy, breaking it up. The power of the clash blows Grandfather back two steps. I fling another heated wave at the dragon.

It screeches when the flames lick its scaled hide. It scuttles backward and shakes its head. More energy snaps around its body. It spirals out like a net in the air toward me.

"Tambrynn, watch out!" Grandfather yells.

"*Stop! Stop this at once.*" Audhild's voice blasts right before the lightning hits me.

Shock at hearing the firedragon's voice is short-lived. The other dragon's magic crackles against the bubble around me. It penetrates and stings. *Burn it,* the voice inside my head implores, *burn it to the ground.* Between the dragon and the unwanted voice, I scream in anger. The shriek bounces off the stone walls, rattling the debris below.

Grandfather falls to the ground clutching his ears.

The dragon shrinks back, its long neck lowered.

Lucas screeches and flies toward it. It raises its head, paying no attention to Lucas's claws, which scratch harmlessly over the hide.

Audhild steps between me and the dark dragon. "*Stop, Magpie. You'll not harm one as great as he. He's from a different kingdom and can't mindspeak as we can. He's either been abandoned or mistreated. He may not trust anything because of this.*"

Audhild turns toward the dragon. "*I welcomed you to my*

nest. You serve no purpose attacking my clan this way. Cease in your actions or suffer my wrath!" Her last words are like a gong in my head, making me wince.

The black dragon stumbles back and shrieks. Its eyes are on Audhild now. It doesn't look happy, but it doesn't strike back at her.

"You're asking us not to attack him? Aren't dragons forbidden by their own laws to not attack lesser beings unless they've been attacked first?" Grandfather shouts at her.

The black dragon hisses and sidesteps.

"Don't yell, Bennett. I'll calm him down and explain everything." A series of clucking sounds and growls come from Audhild.

Lucas, having no luck in attacking the dragon, circles around and joins me in hovering over Grandfather.

Audhild continues clacking for several moments. The other dragon never answers back, but his wings curl around his back.

"There. He's settled." Audhild's long neck stretches so she faces us directly. *"You can change back, youngling and Watcher. There is no threat now."*

Lucas lands easily. I drop less elegantly, tipping sideways. I thrust my wings out to help me balance as Grandfather said, and I'm relieved to find I stay on my feet this time.

"That's the dragon we saw yesterday. I thought it attacked you." I shake my hands out, trying to ease the warmth from them. It does not go away.

Audhild shrinks from her massive size, becoming a woman in form. She's tall, taller than I am, and intimidatingly muscular. "He did. But I don't believe he knows any better. I'm not sure how he got to Anavrin or where he's from. There aren't many kingdoms where dragons still exist. He's either too scared to speak or he's been mistreated to the point he can't speak. Either way, he needs care."

The other dragon watches from the shadows, his eyes eerily reflecting gold.

My necklace stays warm against my neck and my ability continues to hum within me. I remain skeptical of Audhild's claims. Not that I believe she's lying. But I don't trust this new beast.

When I turn away from the black dragon, I can't help staring at Audhild. She's dressed all in red. Her round-neck dress is fitted from the waist up, the split skirt flowing, sweeping past her pants and black boots. She doesn't look a day older than I am. Most surprising, however, is her intricately braided hair which is the color of spilled blood. Her ebony skin glows.

When she glances my way, I notice her eyes are odd, much like mine, having slits instead of the usual round pupils. Not star-shaped, however. Their predatory nature startles me, and I can't help but think of all who looked upon me and were scared. I understand now why it was so unnerving to view.

Grandfather lets out a strangled noise. "What're we supposed to do with a wild dragon without restraints?"

"The same we would do with a firebird who cannot control her fire." Audhild jerks her head in my direction. "We train him."

11

Several hours later, I join Lucas on Grandfather's side of the cavern, as far away from the black dragon as we can get. The chamber is divided in two by a thick hourglass column of rock, separating Grandfather's keep and Audhild's hoard.

Audhild's side, from which the dragon steadfastly watches us, is littered with coins, treasures, and trinkets. All shiny. And all Audhild's, as she'd warned after controlling the other creature.

"Are you hurt, my lady? I sense some unease coming from you." Lucas's hand is warm against the nape of my neck. Though this cavern isn't as cold as the one on Tenebris, I've had to call upon my inner fire to keep me from quivering.

"No, but I wish I would've gotten a good shot in before Audhild stopped us. At least enough to sting a bit." I shrug. "He gives me the creeps and I'd rather he feared me than think I'm an easy target." I picture Siltworth in my mind. I had been too easy a target. Though I'm not sure how effective it is to assert myself against the dragon, I needed to start somewhere. I don't apologize for my actions anymore.

I pull out one of the wooden chairs and sit, facing the dragon. He hasn't moved from Audhild's unruly piles. And though the others are unconcerned over his presence, the golden gaze never leaves me, becoming an itch I can't scratch.

This side is much more organized, with a long table and bookshelves full of weapons, jewelry (keys to other kingdoms, Grandfather informs us), books, and parchments. Four chairs are lined up on one side of the table, and the top is piled neatly with books, papers, and what I assume are writing utensils. But, they look nothing like the quills, ink pots, and blotters I'm used to.

Grandfather hustles back and forth, gathering items and dropping them on the desk. His face is flush and grim. The calm I'd witnessed earlier has eroded to desperation. The black dragon has unsettled him. Another reason I dislike the intruding creature.

I'm unsure what to do with myself. Mother taught me to read basic eldrin and Tenebrisian, but here different languages are displayed on numerous tomes. A handful of books I'd scrutinized had words that I couldn't pronounce, let alone understand.

Disappointment builds in my chest. I am right where I need to be to find the answers I'm looking for, and they're as elusive as ever. I huff and plop my chin on one of my hands resting on the tabletop.

"Is there anything I can do to help ease your frustration?" Lucas gazes at what I'm sure is a sullen expression on my face.

I try to smile away the uncertainty that stretches my nerves thin. It's not his fault. He and Mother had been teaching me when the beasts came the first time. I rub my hands down my thighs. "No, this is a bit more complicated than I first imagined." I wave a hand over the stacks of books and papers. "I can't imagine being able to understand it all."

Lucas rubs my back. "You don't have to understand all of it. No one can. And we're all here to help you find it." He sits beside me, flipping through the papers and perusing several books. "Interesting." He shows me the cover, *'Minerals, Rocks, and Conjuration Use.'*

"What is con-joor-a-shun?" I sound the word out.

"It's pulling from the energy of nature. Some of it you understand innately." He flutters the pages and the book settles on a section that must've been well-used before. "This might be what Bennett is using to hide the keep's doorway."

I smile as if I understand. However, my mind is on other things. My stomach drops despite Lucas's encouragement.

I say nothing as Lucas gleefully inspects everything on the table and then turns to glance at the shelves that are overflowing with more books, scrolls, and papers. I recognize now his excitement when he talked about going to school for the first time after Madrigal found him. His love of books and learning is obvious in the tilt of his head and the easy way he immerses himself in the pages. Jealousy, or is it envy, of Lucas's education creeps into my mind.

I tamp down the ugly emotions. He is truly enjoying himself, and I'm happy for him.

"Go," I tell him when he hesitates. "I'll sit here and wait while Grandfather gathers what he believes I need."

Audhild walks toward me. She practically floats, unlike my shuffling footsteps across the dusty floor. Though dirty and dim, I have to admit this space is much better than the grime that coated the Sanctuary caverns on Tenebris. It's had much more care. Audhild sits at the other end of the table facing me.

"Why are you not looking for the items you need?" It's a simple question, but one that prickles my self-doubt.

Before I can speak, Grandfather drops three books in front

of me. I choke on the cloud it sends flying. It takes a minute to stop sneezing and sputtering.

"My apologies. It's dirtier than I remember." Grandfather pats my arm. "Anyway, I wasn't sure how much you could read. From what I recall of those who visited Tenebris, it isn't a scholarly kingdom." He shifts a book around and shows me an illustrated cover. "The basics of nature and how to summon it. It's taught to our children in their elementary learning classes." He opens it. "It has photos to help with the descriptions. If you have any questions, Audhild or I can help you."

My face heats, but I'm thankful for the book.

Grandfather, like Lucas, is energized in this space. He hurries back toward other shelves and thumbs through them.

"My apologies, youngling." Audhild's voice is contrite. "I didn't realize you may not be able to read."

I meet her animalistic stare. "I can read some." I shift in my seat. "The bigger words confuse me. Anyway, you couldn't have known."

"It is how many wars are started—with some not understanding another's views. I shouldn't have assumed." She stands and chooses the chair next to mine. "I can help. I've learned many languages in my years in this kingdom. Some to keep the boredom at bay." She takes the book Grandfather left and opens it to the beginning. "Let's start here."

Hours later I stretch my arms, my back popping. The room's light never changes, so my eyes grow tired before my body does. Audhild, it turns out, is a wonderful, patient teacher. We'd read and then she'd quiz me on what we'd gone over. Book after book, she'd search and find subjects I needed to learn. My mind is crowded with facts and information by the time we finish.

I managed to create a magical whorl of dust to clean the

table, gathering the debris to a far corner of the room. When my eyes started to bother me, Audhild showed me how to shift the gems in the staff to shine brighter. I'd also managed to call water out of the air, cleanse it with my fire, and collect it into a kettle.

"Here are some notes from the kingdom of Pseminia." Audhild unfurls a parchment, motioning for me to hold one side of it. "Sem-in-ee-ah is how it's pronounced. It's a land of lava and fire where many fire dragons used to live."

My heart races at the thought we may find some answers after all. "Have you ever been there?"

"Once. Long ago." There's sadness in her quiet tone. She does a quick head shake and the light in her eyes returns. "It was quite hot. Humid really. And since it was so torrid when it rained, the water evaporated before it got to the ground." She makes a tsking noise. "I adore flying in the rain, so I didn't much enjoy the atmosphere."

"But they have many fire dragons there?" I caress the parchment's still-pliable tanned skin. The dark ink is blocky and foreign to my eyes.

"Yes, many. I was told they prefer the more arid, or dry, air. But I cared not for it." She peruses the writing, her lips moving wordlessly. "It says here," she points to a section, "that it takes years, sometimes centuries, for firebirds to master their abilities." She continues to mouth what she reads, but I'm unable to understand it since she uses the Pseminian words. "It does say that firebirds are preternatural beings, meaning they are outside the bounds of what is normal in nature. They're highly sensitive and intuitive, attuned to nature on a deeper level than most creatures."

I curl my hands into fists. "I only understood half of what you said."

Audhild pats my arm. "You are unique, which we already

knew. You will be able to sense things others will not, such as when there is danger, and your protection ability surfaces in the form of blue energy. It goes on to say that only a handful of firebirds have existed since the great split. They're born only when a time of great need is upon the land."

She reads further, trailing a long, crimson fingernail across the scroll. "Ah, yes. I recall the stories." She glances up, seeing something beyond me. "There once was a great icebird from the kingdom of Iolneo, a land of ice and snow, naturally. It had a vision of a drought in the water kingdom of Trithis, created by a dark wizard. We call them mages here." She squints back at the writing. "The icebird, a male named Vitru, called upon the great sea guardian."

She mouths a few words. "Doesn't say what kind of sea guardian it was. I only know of one, and she is cursed. Anyway, he called upon this guardian who swam to the ocean's depths to unlock the floodgates. However, the guardian had to battle a leviathan—a massive sea serpent—before he could reach the gates. He managed it, opened the gates, and ended the drought." She flips the parchment over and then back again. "Either I am rusty in my Pseminian, or they didn't believe in details."

My shoulders droop. "Without more details, who knows what actually happened. There's so much I don't know." I drop my forehead to the book open on the table before me.

Rumbling snores resound from the other side of the room. A glance up assures me the other dragon has fallen asleep.

We both giggle at the snoozing dragon.

"We'll search again tomorrow." Audhild yawns. Her teeth are sharp-tipped—dragon teeth. "Now, however, I'm tired, youngling. It's been a long day. I will settle with the drake to sleep. I bid you goodnight."

I understand from the books we'd read that drake meant

the male dragon. I stretch my arms over my head to untangle the knots in my shoulders.

She glides away a step, and in the space of one moment to the next, she shifts to her dragon form.

Her movements startle Grandfather, who stretches his arms above his head with a yawn. "I apologize. I may have forgotten the time. Hard to tell when there's no sun to go by." He places a hand on Lucas's shoulder, surprising him out of his reading.

"Don't worry about them. Dragons sleep like fat, hibernating bears." He sighs and sits down in the far chair. "Did either of you find anything helpful?"

Lucas launches into a discussion about the books he's read so far, his eyes aglow with delight. After the second sentence, I understand nothing, so I tune him out.

Grandfather is so indulgent, nodding and listening, that I can't help but smile. It's a new experience, one I find I'm quite fierce about. It fills something inside me. Taking them both in, I wish we could stay here forever, hidden and safe. Learning new things.

But then I recall the nomads looking for their kin. And the dangerous mer-girl without her crown which would allow her to return to her home beneath the sea. And the eldrin, who are overtaking Anavrin for their own rule. I inwardly groan. This keep is too much of a bubble, not reflective of the outside world. I do, however, fully intended to take advantage of its protection for as long as I can.

"Where should I sleep?" I inadvertently break up the men's discussion.

"Oh, yes. Let's see." Grandfather walks around and stops, his hands on his hips. "Audhild, would it be an imposition for Tambrynn to use your side to sleep?"

Red eyes glower, breaking the murky shadows. "She may."

Rattling sounds along with a huge puff of air, follow her response. "The drake is shackled. You are all safe for the time being."

I have to wonder about her idea of safe.

Grandfather leads me across. "I'm sorry for this, but I fear you may catch the books on fire as you sleep." His words are kindly spoken, though the truth hits me harder than I'd like to admit. "Take nothing. Dragons are known for their hoarding. An addiction, really. It wouldn't matter that you are on friendly terms. If she senses something is missing, her instincts will take over and she'll become aggressive."

"Aggressive?" I whisper, not wanting her to hear me, though I'm sure she does. We've arrived at a bare spot between Bennett's neat hoard and Audhild's unruly piles.

He pats me on my shoulder. "Very aggressive. I don't suggest it. Good night, dear one."

I glance back to where she and the other dragon rest and am greeted by two golden eyes watching my every move. The orbs narrow menacingly, making the heated blood in my veins turn to ice.

———

Though exhausted, I sleep fitfully. I dream of reflective eyes everywhere I turn. Images of Trithis with its underwater towns invade several different nightmares where hands try to drown me. I become lost at sea and settled on the bottom of the ocean floor like a wrecked ship left buried in the watery expanse. A giant serpent wraps around me, with its tail-like arms choking me until I succumb to its strength. I'm almost as tired when I wake as when I laid down to sleep.

Between the flames that lick my skin, I spy two golden orbs watching me again as I wake. I shake my fire off, leaving me chilled. I try to loosen my knotted muscles, but it's no use. I'm tenser than a young maid carrying used bedpans down a crooked staircase.

The drake moves his head, whatever he lays upon shifting and clanking. His eyes follow my progress to Grandfather's keep. I refuse to look directly into his golden stare.

"Good morning, Granddaughter. Did you sleep well?" Grandfather gives me a tired grin. He holds a steaming cup of something that smells earthy and nutty.

"Better than some. Not as well as I'd liked to have." I yawn and stretch my arms, wishing I had something warmer to wear. Or that I could find a way to keep the fire in my veins heated enough so I could stay warm when I change. I sit next to him. Several new tomes lay stacked upon each other, each opened to a different section.

"Would you like a cup of chicory?" He points to a kettle.

"What's chicory?" I ask, taking a cup from a stack at the end of the table. "Some magical brew?"

"Not magic that I know of. It's the root of a flower, roasted and ground up. It grows around the mountain in abundance." He pours some dark liquid into the cup and motions for me to try it. "You can practice using your fire to heat it, which is my favorite way to drink it."

"You watched Audhild teaching me?" I ask, warmed by his interest. The dragon had taught me how to balance flames on my palms for a brief time last eve.

"Of course. You did wonderfully." His smile is genuine, puckering the skin at the edges.

I concentrate and in seconds I heat the cup enough to steam. My smile mirrors Grandfather's as I sniff the concoction. It smells safe. I sip carefully, not wanting to burn my tongue. A bitter earthy flavor invades my mouth. I gag. "Ugh! How can you stand this?" I set the cup down.

He chuckles. "More of a tea person, eh?"

"Water is fine. Where's Lucas and Audhild?"

"They both went out to hunt. Different things, of course. Audhild claims if she feeds the other dragon, he'll start to trust her and may be more communicative." He pours my cup into his and swirls it around. "I did manage to find a book on fire dragons and their kin. I'm reading about the secrets of fire magics now."

I yawn again, trying to hide it behind one hand.

"You do not look rested at all. Maybe you should go out, and get the blood pumping, yes? There's a pool not far from the doorway if you want to wash the sleep away. Take this with you." He hands me the dagger.

I take it while eyeing his cup, wishing I didn't have the flavor stuck in my mouth now. "I think I will, thank you."

I try not to look at the black dragon as I pass. His gaze is on my back as I make my way to the passage and outside.

It doesn't feel as long a trek as it had last eve, even with having to crouch to get through some areas. Maybe because I'm climbing down instead of up. I'm out in the sunshine before I know it, taking a deep breath of fresh air. The sun is bright in the sky, so it's not early morning. However, it's still dewy, so it can't be midday.

Though I search for the pool, I find only gray rock and bristly bushes. In the distance, mountains rise majestically into the cloudless, blue sky. Pine trees cover the gray stone in large swaths.

A low rushing sound catches my attention and I stop and stare at a waterfall, something I've only heard about in stories. I'm close enough that I can see the water froth over the rugged stone edges. Something about it pulls at me. I need to get a closer look.

Glancing back, I ascertain Grandfather's mountain isn't

that far from the waterfall and decide to go. It won't take too long to fly there and back. I shouldn't be missed.

In an instant, I'm changed and flying toward the waterfall. Other large birds call out from hidden limbs as I glide by the pines. Warning me? Beckoning me? Their squawking caws are like a drip in the distance, and I ignore them. I need to get closer to the rushing brilliance.

Then I am. It's magnificent.

There are multiple falls with shelf after incredible shelf boasting lush flowers and foliage. And it's loud. Water crashes, smacking boulders that jut out of the jagged mount. The stream is crystal clear, and I can see the stones beneath the surface, reflecting the pure blue of the sky.

I dive through a curtain of spray and a majestic song erupts in my head. The rush is cold and crisp against my heated body. Energizing. I dart in and out of the torrent, never wanting the song to end. I'm reveling in the beauty of the lilting notes. I haven't been this free and giddy since I was a child playing in the meadows with Lucas. The memories are as clear as the current. I twitter along with the sound while I dip and flutter.

I dodge in and out of the waterfall's spray until I tire. The music of the ebb and flow is so perfect, it's all I hear. My chest bursts with the freedom and glory of it and I make one darting swoop down toward the pool.

That's when I catch sight of the creatures in the water below. Too small to be finfolk or fishkin, they're focused upon me. Blue flames crackle along my drying feathers and the spell I'd been under is lost. I'm wide awake, alert, and more than a bit concerned when I see they also have wings. They jump out of the water at me and I flap hard to get away from them. Luckily, their wings are smaller and less able. Their arc is barely a couple of feet before they drop back down into the clear pool.

Who are they? What are they? Are they controlled by Siltworth? The questions spin through my mind. I turn tail and leave the crashing water with its beguiling song behind flying fast.

I pass the second mount, praying I haven't given away our hiding place. I push my wings harder, willing the space between here and the keep to be gone. I know how cruel the merkin are. What if this is some new kind of vicious water creature? I'm so disgusted I succumbed to the allure of the falls that I could grow another leg and kick myself.

After several minutes of flying, I fear I'm lost. It didn't take this long to get to the falls. My honing ability is no help, I can't tell north from south. I couldn't have flown past the entrance yet, could I? The trees all look the same. Several rocky ledges and outcroppings confuse me. I don't see the crooked tree, but then possibly I wouldn't with Grandfather's stones and other protections in place.

I circle around and around, but everything seems the same. Every mountain, each cliff, all of the trees. I can't even find the pools Grandfather spoke about. Why hadn't I paid more attention when I left the cave's entrance?

Because something drew me to the falls, like candy to a child—irresistible. I hadn't been thinking. I'd lost myself in the call, music, and feel of the water rushing over me. It was a ridiculous, stupid mistake to not get a good look at my surroundings. I know better. My mind is whirling. Should I call out to Lucas?

I'd have to admit that I'd been reckless and left without telling anyone what I was doing. He would have a lecture for that. Grandfather would be so disappointed. And Audhild would surely snicker at my carelessness, as well.

What am I going to do?

12

I zig and zag in a semi-organized pattern, trying to find anything familiar. After several minutes of searching, I think I see steam in the distance. The heated pools? I'm tired of searching. It would be worth a lecture to find the keep again.

"*Lucas?*" I cry out in my mind.

I'm too agitated. I can't sense him. He doesn't answer me. I fly around some more, calling out his name. Panic begins to take up residence in my heart. The only other time our communication failed was when Lucas had been hit with my father's hex. Could there be something wrong with him? Had they been attacked?

All of the possibilities zing through my mind, each one worse than the one before it. My heart thrums so hard I'm sure it will break out of my chest.

"Tambrynn?" Lucas's voice calls up to me. He's holding a hand to shield his eyes against the bright sunlight.

Oh, thank goodness!

I dart beside him and land, without teetering for once, into his open arms in my girl form. His heartbeat is calm while mine beats out of my chest. "I was calling for you, but you didn't hear me. I'm so glad you called out. For a moment I was lost."

Lucas pulls back, confusion and concern clear on his handsome face. He raises one shapely eyebrow at me. "I didn't hear you. Were you out flying around? You know that's not safe. Besides, you shouldn't be out exploring an area you don't know alone." He kisses the top of my head. "Next time wait and I'll go with you."

Beside him on the ground are two rabbits and two small pigeon-sized birds, already cleaned and packed on some sticks ready to cook.

"I'm sorry. I know I shouldn't have gone out, but there was this waterfall and—"

"And you couldn't help yourself. You're not part djinn, are you?" His chuckle is low and teasing. He picks the animals up and starts to walk. "Have you tried the pool yet? Bennett told me about it this morning. I was waiting until I finished hunting to use it. Maybe wash away the sweat."

Relieved to be back with Lucas, I put my arm around his waist as we walk along. "That's where I was headed when I saw the waterfall." I think of the creatures beneath the waterfall. Possibly they were simply fish? I'd been in such a state of bliss that maybe I overreacted to them. So far, however, my gut has been correct in assessing danger. "Do you think it's safe? No water creatures?"

"Bennett never mentioned any." He preens a bit as he raises the sticks. "Let me take care of these first."

I gather sticks and limbs while Lucas builds a fire in the opening of the keep's cave entrance. It's already charred from previous fires. Flying above where we are right now, it looked like the wall of the mountain was closed, quite a convincing illusion. I would never have found it searching from the sky. I try not to revisit the frenzy I'd experienced minutes before. I wouldn't ever leave without making sure I had a good sense of the area again, waterfall or not.

After the fire is blazing, Lucas props the meat over the fire to cook.

"Ah, younglings." Audhild exits the stairway in her woman form. She must've returned while we were gone.

A dark-haired male steps from behind her. He has a strangely cut mustache and beard which curls around his lips and chin. Coal dark rings line his eyes, giving them a smoky, ominous look. His brown eyes glow gold around their edges when the light hits them.

He's handsome as a human, though oddly so. His stare is fixed firmly upon me, so I glance away, but my view stutters to a halt on the fire dragon's womanly form. I blink.

Still dressed all in red, she wears a shockingly tight outfit that shows her arms, cleavage, and long legs. "Bennett mentioned you're going to the thermal spring?"

Neither Lucas nor I speak.

Audhild raises her arms and freezes. The man behind her leans against the wall, staring off in the other direction.

Or biding his time before attacking?

Audhild's laugh is deep. "Have you never seen flesh before?"

"N—no," Lucas stutters.

I glance at Lucas's stunned expression and shake my head. "Not really."

"I forget how conventional and modest you species are. I have a gift for you. Stay right there." She turns but stops. "Oh, and this is the elemental dragon. I have yet to learn his name. His mind is inaccessible. So, I'm calling him Drake."

Drake follows after Audhild, a frown on his hairy face. She leads him past and then behind the stairway. He's never farther than ten steps behind her, so I have to wonder if he's bound to her somehow. He rounds the corner of the stone and stops, then turns to stare at me.

I make a hasty retreat to the cave opening, close enough to escape if necessary. Lucas waits by shifting the poles he's made to hang over the fire. It's unnecessary, but he stays between the dark dragon and me without appearing openly concerned.

Goosebumps bloom across my skin with the intensity of Drake's stare. Will he, like Garrett, attack me if he gets the opportunity?

Lucas, satisfied with the rabbit's position over the flames, walks over to me. "Are you all right, my lady?" he murmurs low.

"No. Maybe?" I kick at the dirt floor. One crystal-white rock skitters out of the cave and into the tall grass.

Lucas leans into me, his arm circling my waist. I tip my head to his shoulder.

A forever minute later, Audhild returns alone with two bundles.

"This is for you." She unfolds it, flicking it open. It's a blueish-gray outfit with shriveled leaves woven into the fabric. She holds it out to Lucas. "The material is plant-based. It's dormant until you enter water, and then it breathes for you. A good thing to have if you ever get pulled into the watery realm. For short-term, that is."

Next, she hands me a grayish-violet outfit, similar to Lucas's. The leaves on mine are smaller, rounder, and look as if they are attached to hundreds of crisscrossing vines.

I take it from her and the leaves, though withered, don't crumble or disintegrate. They're bendable. It's long enough to cover me from my neck, to my elbows, and down to my knees. "Um, thank you?"

Audhild's eyes flare red for a moment. "Lesson one, young

firebird, never ask what should be emphatically stated. Lesson two, a dragon rarely gives gifts. Take them gratefully when it happens." She spreads her hands wide. "Put them on, and always wear them whenever you're near water. I have no doubt they will be useful. You can test them out in the thermal springs."

I hold it, unsure where to go to undress.

She hisses out her annoyance. "You can disrobe in the room behind the stairs. Djinn, use the landing at the top of the stairs." She walks away, her head held high and her steps smooth and soundless against the gritty stone floor. Her hair shines a brilliant red when she steps into the sunlight. "Come along, Drake."

He stares at both Lucas and me with a gleam in his eye.

I step away from him, clutching Audhild's gift to my chest, my eyes never leaving him until he reluctantly exits the cave.

"Meet you back here." A magpie once more, Lucas flies up to the top of the stairs.

I'm not sure why we hadn't thought to do that last eve. It would've made traveling through the winding stairway much easier. I shake my head at that thought, determining to use my wings next time.

Behind the stairway carved into the side of the mountain cavern, is indeed a room packed with chaotic piles. It's as if Audhild had an armful of something and dropped it before bringing another armful in. I think of the piles in the cavern. Who knew dragons could be so messy?

Behind the mess is a carved, wooden wardrobe. Intricate flowers and vines lace the outside of the dark mahogany frame. Metal hangers hang from a bar inside, their contents crooked and askew. The drawers below bulge with clothing that look to be the same thin, silky cloth as the eldrin clothes I currently wear. Shoes and other items litter the floor in a wide arc around the piece of furniture. I start when I see a half-dozen coats of varying thicknesses hung on a rod along the back side.

It's exactly what I've been needing!

I catch myself before I touch something, Grandfather's warning about dragons and their possessions springing into my mind. Instead, I hurry to remove my clothes and the dagger so as not to receive more of the fire dragon's ire. I fold them, put the weapon on top, and step into the one-piece outfit. It's stretchy, and though not necessarily soft, it's comfortable like a second skin. I re-tie the dagger around my waist and keep my slippers on.

Audhild comes around the corner and draws a sharp breath.

I jerk back, startled. "What?"

"You're the image of your grandmother. Except for the hair." She waves a hand in dismissal. "But other than that, you could pass for Madrigal when she was younger." She rustles around in the pile and yanks out a picture in a frame.

It's a woman with dark chocolate hair, warm brown eyes, and a smile that holds secrets. "You see? You're the spitting image of your grandmother Madrigal, and Cadence, too. The resemblance is impressive." Her eyes narrow in thought. "Your silver hair quite suits you, though. Thank the Kinsman for his creativity. If your beautiful tresses were brown, you'd melt right in with the rest of the eldrin." She tsks. "That would have been such a disservice to your firebird heritage." She bends over and hands me a towel and spins around to leave.

As if she hadn't just put a dagger in my heart.

I'd always wanted to be beautiful like my mother. I never thought I looked like her. My appearance had elicited fear instead of admiration. Insults instead of compliments. It had been a curse. And for Audhild to comment so glibly that I would've fit in with the eldrin had it not been for my silver hair? I don't thank the Kinsman for that, even if she did.

Longing for my mother brings me to my knees. It's joined by a new ache knowing I will never meet my grandmother whom I also resemble. I hold the towel close as I dash the tears away.

13

I take a minute to compose myself. I don't wish to alarm Lucas when I meet him back at the fire. He stands in a halo of light shining into the mountain's opening. His back is to me, and he stares into the forest surrounding us.

I can't help but admire his legs. They're thin but well-developed and bird-like. My eyes travel upward, admiring his physique. His body is evenly proportioned, unlike some men whose torso is too short or too long. He's not overly muscular, but there's a lean strength that is striking. Even in strange clothing, he's the most attractive man I've ever known. My pulse quickens, doing an appreciative dance.

Smoke wafts around him to the open air beyond the cave, carrying with it the enticing scent of the roasting meat. The fire pops and my empty stomach growls, catching his attention.

He turns and clears his throat. "I was going to tease you that I fear I look as ridiculous as you do. But you look delightfully brambly."

A blush creeps up my throat and over my cheeks. "Is that a

good or bad thing?" I run my chilled hands down my thighs. I fear my thoughts are evident in my nervous posture.

He crosses his arms over his chest, the blue fabric pulling tight across his shoulders. The color sets off his inky black hair and narrow, dark eyes in the most beguiling way. "It's good," he hesitates, "but in a slightly bad way." His smile is crooked and most dangerous.

My blood runs hotter than a blacksmith's forge, having nothing to do with my firebird heritage. I fear my face is going to ignite at his insinuation.

"Come along, younglings." Audhild reappears, silently, from the stairway—alone.

Lucas stiffens and drops his head. *"Wasn't she outside? I don't recall her passing by me at all."*

Audhild's sharp smile turns predatory. "Rule number three, younglings. Unless and until you learn to shield your minds, I can hear when you mindspeak to each other. I heard you during the storms. Now, let's go. Bennett waits patiently in the spring for us."

Once again, embarrassment slides over my skin, and I'm surprised flames don't engulf me. For a moment, I wish they would. With a bashful glance at Lucas and a flustered grin I can't hide, I follow the dragon woman out of the cave.

Lucas takes my hand and we head outside. He squeezes it. "So much for keeping our conversations private."

I work hard not to laugh and draw the fire dragon's attention once more.

The pools are closer than I first imagined. Hidden behind stark gray walls, bushes, and rock, it's close to the mountain entrance, not far from where I walked earlier. Like the waterfall's pool, the springs are clear and blue. I slow my stride to spy for creatures in the water, but there's nothing there. It's as clear as the air. Is it there at all? But yes, I see a ripple along the edges.

And thankfully, no song to lure me in.

Lucas takes a deep breath. "It's stunning, isn't it? I've never seen water as crystal clean before."

I agree with him.

Hot springs, more than one since there are multiple rounded sections, span the length of the mountainside. Steam wavers off it and the sky reflects brighter than a mirror on its still surface. Knee-deep grass gives way to patches of weeds that grow around the rocky ground. A mild scent of rotten eggs drifts upon the breeze, but it's not near as twangy as fresh pig and chicken droppings on a hot day. Cleaning the pens had been one of my most despised jobs, and one many of my employers deemed me worthy of doing time and again. Anything after that is tolerable.

Plant life near the pool is coated with a layer of white, creating an outline around the numerous springs, some too shallow to sit in.

Grandfather sits inside the closest and deepest pool by the mountainside. He wears an off-white tunic that billows slightly at his neck. It's steaming, as if he's cooking inside of a pot. I work not to smile, remembering when I'd threatened to put Lucas in a stew. I sober as I recall Cook placing my hand over the sizzling pot.

The steam makes Grandfather's face hard to see clearly. "Hello! I thought I'd be the last one in." He waves a hand over the water. "Come, relax."

"Sorry, I went exploring instead of heading here this morning. Then after I returned, Audhild gave us gifts."

"Ah, she did?" He glances at the dragon-woman.

"I don't tell you everything, beggar-thief." She slips into the water with a long sigh and swims easily over to the far side where it seems deeper. Once there, she lazes with her eyes closed.

"Where's Drake?" I inquire, curious. I'd brought the dagger to defend myself against him and I don't see him anywhere.

"Chained in my lair. You're safe." Audhild sinks into the hot water up to her chin.

"Have you seen the Enchanted Falls?" Grandfather points to the side where I can spot the water rushing down the mountainside from a different angle than what I'd seen earlier. I can almost hear the music in my ears still.

My heart quickens.

"I flew around it briefly this morn. I should've paid more attention to my surroundings, though." My throat is tight as I recount my outing with them. I don't look them in the eyes but set the dagger on the ground. Since the other dragon isn't here, it should be safe. I wrap up my adventure and climb in, slowly at first. I'm unused to heated water, and it's disconcerting at first.

Grandfather lets out a sound that's part grunt and part laugh. "You went to the falls? I should've warned you. It's a wonder you got free. They were enchanted by the grand dame of sirens, Thexia, when she could no longer dwell in the sea. Most who go there can never leave. Take a closer look at the base of the mountain and you'll see all who happily perished, their lifeforce having fed her song that still lingers long after her death."

I frown. "That explains a lot." I stick my toes out of the water, surprised by how cool the air is against my heated skin. Thankful I wasn't scolded, I creep closer to Grandfather. The dead leaves I'm wearing perked up once I sit in the water. They turn a brighter purple-gray. After the initial shot of heat, my body adjusts. I relax neck-deep in the basin and lean comfortably against the smooth rim.

I inhale deeply and notice a significant difference. Instead of the air struggling to enter my lungs, it comes easily. The constriction loosens. "Oh!" I exclaim. "How delightful. I hadn't realized how difficult it had become to breathe!" I take several hearty chestfuls of sweet oxygen, rejoicing at the ease.

Audhild glances at me. A corner of her shapely lips curves upward.

Lucas splashes in beside me. His outfit perks up the moment he enters the water as well. Colorful blue-green leaves unfurl like tiny ferns. They move with the motion of the water. He, too, exclaims in surprise before lounging back. "I haven't had a hot bath since Tambrynn dunked me in a kettle full of dirty water."

My mouth drops open. "You deserved it for chasing me around that forest and then trying to get into the cottage! And you ate my only food."

His laugh echoes off the stone walls around us. "I was starving. You can't expect your knight in shining armor to save you on an empty stomach, can you? Besides, I made up for it with my hunting trip today."

Grandfather laughs at our banter. His skin, usually rigid across his snout and mouth, is relaxed, showing fewer teeth. He also seems to be quite serene. "It sounds like Tenebris wasn't all bad."

I wave my hands back and forth in the water, delighting in the luxurious feel of it. Lucas is sitting close, but not too close. He catches the side glance I give him. "Not all, no. There was enough that was, though, that I wouldn't want to go back there."

"Not even if you were to go on a quest like my trials?" Despite the humor I sense in his tone, there's an undercurrent of gravity in his words.

Though I'd traveled from one kingdom to another, I'm

unsure if it's something I would like to repeat. I stare at the bushes that line the way from the cavern opening around the curve. They're the same type of foliage that grew around the nomad's mountains. Could it be that there's kinstone in this mountain as well? I turn my mind back to ponder Grandfather's question. Would I want to go back to Tenebris?

"What kind of relic do you think we'd find there?" Lucas asks. He's floating with only his head and toes sticking out of the warm water. It's clear enough to see the rest of him, but he's distorted. It's intriguing and reminds me of the illusion I found the nomad women stuck in. I have to wonder if that's part of the redirection of energy I'd studied with Audhild last eve.

Grandfather shifts in the water and his tunic clings to his chest. The skin beneath it is puckered and scarred. Was it from my father's spell or the eldrin 'turning' him away?

"There have been few trials to Tenebris that I recall." Grandfather breaks me free from my thoughts. "So, I'd be surprised if there wasn't something there to find. The rings, for instance. There should've been a couple of rings from the Kinsman's first Council who formed Tenebris. Then there's the maps and books, of course." He sends Lucas a sympathetic look.

"Yes, well, the ones we brought are gone for good. If they weren't stolen, they'd be ruined by the rainstorm." Water sloshes as he sits back up and rubs a hand over his face, leaving droplets behind.

Lucas's hair curls at the ends while wet. My hands itch to run through it, but this isn't the time or the place.

"You may still be able to retrieve them. Maybe not today. But sometime in the future, perhaps." Grandfather turns to me. "I did learn, Tambrynn, that your ring might not be lost. It was in the Dragonology book I retrieved from Far Starl. It had been hidden by a rogue cleric there whom I befriended."

I smooth water over my arms, loving the play between cool air and the heated water on my senses. "What do you mean?" I'm startled to catch Audhild's glare.

"I—" Grandfather is cut off by Audhild.

"The Kinsman's chosen don't need such tools to get from one kingdom to another. We simply are the key. Our essence opens any of the doors."

"Any dragon?" I ask, thinking of Drake.

Audhild swims back to where she stepped in. I can now see the uneven ledges she uses to gracefully rise out of the spring. "Any dragon," she confirms.

Lucas frowns. "So, you're saying that dragon *could* be from any of the kingdoms?"

Audhild doesn't respond. Her movements are stiff.

Grandfather nods. "Technically, yes. Though *some* believe all dragons to be noble, I am not completely assured of that fact. Despite the abuse the dragons experienced on Far Starl, some were true rogues. Obedient one moment, violent the next. We may never know where he's from. Or what, if any, purpose he has."

Audhild stands, water dripping off her body. She turns to speak, but Drake surges out of the tallest bushes along the mountainside's base.

The dagger Grandfather gave me glints in his hand as he holds it tight to Audhild's throat.

"Don't anyone move." Audhild grinds out through gritted teeth.

14

G randfather rises, the water rippling around him. "Audhild!"

My hands are alight with blue energy. When did the dark dragon get the dagger? I try to think back to when I last had the weapon.

I'd dropped it when Audhild had mentioned he was chained up. Another stupid mistake. Now her life is in danger.

Audhild's eyes flash and then flutter. "Don't. Move." She breathes heavily. She's scared, which terrifies me. "Drake, don't do this."

My pulse races as a slight line of blood trickles from where the sharp blade is pressed to her artery.

My stomach roils and my eyes heat up. "Stop!" I push every ounce of power into that one word.

The drake simply shakes his head and glares hatred at me. He yanks Audhild to the side.

Frustrated that didn't work, I move to get out of the water, and Lucas's hand stops me midstride.

Grandfather grunts. "You want something or you could've murdered her already. What is it?"

He dips his head at us. No, at me.

I steel myself to look him directly in the eyes. "What do you need with me?"

A strange kind of grunting-clicking noise comes from his throat. He beckons me with a jerk of his head to come closer.

"He says you can help him." Audhild's voice is breathy.

"Don't do it, my lady. We have no idea what he wants." Lucas switches to mindspeak, *"He's dangerous, Tambrynn. Too dangerous."*

I frown. *"What else am I supposed to do? It's Audhild's life in his hands. She at least has the power to save me. He shook off my order to stop like it was a fly he was avoiding."*

Drake grunts louder, his motions jerkier, impatient.

"He wants you to come now." Audhild translates. *"You can do this, Tambrynn, but be careful."*

Lucas frowns, but he doesn't disagree with the fire dragon.

Audhild's confidence bolsters me. I hold my hands out to appease him, my eyes on the blood flowing down Audhild's neck. "Fine. I'm coming."

Lucas takes my hand and helps me out. I know he doesn't want me to do this, he clings tight to my hand. I squeeze it. *"Stay here, Lucas. Please."*

My Watcher reluctantly agrees and releases my hand. Anger radiates off him hotter than the springs. Water swishes. Grandfather must be getting out as well. I don't dare to break Drake's stare.

I step up to Audhild's side, but he turns to face me. With a blindingly swift motion, he lets her go and grabs my hand.

Instantly, I'm immersed in a vision. A different kingdom. Many dragons. What must be guardians. Beatings. Loneliness. And Thoron. Then pain, so much pain. I barely recognize that my knees hit the ground. Everything blurs, except the pain, until finally, I catch sight of a magical battle. Drake fights off Thoron's attempts to kill him. And then, when that doesn't work, my father's attempts to turn him into a beast. Like my order, it flows off him. If it weren't for Drake's thick scales, he'd have been doomed. He flees, stumbling across an old tree. A Zoe Tree? A blinding light. He stumbles, injured, into the Passage that I recognize from the strange light and the different sections of plant life that grow abundantly.

Thoron is there again, trying to stop Drake from entering the first and second doors. Magic explodes everywhere. I don't recognize anything for certain. The battle wages on through the Passage that increasingly becomes unstable. The radiant light turns stormy. Wind whips at the dragon. Drake manages a successful attack on Thoron, who's left bleeding—darkness leeching out of him.

But Thoron rallies. The light in the passage brightens and then dims. Lightning zags, hitting trees. They're uprooted and crash down. Drake arrives at a blackened door, bracing himself as he falls through.

He's disoriented. It's night, too dark to see and a light keeps flashing and then is gone. The lighthouse. He's drawn to it, but Thoron is there. Desperate, Drake takes off into the sky. There's an awareness of another dragon, and then the storm comes, ripping across the skies and drowning anything not strong enough to fight against it.

I'm yanked away. My head swims as the images settle and I try to make sense of it all. When the dizziness stops and I can open my eyes again, it's to see Audhild standing over Drake, my dagger in her hand and anger glowing from her eyes.

"Are you all right, youngling?" Her eyes are so bright I look away.

My head is pounding. "I think so."

"What is it that you saw?" she asks.

"Thoron."

———

We gather around the fire where the meat is sizzling. Grandfather ties a silver chain around Drake, leaving him unconscious against the inner wall of the mountain. "It's infused with Kinstone. Should keep him from breaking out again." He gives the other dragon in the room a look. It's not a happy one.

I sit with my arms crossed, soaking in the heat of the fire. Lucas has his arm around me.

"Drink this." Audhild gives me something she mixed with dried leaves and steeped over the fire. "It will help with the disorientation."

I sniff it first, hoping it's not the same drink Grandfather had me taste earlier. It smells different, more like tea. "Thanks." I take a sip, letting the heat rekindle inside me as it slides down my throat. Spices and flowered honey make it delicious if a bit sweet.

"Now, what did you see?" Audhild has changed back into her pants and split skirt outfit. She sits across the fire from me. She's being kind, but I can tell she's keen to get the answers to why Drake attacked me.

I blow out a breath and start to relate the flashes of things I saw starting with the strange kingdom. All caverns and flat red rock mountains. Grandfather's face turns grim as I continue to describe the place.

"It sounds like Far Starl to me," he mutters into his mug of steaming liquid. "It's arid with iron-rich soil and mountains. That would explain the red rocks."

Lucas turns the sticks one more time, settling the last

uncooked hunk against the flames. Juice drips and fizzles into the fire. The scent is alluring, but my stomach is unsettled.

"The men, guardians maybe, attacked Drake and he fled to live in a desolate place. He was alone, as far as I could tell. Then Thoron showed up and attacked him. He tried to kill him first, then tried to change him before the dragon fled into the passage."

Audhild sends me a sharp gaze. "Then what?"

"Thoron attacked again. He's still using a ring to get into the passage and other kingdoms." I take a deep breath. "The passage was thrown into chaos. Drake fought Thoron off until he found Anavrin's doorway and that's how he got here. Right before the storm came." I glance at Lucas, who has remained broodingly silent.

"So, I was right." He pokes at the spent logs with a twig. "It was the same on Tenebris. The storm wasn't natural. It's because of Thoron and his accursed games." He turns to glance at me. "Did Thoron change him, then? Is that why he's attacking you?"

"You pulled him off me too soon to know, but I don't think so. He resisted until he was able to fly off when he got here. He sensed Audhild. I doubt Thoron found him during the storm, and it wasn't too long after the storm that we first saw Drake. Audhild got there fairly quickly after that. I'm not sure what he wants, but I don't think he wants to hurt me." I watch his unmoving form on the ground.

"Regardless." Audhild sniffs. "It goes against everything a dragon is to attack as he did. Rogue or not, he must be held accountable."

Grandfather's laugh is derisive. "I thought we were going to give him the benefit of the doubt and work to train him in the way he should go."

"Don't try using my wisdom against me, old man. He

attacked the Kinsman's chosen one after he was given leniency. There is no doubt left." Audhild stands and strides off toward the doorway. "I need to clear my mind. I'll be back later."

With a swing of her arms, she changes into her magnificent red form and flies off.

"And what're we supposed to do with him if he wakes up?" Grandfather spits out angrily to the empty air.

Fear skittles along my spine. "Will those chains hold him?"

Grandfather pours out his drink on the flames, almost extinguishing them. "They should. They're from Far Starl and used to confine the more violent of their species. But, then again, he got free once already. I need to check on something in my library." He takes a hunk of meat off one of the rabbits and leaves, heading up the stairs.

Lucas and I glance at each other. His face is as tense as his posture. "Hungry?" he asks as he removes the sticks and browned meat.

My stomach twists, though I'm not sure if it's with hunger or something else. However, I refuse to reject what he was so proud to catch. "Yes."

I choke down as much as I can handle while watching Drake. Before I finish, he wakes. He tries to raise his hands to his head but is surprised by the chains. He swivels around and catches sight of us watching him.

"He's not too happy about this turn of events, is he?" Lucas almost gloats. "Serves him right for attacking you." He throws a bone into the embers of the pit.

An idea starts to form. "I'd like to try to see into his mind again."

Lucas slides around on the ground to face me. The dried leaves of his gifted clothing tickle my arm. "No. He's too dangerous. What if he can break out of the chains? I can't stop him."

I reach up to caress his cheek. "He can't do anything with those chains on. Grandfather wouldn't have left us alone with him if he was dangerous, right? If it seems like something's wrong, I promise to stop. Okay?" When he doesn't appear to be giving in, I try again. "I have to try. I may be able to figure out what he wants."

He frowns and then seems to come to a decision. "Fine. But I'm going to be right beside you." He picks up the dagger Audhild had dropped by the fire.

We walk over to the dragon, who doesn't look happy. I reach up to touch his face and he flinches away from me. "I won't hurt you unless you do something you shouldn't." My hands are alight, and for once, I don't wish it away. I want the dragon to know I have some power left.

I reach out once more, and when my hands come into contact, I'm back in the vision. Dragon kingdom. Thoron. Magic fight. Passage. I'm trying to take in other details I may have missed before and I'm certain I see shadows of something moving in the background in the passage. Hunched figures, long, webbed feet. But I don't get a good look because I'm in Drake's point of view. The tree is less vibrant. Then, the vision swings to the doorway, and I—we're in the storm again.

Drake searches for the other dragon that some inner intuition tells him is there, and he comes upon me in my firebird form.

I've never seen myself as a bird. I've seldom seen my reflection. It's strange to be viewing myself from someone else's eyes. I'm much larger than I feel when I'm flying. My feathers gleam silver as if they have their own light. Lucas is with me, and though I see his light-filled aura, he's not nearly as bright as I am.

The mer-girl's words about me shining like the sun make more sense now.

An intense need to get to me overwhelms the male dragon. I'm the one. I can set him free. I'm the only one who can.

Understanding dawns. I open my eyes and murmur, "Release, be free."

The chains drop to the ground beside him.

Lucas shouts, but I don't hear what he says. Light encompasses Drake, and he's lifted from the ground and into the air. His arms spread wide as he's suspended. Light glimmers from his eyes and a magical barrier like a snakeskin sheds off him. It disappears like mist into the air and Drake drops to his feet on the ground.

"At last!" his voice is deep and resonant. He grabs me and pulls me toward him.

Lucas roars in anger and I'm flung to the ground. My ability hums in my gut and then is yanked from me, leaving me chilled. When I glance up, Lucas has changed forms but he's as big as the dragon-man is tall. His inky black feathers are as long as my arm. He stands with his white bib against Drake's chest.

My mouth is wide with a silent scream at the change in Lucas.

15

Drake holds his hands out in a placating manner. "Whoa, whoa! I meant no harm or dishonor." The grit on the ground crunches as he lowers himself to his knees and bows his head. "Please. She freed me. I was overexcited."

I put my hand on Lucas's strained neck.

He lets out a shrill shriek.

"It's okay. He wasn't trying to do anything except thank me."

Lucas fluffs his feathers and, with a snap of his beak at the dragon, is changed back into a man. He runs a hand across his shirt, which is stretched tight across his shoulders. "There are other ways to thank someone."

Drake glances up at him, and though he tries to look remorseful, I can tell he is bursting with pleasure at having the spell removed. "My deepest apologies. I didn't realize."

"Realize what?" I ask.

Still kneeling, Drake lowers his head more. "It is dangerous to come between a dragon and their bonded mate. That was not my intention."

I flick my hand up to stop him. "Uh, hold on. Mate? You don't mean what I think you do." I agree that Lucas and I share a unique bond. But we weren't *mated*. Heat steals across my cool cheeks.

Lucas places a hand on my tense shoulder. "I don't believe Drake meant mate in the intimate sense. Did you?" An underlying threat darkens his voice.

Shock spreads across Drake's face. "More apologies. With dragons, those who are bonded are soul mates, matched for life." His lips twist. "It's hard to know how to say something when your traditions are different. I mean no offense."

"Fine." Lucas stretches the collar of his tunic. He still stands ramrod straight, leaning over the other male. "Our tradition is to keep our hands to ourselves unless we have permission. Find another way to express your gratitude."

On one hand, I've never seen Lucas so jealous. On the other, I like the fact he stood up for me. The tension, however, is too thick for my liking.

"Please stand, Drake. You're making me uncomfortable." I turn to Lucas. "Are you okay? I've never seen you change into such a large bird."

"I'm unsure." His face is still red, but the color is waning. *"We'll have to discuss it in private."* He mindspeaks to me without taking his eyes off Drake. "But, I'm fine except I feel too big for my skin right now."

I rub my hand over his arm, concerned. "You do look like you've grown. Is that normal?"

"Not that I'm aware. But, having had my abilities delayed on Tenebris, this could be normal. Like a growth spurt. We'll have to ask." I notice that he doesn't apologize, however.

Turning to Drake, I try to keep the worry over Lucas's sudden change out of my mind. He's still bent over and avoiding our gazes. "The mage that attacked you and forced you into the passage. Was that his spell?"

Drake slowly stands, his hands still out appeasingly, his eyes on Lucas. "Yes. It surprised me as our guardians spell us to keep us docile, unable to use our abilities when we hatch. I was one of the few who were resistant and I was supposed to be killed, but I managed to escape and become rogue. However, this mage's spell bound me to my dragon form in a way that shouldn't have worked. He is not someone I want to meet again."

His mustache twitches. "And then Audhild broke through the power keeping me in one form. It was wonderful. I still couldn't speak to you, however. So, you see? I had to get your attention."

"Audhild does have that unique ability to force the change." I agree with him. "That doesn't explain why you attacked us."

"You broke it. The mage's spell is gone!" Drake grows excited again. "I can't thank you enough."

My patience grows thin. "But why did you attack us? You risked so much. And Audhild is cross with you." I move aside while he dodges for the last of the meat on the sticks and begins to devour the last scraps on the bones. I knew he was slim, but he must be starving as well.

"Oh, this tastes so good. I haven't eaten in a unicorn's age." He drops the bones into the fire as Lucas did. "Is there any more?"

Unicorns?

Lucas steps in front of me. "Now hold on. Why did you attack everyone?"

Drake shrugs. "To break the Perdant spell the mage put on me. So I can talk with you." He holds a finger up. "And it worked, didn't it? It's glorious being set free." He turns a circle on the stone floor and then stops to face us. "By the way, my name is Rekspire, not Drake. Is there any more food?"

"*Audhild? You need to return to help us with your other dragon.*" I send out with my mind, hoping she will return to help with Drake-Rekspire. To the dark dragon, I ask, "Why would I not touch you unless I thought you were dangerous? Isn't that the opposite of what would happen?"

His face scrunches up. "Because guardians don't touch you unless you're violent and then only to put the trackers and spell marks on you." He turns to show me a raised mark on the back of his neck. It's a circle with a symbol inside of it that reminds me of the brands farmers would use on their cattle.

"Spell marks? Do you have a tracker?" I recall how painful Nyle's tracker had been.

"No, they weren't able to. But this is the mark they put on me when I hatched to keep me from changing into a human. It keeps us compliant, but it doesn't work after we change. So, immediately after we hatch, it's placed on us."

"What happens if a dragon changes first?" Lucas questions him, holding the dagger as if he doesn't fully trust Rekspire yet.

"They're killed and disposed of." Grandfather answers from the stairway. His eyes are intent upon the dragon man.

Rekspire blanches and then recovers. "Yes. I escaped. I was one of the stronger ones. I fought the handlers and the guardians, injuring them so I could get free. The other three rogues with me didn't make it. I mourned them before I went into hiding among a dozen others of my kind."

I'm appalled. "That's awful." A thought occurs to me. "How old are you, Rekspire?"

"Old? I don't understand. I have been in hiding for many rotations of the wintertide."

Before I can ask, Grandfather answers my question. "Wintertide is the cold season on Far Starl. A dormant season, it happens once a year for three months until the Springtide brings the thaw. That's when the dragon eggs are hatched. Then they're fully trained by the next wintertide."

"So, if you were in hiding, how did my father find you?" I ask.

Rekspire frowns. "There was a battle for dominance among the stronger dragons. Many were killed. I hid until the newly crowned junta, our dragon leader, and his followers left for the fertile valley. The guardians never check the bone yards. No one ever goes there. I sensed him before he showed up. He was gathering bones. He attacked when he saw me, but my hide doesn't take magic signatures. At least I didn't think so. I fled to the mother tree and fell into it while trying to escape. I didn't know where I was, only that I needed to get away from the evil man. It was there that he put the Perdant spell on me. Next thing I knew, I ended up here."

Grandfather whistles low. "You're not safe here."

"And I was safe before?" Rekspire's deep voice rumbles.

"What is going on? Why am I being summoned?" Audhild lands outside of the mountain opening, turning immediately into her woman form. Her footsteps grit against the stony floor and her eyes snap a dangerous red.

Grandfather steps in front of us. "Tambrynn released your drake from Thoron's Perdant spell."

The fire dragon huffs past him with a swish of her partial skirt on her way to Rekspire. "Explain." She levels a finger at the dragon-man.

Rekspire's adam's apple bobs before he speaks. "I only wished to be released. I meant no true harm. I wouldn't have done anything. It was only a threat." His last words end in a small voice, choked, like a child who's been reprimanded.

"You raised a weapon to a Sovereign, an action punishable by death, and you threatened the Kinsman's chosen."

Audhild's eyes flash, her dark skin brightening with an angry flush. "Even rogues have laws by which they live. Do not tell me you are ignorant of those laws. There. Is. NO. EXCUSE!"

Power flows from her words, rattling the cave walls. Rocks and dust tumble to the ground. My eyes widen as smoke leaks from her nostrils. Rekspire, for his part, is chagrined. His head hangs low, the excited energy he'd had earlier dampened by Audhild's reprimand.

"I hate to be the voice of reason here." Grandfather moves slowly toward both dragons, but far enough to the side to remain out of reach.

"Then don't," Audhild roars at him.

I flinch even though I'm farther back. I knew the fire dragon was fierce, but until this moment I hadn't witnessed exactly how powerful. I'm glad now that I've remained in her good graces.

Grandfather seems unaffected by the dragon's ire. "Even so, I feel I must intercede. He has given us new information about Thoron and his latest actions, which may prove helpful. Should he not be acknowledged for that?" Grandfather stops a couple of steps away from the two.

Audhild takes a visible breath before turning back to Rekspire. "What news is this?"

Rekspire's hands shake as he wrings them. "H—he was stealing bones from Far Starl. Using some strange form of ceremony to extract the magic from the marrow. It was shocking to watch and I'm afraid he caught me witnessing it. He attacked, chasing me through the mother tree into the passage and then here."

"And this is significant why?" she demands, some of the redness leaving her cheeks. "We already know he uses dragon's magic to stoke his dark powers."

"We now know where he's going to replenish."

Grandfather's shoulders droop. "Which—" He hesitates. His eyes turn watery. "I believe I know who Thoron is and how he got the key."

Audhild narrows her gaze at him. "Elaborate."

"It all started—" Grandfather doubles over, crying out in pain.

Howls sound. It's loud enough that they are within sight of the mountain opening.

Something tugs at my stomach. I clutch my gut. I remember this sensation—a hostile beckoning. My father used it on me in that cottage on Tenebris. "It's Thoron. He must be close by."

Lucas cradles me to his body. "Are you okay?"

The pulling intensifies and I'm bent over panting. "I've been better."

"What do we do?" Panic fills Lucas's voice.

"How did you escape him the last time?" Audhild asks.

I push out with my ability, slapping at the force in my mind and directing it away from us, much like knocking an arrow away from its target. I'm released and the pressure is gone. I heave out a breath. "We surprised him by flying away. I'm sure that wouldn't work a second time. He'd be prepared for it. So, I tried to lead him away by pushing against his magic." I turn toward Grandfather who seems to be recovering as well. "Will the stones and your displacement spells work in case I'm not powerful enough?"

His strained face is pale. "They should." He shakes his head. "But his presence shouldn't have bothered me so much behind these barriers. He's getting stronger. He must've refueled after losing track of Rekspire. And with all of those bones, he has an endless supply."

Audhild clears her throat. "You were about to tell us who he is?"

Grandfather hastens by her without answering. He has a slight limp in his walk. "We need to check to be sure everything is in place."

I hurry after him hoping to help in some way.

Grandfather inspects the walls, where there are symbols much like the ones on Tenebris's cavern walls. He then checks the stones. Now that I concentrate, I can feel the vibrations they make. Curiously, I hadn't noticed it before.

He stretches, grunting in relief. "Everything's in place."

"Why do you think he's here? How'd he find us?" I ask no one in particular.

"The magic you used to access Drake's memories." Audhild cranes her head at the edge of the displacement spell. "I don't see him or sense him now. You don't think he has one of the eldrin's apatestone necklaces, do you?"

Her words make fear crawl up my spine. Thoron could travel almost anywhere if he had one.

Lucas steps by me and glances outside at the bright, sunny landscape. "I could do a fly-by and check."

Panic joins my fear and they dig in with claws that show me no mercy. "No!" I hadn't meant to, but I push my ability into that word. I take a moment to collect myself. "I'm sorry."

Lucas brushes his hand across my cheek. "It's okay. I understand your hesitation." He chuckles. "I used to feel it all the time when I was your Watcher."

I try to smile convincingly back at him. "You're still my Watcher."

Grandfather pats Lucas on his shoulder. "But she's probably right, my lad. It wouldn't do if Thoron spots you. If he's fueled up on dragon bones, he'll sense anything magical nearby. We'll have to wait him out. It's not like we won't know when he's close by. And I don't think he's patient enough to wait long."

A small measure of relief releases the claws of terror on my spine, and I can breathe easier.

"Now that's decided, tell me all about who you think the death mage is and how he has access to Far Starl." Audhild spins and dashes back inside the cave. "I'm anxious to figure this mystery out."

16

We all settle around the table on Grandfather's side of the keep. An apologetic Rekspire hangs out on the staircase to warn us in case Thoron or any other creature comes near the entrance.

"I am assured he can't get through the protections. He was probably probing the area. We will need to be most careful for a while, though." Grandfather stirs some of his ground chickory into a mug of water. I grimace at the concoction and take a drink of lukewarm water from one of the canteens instead.

"About Thoron?" Audhild taps her pointed fingernails on the wooden tabletop. They share some sort of mutual look, and she takes his mug in both her hands. Red glows from them and the liquid bubbles inside the cup, its steam escaping into the air.

"Thank you." He takes a cautious sip of it and then sits down beside me at the table. "It all started the year I did my trials." Grandfather recounts all of the details he'd told me about his trip to Far Starl with the other council hopeful,

Jarmon. "And when I left, I tried to find Jarmon, but he had worked his way into one of the guardian's confidences. I couldn't get past their security to let him know I was leaving. It was then that I knew he planned to stay."

"What has any of this to do with Thoron?" Audhild starts to rap her fingertips on the table once more.

"I was getting to that, your scaliness." He disregards the fire dragon's glower. "Many years later, Jarmon turned back up on Anavrin. He'd been blacklisted on Far Starl and had lost everything. Except for his necklace—the priceless key to the kingdom of Far Starl that allowed him back into Anavrin. He chose to come home and try to reposition himself as a Councilmaster since he had spent years enmeshed in Far Starlian politics and had learned a great deal about their history. He wanted to spill all their secrets for a price."

"So, he became a traitor to Far Starl after he betrayed Anavrin's Council. Go on." Audhild's dark forehead creases and she shifts in her seat.

"Stop interrupting me and I'll get to the point." Grandfather turns from the fire dragon to me. "Jarmon confided in me that he had brought a woman here shortly after our trip to Far Starl, around the time Madrigal was pregnant with Cadence. This woman was also pregnant with Jarmon's child. On Far Starl only those sanctified in reproducing had the right to have children and there were no means available to end the pregnancy. At least none the woman would agree to."

Grandfather's eyes stare off. "He would've been punished when the woman revealed he was the father. And I have no doubt she would have. They didn't love each other. I don't think Jarmon could love anyone but himself. He had grand aspirations on Far Starl." He shakes his lowered head. "He was always too ambitious. I threatened to tell the Counsel, who would've banished him. He didn't care. He still had his key when he left me."

He takes a drink of his obnoxious brew. "Anyway, years later Jarmon was searching for this child. Wanted to get to know them, he said. A week later he was dead and no one ever located his necklace. As far as I know, there had only ever been two necklaces. Mine and his, which is why his betrayal would've cost him any position on the Council. That was about five years ago, almost six now. Right before Thoron attacked the Sanctuary city."

"Does that mean Thoron is Jarmon's son?" I ask, trying hard to follow.

Grandfather spreads his hands out on the table. "It is the most likely explanation for how Thoron would have the key to unlock the Zoe Tree to Far Starl. It could be a fluke, though. Thoron could have come across Jarmon, who was quite boastful, and he could've attacked him then and got the necklace."

"Or it could be nothing at all." Audhild considers, a far-off look in her eyes.

"It could."

I consider his words. "If my father is Jarmon's son, does it change anything we know about him?"

"I'm unsure. I never found out anything more about the pregnant woman. I only knew that she was from Far Starl and that Jarmon deserted her in this kingdom without much ceremony or support. She would've had to raise a child on her own in an unfamiliar kingdom that is unfriendly to half-breeds, which Thoron would've been, even though dragon guardians are considered eldrin overall. Without Jarmon there to prove it, the woman and child wouldn't have been accepted into the Sanctuary."

He rubs his cheek. "If this hypothesis is correct, it would

explain how Thoron knew how to harness the power of the dragons. It also answers the question of why he attacked the Sanctuary. Jarmon had been tortured—" Grandfather's shoulders curl in and a look I can't decipher crosses his face. "He may have revealed some of the eldrin's secrets to his son to appease him. Knowing Jarmon, he would've thought he could handle any situation, bargain his way out of it."

"You mean his cowardly instincts of self-preservation above anything else." Audhild huffs.

Grandfather's silence speaks to his agreement. "Thoron is already dangerous and growing more so if he's allowed to keep returning to the dragon kingdom."

Lucas breaks his silence. "So, how do we stop him?"

Grandfather gives him a direct look. "I wish I knew."

Audhild pounds the table with her fist. "That is not helpful. We need to make a list of the things we know about Thoron and start from there." She gathers a stack of white parchment sheets. "One, he was a death mage before his father returned." She writes in elegant penmanship on the first page. "He clearly knew some secrets, possibly from his mother who could have told him about dragons and their significance."

Grandfather breaks in. "The only problem with that theory is that Far Stralians don't believe that dragons have magical blood and bones."

I clear my throat. "His mother might not have told him. What if growing up here he was told fairy tale stories as a child? Could he have figured it out on his own?"

"The myth of the fire rocks." Lucas snaps his fingers. "Remember, Tambrynn? I told you about how they traveled from the Bloodthorn Forest down the Stream of Marmara and past the Capricious Falls. The light on the Zoe Tree's island is supposed to be from a fossilized bone."

Audhild clicks her tongue. "Even if he heard stories, there's a gap between hearing stories and turning into a death mage."

We're all silent for a moment.

Grandfather takes another sip and swallows. "The motive is what we're missing."

I think back on all of the events in my life and consider the ones that I wanted revenge for the worst. "Farmer Tucker's son."

"What?" Grandfather asks, his thick eyebrows furrowed.

"There were many people who did things to me over the years. But Farmer Tucker's son's lie was the reason for my first beating. Because of him I was first declared cursed. I wanted revenge against him the most."

Sadness and understanding glimmer from the dark depths of Lucas's eyes.

Audhild's expression doesn't change. There's no pity, but there's also no judgment. "How will that help, youngling?"

Grandfather leans back in the chair. "Perhaps if we figure out the genesis of his evil it might give us some insight into why he does what he does. Maybe find the source of his power and remove it."

Source of power? "I don't understand."

"It's quite simple." Audhild almost smiles. "Like the froggen's pearl, the mage has a talisman, a source that he used to become what he is today. Destroy it and you will eliminate enough of his power to defeat him."

I blink. "That sounds more hopeful than anything. Does it have to be jewelry like the necklace the froggen wore?"

Audhild snorts. "It could be anything. A rock. A shoe. A mirror. But usually, it is something of value or has special meaning. You wouldn't want to forget or misplace your talisman, now would you?"

Grandfather sits up straighter. "That's it. We need to go

back to where I confronted Thoron all those years ago. At Lowborn in the Marshlands." He hesitates and his hands shake. "Maybe we can find some sort of clue there."

"Are you sure?" I ask. "Is it something Lucas and I can do on our own?"

He taps his hand against his mug. "I'm grateful for your concern, Granddaughter. It's been many years since I faced Thoron. I've hidden for far too long. Besides, I'm the only one who knows the paths that lead to the tree village where the outcasts lived. Might still live, for all I know. There's no map I could give you or draw you. I will have to go by memory alone."

"What of the effect he has on you, old man?" Audhild's words are tempered by a softness in her tone. Perhaps she is as concerned as I am.

His chest raises with a deep breath which he slowly lets out. "I always knew I'd have to face him again. I assure you the thought isn't welcome but necessary." He downs the last of his chickory and clunks the cup on the table. "We'll spend the rest of the evening researching shields and powerful protections. I believe I have Cadence's papers and books for reference. The Shadowlands where the marshes are located is about a day's journey from here. We can leave after first light and should reach them by nightfall."

———

"So, what exactly are swamps?" I ask Audhild while searching in a book titled, *Fasting, Prayer, and Supplication.*

She flips a page on her volume. "They are large, wet, and muddy."

I picture the nomad women rolling around in the illusion's muddy stream. "That doesn't sound so bad."

Her glowing red eyes settle on me. "They are miserable.

Brackish water for miles. Trees grow right up out of the sluggish mess while the depths hide land like a treasure. The only place to survive is in the trees."

"Like bird's nests?"

"Something similar. Houses in tree villages are built among swaying walkways. They aren't easily spotted due to the curtains of moss that grows from the limbs." She makes a guttural clicking sound. "Not to mention the ghostly fog that comes off the water."

"Don't scare them." Grandfather interrupts her. "The villages aren't that doom and gloom. Plus, there are no such things as ghosts. It's nothing more than swamp fumes."

Audhild lets out an agitated snarl. "Is it too much of a stretch for you, former Councilman, to believe in something you cannot see? Must you cling to your absurd traditions and doctrines? I thought you'd moved beyond them." She slams the book shut. "You have no spirit sight to know the difference between mist and specter, so let me confirm that there are lost souls in that swamp. There are also spectral guards we must get past to even enter the area. Tambrynn will be able to sense them. Do you not want her forewarned before we arrive?"

I hold my hand up. "Hold on. There are ghosts there?"

"No!" yells Grandfather.

"Yes!" Audhild roars at the same time.

Lucas is wide-eyed. "I've heard stories of the swamp witch, Haga—something or other. Is that what you're talking about?"

"The Hulda, guardian of the swamp crypt." Audhild snaps in Grandfather's direction.

Grandfather's face darkens. "There is no such creature. It's a child's tale to keep the young ones away from the dangers of the murky water."

"On Far Starl, there are places where the spiritual realm, particularly malevolent beings, reign." Rekspire answers from the stairway, startling all of us. "Beg your pardon, but I overheard your conversation, and it's getting dark out. I didn't think there would be any more concern to watch the entry."

Grandfather blows out a frustrated breath. "That dragon needs a bell around his neck."

"What do you mean 'malevolent beings reign'?" Lucas asks. Trepidation seeps through our bond.

Rekspire clears his throat. "Dragons, not the domesticated ones since they're mindless slaves, but the rogue ones, can sense the presence of evil. Often there is nothing there, so it goes to reason that when it's not physical, it's something beyond. If it helps, the Far Starlians don't believe in it, either."

Audhild's expression is triumphant.

"It does not help. Are you two mindspeaking? Conspiring against me?" Grandfather's face is as red as Audhild's dress now.

I have to wonder again about their alliance since it seems as if there is more animosity than friendship or agreement.

"We've done no such thing." Smoke trails out of Audhild's nose. "You, old man, still have room to learn instead of believing along a narrow line. I've been alive ten of your lifetimes. There are many insights lost through the ages. You know this, yet you doubt my intelligence? There *is* more to life and death than this transient world. Belief in a greater being such as the Kinsman should convince you of that. He places guardians where his wisdom leads for reasons we can't begin to fathom. Or do you think the Kinsman is simply a man or a fairy tale?"

"No," Grandfather grunts. "But I don't for one minute believe souls are floating around in the hither and nither. Nor do I believe in malicious forces being tied to any physical realm. Nothing will convince me that the Kinsman would have an evil force guarding anything for any reason. It simply isn't so."

Audhild's face glows as if it's going to explode into flames. "Then you are more of a fool than I took you for. Good luck, youngling, Watcher. You're going to need it if you rely upon his limited comprehension." With a flip of her split skirt, she strides by Rekspire and out of the keep.

17

Rekspire's gaze turns golden for a moment and then flickers back to his manly, dark one. He dances from one foot to the other. "I am unsure what to do without Audhild's presence."

"Stay on her side of the keep." Grandfather brushes the air with one hand, indicating the direction he should go. "We have much to do. I don't want you filling our heads with dotty tales and myths."

I send the elemental dragon a sympathetic glance. Having been disliked for being different, I understand the dragon's hesitation at the cold dismissal.

My mind whirs with how to address it without making my grandfather cross. "You once told me that years ago you wouldn't have believed many things that have come to pass. Is there a chance that Audhild is correct or that she understands things you don't have access to as an eldrin?" I rest my hand atop his and speak carefully, kindly.

He takes a deep breath and blows it out. "I'm unused to

being confronted by you. I find I can't fight you like I can the dragon." He chuckles. "She is prickly and fiery in temper, isn't she?"

I smile back at him. "And you're not?"

"Certainly not!" Humor shines from his face. His ears, which have been pricked to attention during his discussion with Audhild, lower and relax. He tops my hand with his other one and squeezes it. "Now, let's get to researching, or we'll never be prepared."

I glance up to see a fond expression on Lucas's face. He hugs me when Grandfather walks off in search of Mother's books and papers. "I know that was hard, confronting your grandfather. You did splendidly. He's fond of you."

"As I have grown of him." My throat constricts, making it hard to swallow. "It is hard. I've longed for a family for so long that I fear I'll do something to ruin this chance I've been given. It's been wonderful having him with us." I lean into Lucas's embrace, relishing the moment.

"If only time could stand still and we could stay and learn everything that's here to know." Lucas's whisper tickles my ear.

The hair at my nape prickles, sending sparks down my body, and I'm reminded once more of my desire for my Watcher. However, Grandfather is mere steps away, so I stifle the heat blooming in my heart.

"What was it you were going to tell me in private after you confronted Rekspire for touching me?" I speak low.

Lucas takes a deep breath and gazes around. "I think—I wasn't trying to. I may have used some of your ability when I turned into the giant bird." He scrubs a hand through his hair.

"Oh," I say, surprised. "I did feel something when it happened, so I think you're right. What do you think it means?"

Lucas clasps his hands and squeezes them. "I'm not completely sure. It might mean we can share power. The thing is I don't remember how I did it. If indeed I did. My emotions got away from me. My apologies."

I place my hand on his cheek. "It's all right. I don't mind you standing up for me. Taking care of me. I endeavor to do the same for you."

He kisses my palm. Pleasure zings up my arm.

We sit in companionable silence for a moment before Grandfather drops a parchment pad on the table in front of me. "This was Cadence's journal. It might give some insight. I'm going to read through her old textbooks to see what's there. Would you like to join me, Lucas? There are several."

Taking the hint, Lucas joins Grandfather, and I flip the journal open. I recognize Mother's penmanship immediately. We'd had little access to parchment, but mother would write in dirt and use coal on treebark when we had the chance. I'd always admired the swirling, curvy letters she'd create. The writing blurs as tears gather in my eyes.

I sniff them back and wipe my eyes dry. I start to read and most of it is about her friends and the outings she had during school. I marvel that even though the eldrin may have done many things wrong, they allowed women to have an education —something unheard of on Tenebris. Yes, the fine ladies had tutors in music, art, and sewing. But peasant women had to learn at the feet of others who had perfected their trades before them. I never understood the inequality, especially when some women worked doubly hard as some of the men. And yet they would be paid less than a quarter the wages.

I'm halfway through the book before I find some information on the protections she had been studying.

"I believe I found something," I call out to the others, my eyes never leaving my mother's notes.

"What is it?" Grandfather's hand is warm on my shoulder.

"Something Mother made to wear for protection." I read: "Take these stones and weave them into a bracelet which you place on your wrist for protection. Obsidian to block the negative, smoky quartz to ground you, amethyst to purify, pearl to seal your faith, and finally, a tourmaline to shield. Set over a fire in a ceramic bowl and sprinkle the flames liberally with the grounded star of kinsman blooms, bark from the eternal tree, and an oyster shell from the sea. Repeat seven times, *sanco – sciath – nequitim – maligna – perfecator*. The smoke will infuse the stones with intent as you speak the incantation. When the fire is out, wash the stones in purified water to cleanse and establish their purpose. Set them in a metal chain mold with the melted extract of kinstone so no magic will deter them. Wear the bracelet for protection wherever you go."

Grandfather's smile is wide. "I recall this was the first project she made during her tenth level. She was so accomplished that she'd moved ahead two levels and was the youngest girl in her class. I had to find several of the ingredients with her." His grin slips. "It took us two weeks to finish it."

My heart sinks. "Oh."

Lucas pulls the chair on my other side out and sits down. He has a serious-looking textbook in his hands. "You found this, though. I'm sure there are many other more advanced protections you have yet to find."

Grandfather's next squeeze is more consolation than comfort. "Right. I'll keep looking."

The room grows quiet again as we search. There are many different protections in the journal, but as with the first bracelet, there are also many elements to acquire to put it together. I sigh heavily. "I didn't know creating a protection spell was so complicated."

Grandfather rubs his eyes. "That's because you are so powerful already, you don't need much in the form of protection. And somehow Cadence's prayer, when we were being attacked by Thoron, imbued you with some of her essence. I believe it is the shield you manifest when attacked. It's very similar to Cadence's magic."

"It is?" I ask. Both of them bow their heads in agreement. "I suspected, but I don't remember seeing her use her protection magic except when the beasts attacked and killed her. And I don't remember much then since I was crying and Mother was trying to hide me behind her."

Tears prick my eyes once again at the memory of the attack and the time since. "If only I could use my ability to call everything I need to make the bracelet."

Grandfather's head pops up from the book he is reading. "I hadn't thought of that."

Lucas's brows are furrowed. "Wouldn't Thoron sense her magic again? Maybe come back?"

"I do have some of the items in this room. I'd need to find them." Grandfather glimpses around, then back at me. "Or you could call them."

"Which ones?" I ask, my heart beating faster.

"The stones in particular. The Star of the Kinsman and the bark are outside of the mountain entry so we can gather them quickly. Also, I can purify the water from the springs. Most of the work is already done on it. The last element is the incantation." He frowns. "The only thing I don't have is the kinstone chain and the shell."

"Excuse me." Rekspire breaks into our conversation. "I have a shell. I thought it was pretty." He takes something from his pants pocket and holds it out. "Is this what you need?"

The chair Lucas sits in rubs against the floor as he stands up. "Aren't the shackles used on Rekspire kinstone? Could we somehow make a crude chain by melting it?"

Grandfather's eyes gleam. "Possibly. Tambrynn, work on the stones first."

I wasn't sure what all of the stones were, but it was never completely necessary to understand what I needed when I called. It was the purpose behind it that came through.

Hands held loose in my lap, I close my eyes and focus. I *call* out in my mind, picturing Mother's bracelet to call on the stones. There's a pull of some kind, like a whisper. I turn my head to the left, my eyes still closed. I continue seeking the protection stones, and I sink into a deep sense of awareness. They're there, on the edge of my consciousness. The scent of lavender and roses brushes against my nose. Mother used those flowers to make lotions which she used all of the time.

"Mother?" I *call* out, yanking at the invisible thread that speaks to me in words I can't understand nor truly hear. It's instinct, much like when I was in danger and would call out. Something pulls back, though. Dark and angry, it probes my ability. Hand up, I push away the energy holding the stones hostage, keeping me from having them.

In a rush, the black presence forms a face. It's Thoron, and he's furious. Red glows where his eyes should be. He screams and the shadow around him breaks into pieces, reforming into insects that squeal and scuttle toward me.

I shriek as the darkness jabs at my protective sphere. All the detestable flavors I've ever tasted mix together and flood my mouth. I gag. The presence coats my body. I jerk to get free of the assault.

"Join them. Let them in. Let *me* in." The voice is back, confirming its evil source. It's not coming directly from

Thoron, but it is connected to him. I focus on it. "Go away!" I push as much of my energy into my intentions as I know how. Like a worm, the bleak shadow slithers back toward my father, who becomes more incensed. His creatures eat at my glowing, blue circle like ravenous bugs, binging on my power like ticks. They're almost inside my light now. Horrified, I push with what's left of my might to keep them away.

Grandfather and Lucas yell at me from a distance and I bound back and away from my father's reach. He's still howling in anger when I fall backward.

Tears soak my face when I open my eyes. My heart is beating so fast it hurts. Something touches me and I yelp and scramble away before realizing it's Lucas's hand.

"Tambrynn? My lady, are you okay?" He's also breathing hard, reaching shakily toward me.

"Mmm." My stomach seizes. I whimper before heaving air out of my chest. A pot scrapes across the floor toward me. I bend over it and throw up. Rancid-tasting bile burns my throat and makes me gag once more, remembering the horrid taste of my father's magic. I cough until there's nothing left.

"Here. Drink this and wash your mouth out." Grandfather's voice is shaky despite his calmness.

"Thank you." It hurts to speak. I rinse well, spit, and then drink. The liquid soothes my raw throat. I'm glad of the small relief. "That was awful. What happened?"

"You tell us." Grandfather lifts my hand. I'm clutching Mother's bracelet.

"Wh—where?" I stammer. Had I called *the* actual piece of jewelry?

"That's Cadence's." Lucas's voice is as shocked as I feel. "How did you call it? It would've been on Tenebris. Possibly buried with her. Did it cross kingdoms?"

"No." I twist it so I can see all of the stones. "It can't be. This one is held together by a cord." I pull my necklace out. It's the same kind of twine-like material, but cruder. I glance up at Grandfather.

Confusion puckers his stretched features. He gently takes the bracelet from me and examines it and glances back up at me. "Tell us what happened."

"I—I was calling for the stones. I could feel them. It's like they wanted to come to me. I thought they were here, in the keep. And then—" I falter, recalling the scent of roses and lavender. "I don't know. It's almost too strange to say."

"You can tell us anything, my lady."

I find strength in Lucas's steady stare. "I think I sensed Mother. I could smell her. It was like she was there. And then a shadow of Thoron emerged. He was angry, pulling back against me. There were insects, and I could taste his evil aura." I cough back into the bucket and take another cleansing drink of water. Both my head and my stomach ache.

"He couldn't have been physically nearby or it would've affected me." Grandfather rolls the stones between his fingers. His breath catches and he chokes. "These are the same stones she and I found." He holds a brown and black stone with a hole in the center. It was larger than the rest of the gems. "She tried to break it in half before I stopped her. It would've negated the grounding effect had she done so."

"But I don't understand how?" My eyes blur once more and I swipe at them so I can see clearly.

"Did you get your mother's effects when she was buried?" Grandfather asks, his voice softening.

"I wasn't allowed. I was told anything of value was sold to pay for her burial. I didn't attend her funeral if there was one." I think back to those blurry, grief-riddled memories. "I don't recall if she was wearing it when we were attacked. I know she had the ring on a necklace. I never saw it again."

Grandfather's shoulders slump and his demeanor becomes grim. "Perhaps his beasts took it from her when they attacked? That would explain how Thoron got it. It doesn't explain how you could've retrieved it from him. I can't imagine he'll be happy about it."

18

Grandfather closes his hand over the bracelet. "We need to cleanse it in case it took on any of Thoron's essence. I'll have to gather some of the spring water." He grabs an empty bucket and hustles toward the stairway.

Lucas and I choose to fly across the maze of stairs and tunnels. We change back and wait for Grandfather and Rekspire to join us.

The fire is banked and cold, and the sun is setting low in the sky. Audhild is nowhere to be seen, though it doesn't surprise me.

"What do you think it means that I could call the bracelet from so far away?" I ask Lucas.

"Was it far away?" His eyes narrowed in thought. "I'm unsure Bennett should go out to get the water in the spring. What if Thoron shows up?"

"I'll be careful. And as for your question, Tambrynn. It means you're more powerful than your mother ever was." Grandfather emerges from the stairs, his chest heaving. He turns to Lucas. "Gather some more sticks and wood and rebuild the fire." Rekspire almost topples into him in his haste to follow.

"Dragons," Grandfather mutters as he rushes for the entry. He hesitates at the edge of the stone barrier, his glance sweeping the area. "Do you sense him, Granddaughter?"

There's no pulling sensation. No darkness anywhere. "No."

We all hurry out to the springs. Rekspire and I keep watch while Grandfather and Lucas gather.

Grandfather dips the bucket into the steaming liquid. "Tambrynn, pick the silver-white star-shaped flowers. A handful should do. And Rekspire, if you insist on being here, gather a handful of the bark on the Wehyah tree at the entry. Crumble it up and meet us back at the fire."

I jump to follow his instructions, though I continue to scan our surroundings to find the flowers. I locate several that bloom around the base of the mountain, but the silver-white ones shaped like a star are easy to spot. In no time, I have all we need.

Grandfather dunks the bracelet into a spring, muttering something I can't hear. I dance from one foot to the other as I watch over him and his ministrations.

He wrings the cord out when he's finished and grabs my hand to lead me quickly back to the entry. Once there, he takes the flowers and crushes them on a palm-sized, mortar-shaped stone. He adds the shell and bark and grinds them into the flower pulp. On top of that, he wrings the last drops of spring water from the bracelet's cord. The bracelet itself he drops into the mixture and chants words similar to the ones he muttered at the pool.

"Now Tambrynn, take it in your hands and use your flame to burn off any of the corruptions." Grandfather holds the cupped rock out to me. "Clear your mind and think of Cadence. Your motives will purify it back to its original state."

I take the damp jewelry. "What about the cord?"

"That was added after your mother had it. Possibly by Thoron himself. We want nothing left of him or his influence."

"Okay." I hold it to my chest and visualize Mother. Her chestnut hair. The creases around her eyes from smiling and laughing. Her hands always seemed to be dirty from working with plants. I smile to myself, recalling the more favorable memories. Inside, my flame wakens, and I gather it in my hands. It's hot, but it doesn't burn me.

I open my eyes when the heat dies. The cord is ashes in my palms. The stones are glowing with a luster that wasn't there before. I glance up at Grandfather to check and see if it is complete.

He's smiling at me. "You may not realize it, but you controlled your fire most extraordinarily." He pats my shoulder. "I can't help but be hopeful that you are on your way to fully mastering it. Now, let's get some of that kinstone and see if we can restore a makeshift chain."

Rekspire drops the shackles at my feet. Unlike the cruder sets the nomads had, this pair is heavy and well-made. "What do I do?"

Grandfather picks the chains up, rattling them, and studies them. "Hand me one of the stones."

I give him the smoky quartz since it's the biggest stone.

He turns the metal around and studies it and the stones. A bristly scratch to his chin and he hands them back. "We're going to test your abilities. It may not work, but it's worth trying. Take one stone and put it in a hole like the Sacratus staff." He shows me and I take it all from him.

I close my hands around a chain's link and the gem and close my eyes. I picture the metal shrinking down to settle around the stone like Mother's original piece. My hands warm and I squeeze hard, then harder to infuse my will upon the metal. Something warm seeps through my fingers, which are clasped tight. With a final exertion, I open my eyes.

The metal has affixed itself around the stone like a fine piece of jewelry and has melted off the excess kinstone. It pools on the cave floor, cooling into a hardened glob. It is no longer attached to the shackles but is separate and gleaming silver. My heart leaps to realize I've almost completely restored how it looked when Mother owned it. I grin up at Grandfather, Lucas, and Rekspire.

"Ah-yeah. You did it!" Pride flickers in Grandfather's eyes.

"Well done, my lady!" Lucas pats my arm.

Even Rekspire has a grin. He bows. "Well done, Protector and Chosen One."

I blanch at his titles and deference. "Tambrynn, please. And bowing makes me uncomfortable."

The dragon-man starts. "But—you are the Chosen One. The Sovereign decreed it."

Before I can react, Grandfather chuckles low. "She is, but she's unused to such reverence." He holds a hand up before I can argue with him. "Let's not squabble about trivialities. Do you think you can do this four more times?"

My lungs expand as I take a deep breath and blow it out. "Let's get on with it."

I repeat the process, and in the end, I have finished five sets of stones that I link together, making them large enough to fit around my wrist with a simple clasp. "Should it be bigger?" I hand it to Grandfather.

He hooks it around my hand. "It fits. A bit stiffer, perhaps. But it will do the job of protecting you splendidly. Since you mastered that so well, let's see if we can make a couple more, shall we?"

By the time the sun sets, I have located several more of the stones from Grandfather's keep. Grandfather does his part and then I take over once more, making the next bracelets big enough to fit over his and Lucas's wrists. Only four stones are left—obsidian, tourmaline, amethyst, and a shard of pearl for the last attempt. I make it so it fits Rekspire, though it has been soaked in the least amount of the ground-up mixture.

"Are you sure it will work?" I ask as I grasp the metal and attach it to the dragon-man's wrist.

"If it doesn't work fully, it should give him some protections. Being a dragon affords him some security already." Grandfather assures me. "It will enhance his Kinsman-given abilities."

Lucas flies in through the darkened doorway and drops down to the ground. When he changes back, he has several more animals cleaned and ready to put on the fire. "A thanksgiving feast?"

I'd been too wrapped up making the jewelry to realize he'd left. My heart pinches for a brief moment. "Did anyone or anything see you?"

His chest sticks out. "You'd be proud of me. I used all the tricks I know. Nothing saw me, I'm positive." He takes a couple of eggs from his pocket. "And now we can have a real send-off."

———

Morning comes too quickly. I wake to the scent of Grandfather's chickory. I intentionally keep my eyes closed to test my fire. I pull back on the flames, ordering them to leave. When I do open my eyes, I'm heartened not to see my fire.

Grandfather is loading his pack with items. I'm unsure how he can carry it so far when it must have the weight of another person by the time he fills it.

I walk over to sit by him. "Where are Lucas and Rekspire?"

"Good morning, Granddaughter." His smile is genuine.

"They are gathering more canteens. I'm also having Rekspire gather items that should be beneficial in the swamp."

I'm still confused as to what it is we're about to set foot in. "Such as?"

"He's making some lotion from some flowers and herbs to help repel some of the flying insects that plague the bogs. He mentioned to me earlier that though his scales keep most pests away, the area around his eyes, ears, and underside is vulnerable. I thought it might help ease some of the discomfort and protect us from the diseases the bugs carry."

I inwardly blanch, not liking what he's describing. "Shouldn't our bracelets keep us safe from them?" I joke, but there's some hope behind the question.

Grandfather laughs. "If only it were that easy." He finishes packing and gestures toward the dagger on the table and the Sacratus staff leaning next to it. "You might need them for real this time."

Again, I am not inspired by our newest mission. "Besides insects, what dangers do we face?" Not wanting to kindle his anger, I don't mention the ghosts and evil presences we'd discussed briefly the day before.

"Poisonous snakes. A few reptiles to be sure. Stinging plants. That kind of thing. I'm confident you'll manage splendidly." Something about the way he says it doesn't convince me he's being completely truthful, or possibly he's hedging the truth so it doesn't scare me. "Come. We have a long day of travel."

"Would you like me to take this?" I motion to the bag.

"Thank you for your consideration, but no. I have many items that I hesitate to let anyone else near. I can lighten it for short periods." He pats a couple of worn bronze buttons sewn into the fabric I hadn't noticed before. They're hidden on the bottom and in the creases. "Don't tell Audhild. She'd claim I was cheating even though they're eldrin-mandated on each mission pack."

"Grandfather, can I ask you a personal question?"

He stops and peers at me. "Of course."

"What is your relationship with Audhild?" I say quickly so he doesn't get the wrong idea of what I'm asking. "I mean, you're friends one moment and the next you're arguing. I—" I hesitate. "I sense something neither of you talks about."

His smile is there, but it doesn't reflect in his eyes. "You're much too perceptive, Tambrynn." He takes a couple of quick breaths before continuing. "It's a long and complicated story, one I may tell you sometime in the future. Until then, I am not at liberty to divulge our history."

I regret asking immediately. "I'm sorry. I didn't mean to pry."

The tension around his eyes softens. "You are curious and inquisitive. We fail when we stop being so." He pats my hand. "You didn't overstep. It's not only my tale to share. And without her here, well, I don't think it's appropriate to get into. Okay?" He gives my hand a last squeeze, his attention back on securing his pack.

Sensing the conversation is over, and feeling some relief, I grab the Mortifer blade and the Sacratus. I change and fly down to the entry, leaving Grandfather to make his way with his pack.

Unfortunately, his words only make me more curious. Why the fear, or was it anger? It has to be more than just Audhild's permission. It goes deeper than that. It could be personal, something that's embarrassing. But, no. He's already shared several sensitive things with me.

No matter. I acknowledge there's a boundary that I shouldn't cross. And I'm unsure how it makes me feel.

19

Lucas is dousing the fire when I land in the cave. The smoke wafts to the doorway and outside, but the smell lingers. He's put on the leafy clothes Audhild gave him yesterday. Over it, he wears a sleek-looking, hooded cloak, and boots that go up to his knees. He reminds me of a fisherman from Tenebris's North Sea, making me giggle.

He grins back. "Don't laugh too much. You have much the same thing to wear."

I glance to where he points and see the same viny outfit that Audhild gave me, another slick cloak, and a smaller pair of boots. I can't help a quick frown.

"You'll need them." Grandfather's voice echoes before I see him exit the stairs, wearing the same. "We'll be slogging through mud and muck before we can get anywhere near a place to use a boat. Trust me, you'll be glad of them before the day is over."

I cringe at the thought of another boat ride. But, chagrined, I take the clothes and change behind the stairs again. The boots are a tad bit big and, for the first time since losing them, I wish I had my old wool stockings. I glance back at the slippers and decide to put them back on. It's not a perfect fit, but it is better. Hopefully, enough to not wear sores on my feet as the hand-me-down shoes on Tenebris had.

I step back out and find the cave empty, so I walk to the entry and peek outside. All of them stand inside the protective border, surveying the distance, possibly for signs of danger. I'm unsure what they see, or could see, with the sun rising and barely shining across the great landscape beyond the mountain.

Out of the three, I recognize Rekspire, also wearing a dark cape. So, I don my disguise—picturing Mrs. Calvin with her severe features and black hair in a bun at my nape. Perhaps if we're stopped, it will keep me from being seen as infirm again, though being seen as such had had its benefits in Anatolia. Then I turn my mind's eye toward my clothes. Dark brown to match the woods would do, with pants instead of a dress, so I fit in.

A glance down reveals that I changed the look of my clothes this time. I almost squeal with excitement.

"Ready," I state to the men who have their backs to me. I almost laugh at the surprise on their faces. I tap the staff on the gritty ground.

Grandfather is the first to recover. "Well done, Tambrynn! Your disguise is so good, one would think you have djinn blood running through your veins."

My cheeks flush with warmth. "Thank you." I turn to Lucas.

He appears different than he has before, with honey-colored hair, cut short, and a beard a shade darker than his head. "I will never tease you with Farmer Tucker's son's resemblance again." His voice has a thread of gravity to it.

I take his hand, and I realize it's colder than my own. "Have I shocked you?"

"Not at all. You're getting better and it shows." He links our fingers.

I double-check to be sure the dagger is secure about my waist. "Please tell me the trip to the swamp won't wind me as much as the trip to the mountain."

"Your body should have adjusted to the lightness of the oxygen in the air by now," he states as if that answers my question. I take it by his non-answer that it is as far away.

Grandfather collects the stones one by one until they're all gathered into the pocket of his bag. At once, the wind whistles by the old, gnarled tree.

We set off, Grandfather in front with Rekspire taking up the rear. Though it's easier to breathe, I still find that using the staff is helpful to get over the rockier incline.

The sun's brilliance blinds us for the first few hours, and I pull the hood to shade my eyes. By the time we stop to rest, clouds gather on the far horizon behind us.

My bones ache more than I'd like to admit. Our canteen's water is warm but helps quench my thirst anyway. There have been no streams along our path, so no way to cool down. So, any liquid, no matter the temperature, is quite welcome. The sky darkens in the distance. "What do you make of that?" I point.

"Nothing good." Grandfather's eye twitches and he glances away. He sits gingerly on the edge of a downed tree.

"Are you in pain, Bennett?" Lucas asks, his brows furrowed in concern.

"Can you not feel it?" Grandfather grimaces.

Lucas considers. "I do, yes. I had hoped I'd sprained something crawling over the rock-strewn hillside this morn. But with the storm—"

Rekspire wipes his mouth off with his sleeve. "What? What with the storm?"

"Something is happening again. I fear what it means." Grandfather's head is bowed and he stares at the ground. "What I do know is that we need to pick up the pace to get to the edge of the swamp before whatever is pursuing us gets a chance at catching up."

They're right, it isn't achiness from climbing, but something is pressing upon my bones, making them hurt. My necklace shows no signs of threat. I raise my hands, but there's no blue energy. Nothing to indicate danger, though now that they mention it, I can tell something is coming. Ever since last eve when I saw my father, a foreboding has itched along my nerves. "Thoron, you mean? Is it him?"

"I sense … something. It could be another problem we don't know about. Your father isn't the only hazard in this kingdom. Be on the watch and report anything that seems out of the ordinary." He hooks the last canteen onto his pack. "Let's go."

We hustle across craggy hills thick with boulders and brushy undergrowth that scratches at our boots. Although birds chitter among the limbs, they and our breathing are the only noises that accompany us.

The storm, however, is moving faster than us, and soon large drops fall, steaming under the heat of the sun, then a stiff wind steals the warmth. Clear blue skies clog thick with clouds, like curdled milk, in a sickly shade of green-gray.

I know what that means. It's from a children's book on Tenebris which serves to warn children. *Gray skies at night, rain's your plight. Growling winds ya hear, tornado's very near. Skies of gray-green, hail's soon seen.*

Lucas jerks his head in my direction. He must've heard my thoughts. We share a frown.

Rock dust turns to an ashen mud color as it becomes harder and harder to see and the rocks grow slick with wetness. We make it out of the mountainous land and into a lusher expanse with trees when the first explosion of lightning startles us, cracking a few seconds later.

"We have to find shelter," I yell at my determined Grandfather who continues to trudge, oblivious to the weather. It could be that he can't hear me over the drone of the rain. I yell once more with no luck. I clutch the hood of my slick cape tight around my face, trying to keep the water from flying in my eyes.

Another roar of thunder rumbles. Streaks of light zag across the sky and rain falls harder around us.

There's a hiss and a crack. Fire bursts and a large limb breaks off not far from where we shuffle. "Grandfather!"

Rekspire changes, taking flight in his dragon form. Rain batters my face as I turn to see where he's headed. It's thick and too hard to see far ahead, so I concentrate instead on the ground. Water drips inside my boots and I shudder with the violating dampness.

A screech, and then Rekspire grabs hold of Grandfather. He takes the old man, kicking and wailing, up in the air.

I'm instantly changed, Lucas as well, and we dart after the dragon and eldrin. It's instinct. A reaction to danger. But what danger is there besides the storm?

Rekspire is having a hard time holding on to Grandfather and the hefty pack on his back. Grandfather's mouth opens in yells, but the storm is too loud to hear him. All I can do is follow bleakly behind them, hoping for the best. Praying the drake knows what he's doing.

Wind whips at my wings, tearing at my muscles and sending me sideways. If I had teeth, I would be gritting them. Lucas is having much the same trouble, fighting to stay aloft and struggling to stay on track. *"Oh, Kinsman. Please help us!"* I pray over and over.

The pain is back in my bones and though I can't see it, my ability sparks to life, tingling across my feathered body. There's danger nearby. Could it be Thoron traveling in the storm? I twist my head back and forth, the motion taking me down and out of my path. There's no danger to spot.

"Can you see anything? Any threat?" I ask Lucas in my mind.

"No, but it's near. There's a heaviness on the edges of my senses. Whatever it is, it's big and bad."

A gust hits us, and we're tossed like leaves in the wind. I lose sight of Lucas. *"Lucas?"* I call over and over, but there's no answer. I work to circle back, but I'm unsure what direction I'm going as the rain turns icy, stinging. I blink against the onslaught. I recall the snowstorm on Tenebris and how the shadows seemed to chase me. Now there's no moving darkness that I see, but I feel it. Like the illusions I can catch in the edges of my eyes, I sense it. It's there, hiding. Watching. Waiting. I push harder, *calling* out with my mind for anything.

But it's only me and the storm. It rumbles and grumbles across the expanse, as if hungry and wanting to consume whatever is in its path.

At last, I spy the dark outline of a tree ahead, so I make for it. If nothing else, I'll tuck near the trunk and let the branches shield me, until the storm passes. In my experience, storms that blow up suddenly, pass as quickly. Even the blizzard on Tenebris soon ran its course.

But the sleet changes to hail. I'm pummeled mercilessly. Body throbbing, I muscle my way through the air, stroke by stroke, and finally make it to the tree. I collapse when I land, my body aching. I drag myself to the innermost part of the limb and cling to the bark as the tree shakes with the icy, pounding chunks. It rips and tears at the outer part of the tree. Debris falls not too far from me, but I'm safe enough.

"Lucas? Where are you? Are you okay?" I *call* out with my mind. My bird body cannot hold on, so I change back, balancing on the thick branch and holding tight to the trunk. The staff is cradled tight between one shoulder and the tree. The sheath around my waist strains with how I sit, the dagger biting into my side. I ignore the discomfort.

"Youngling? I hear you. Where are you?" Audhild's voice is scratchy like she's parched. Or injured?

I'm about to answer her when my mind is assaulted. Prodded. I *push* it away. Is my father near? I shift on the branch trying to get a glance, but it's too verdant, the leaves too thick.

"Oh, youngling. Where are you?"

A foul stench overpowers my senses. It's the same kind I experienced when finding the jewels last eve. Sickeningly similar to my father's beasts. Shock steals what's left of my body heat. I open my mouth, spitting to rid myself of the imagined disgusting funk.

Blue energy bursts to life in a circle around me, answering my panic. The bracelet I wear tightens against my wrist and my necklace warms. It must be my father. But, where? *"Audhild, get to safety. Thoron is near."*

"Of this I know. But it is not shelter I seek. I seek you." The fire dragon's voice changes to an angry, gravelly menace.

The stones on the bracelet dig into my skin, almost as if they are trying to become part of me. The pinch is painful, but it's not as awful as the realization that something is very wrong with Audhild. More pressure stretches against my mind, like a headache that presses and moves on, probes again, and on and on.

I envision a wall blocking my mind from her like in one of

the books she'd helped me read in the keep. I'd tried it then, but it hadn't worked. I squeeze my eyes shut, working to obscure my thoughts, and possibly my location, from her. I picture places I worked at on Tenebris, different villages, or imagine the dull countryside. Anything else but where I am.

The hail increases in size, breaking branches that crack and drop to the ground, splintered. I will myself to become part of the tree, envisioning the thick bark as a cover, a barrier to keep me hidden. Safe.

Thunder rumbles in the distance, from what I suspect is the direction I'd been headed. I hope it is. That would mean the storm is moving past me. Its suddenness is as suspect as the blizzard had been on Tenebris. Dangerous. Devouring in its ferocity.

I continue to picture the tree as my safe haven, willing it into being. It's not like the other times when I have demanded something and the energy around me accepted it, allowing it to happen. There is resistance this time, but my request is powerful enough and the tree remains protected enough to shelter me.

The pounding lessens as the hail subsides, turns smaller, then stops.

"Oh, little thief, you can hide, but we will find you. And we will destroy you."

We. Though there's no doubt Audhild is on the side of my father now, my inner senses tell me it is more than the two of them. What has my father done now?

Then, I spot her red form in the brightening sky. Her wings are curled, not straight, her head is misshaped, and her body is no longer plump and healthy. I'm unsure how she can fly this way. She wobbles back and forth, up and down, staying airborne. However, the ground is not far below where she darts crookedly around.

My nose stings with tears that I refuse to give in to as my mind struggles to comprehend what's happened. Did she say "little thief"? Thoron had been furious with me for stealing my mother's bracelet back. I expected him to come after me. Instead, somehow, he'd found Audhild. Is it my fault he took the fire dragon instead?

How could it have come to this?

My heart tells me to go to her, save her from whatever foul, wicked hex that's befallen her.

My head is spinning. I struggle to breathe around a lump in my chest. I concentrate on keeping my illusion of being one with the tree tight. I don't want Audhild to spot me.

Once again, I wonder what happens to a person's soul once my father's magic consumes them. I've believed for so long in the sovereignty of the Kinsman because it's how Mother raised me. But how could the Kinsman allow such wickedness to destroy without retribution? It makes no sense to my mind, which wants justice and loves fairness and mercy.

Audhild's red tail snakes past the tree below me. I tuck my face in the space between my shoulder and the hard bark, letting the questions drop from my mind. I have other things to worry about, like surviving right now.

I'm grateful that the tree I clutch is a lighter gray. If my disguise doesn't hold, the coat and boots will surely blend in. Possibly even the viny outfit.

I continue to hold the vision of a barrier over my thoughts. *"Please, Kinsman, hide me. Hide all of us from this new monster."*

A black blur hits Audhild from behind. It roars, and the sound is familiar.

Rekspire.

He sends lightning at the defiled fire dragon. His ability crackles around her, making her squeal in pain. He lets go and she falls toward the ground.

She stops before she hits, what's left of her wings flung wide. She spins awkwardly back around with an echoing screech. Her prey in sight, she attacks the drake that hovers nearby.

They battle in the air. Unfortunately for Audhild, Rekspire is in full control of his elemental ability and has the upper hand. Though smoke trails from Audhild, there are no flames, no power that exudes from her as it has before. My father has stolen the essence of her magic and has left but a shadow behind. She's emaciated. Even her tail is but a whip compared to what it once was.

My eyes burn with unshed tears and from my ability pulsing through me, lighting me up a vibrant blue. Distantly I feel the urge to burn them both down, but the bracelet snaps my wrist, stinging, and distracting me from the dark whisper. I rub the offended skin against my leg. Is it my father or some other force?

Released from the invading voice, I watch as the two dragons battle each other. I can tell Rekspire doesn't wish to hurt Audhild, his lightning doesn't crackle as strong as it has in the past. I'm torn. I don't want either of them hurt.

Audhild has saved me. She helped me to read through the books in Grandfather's keep. She was teaching me how to be a firebird, and how to quench my fire. She even gave me these ridiculous clothes in case I fall in a stream again. And they're a gift most treasured because they were Madrigal's, my revered grandmother's belongings.

The fire dragon wasn't kind in the regular sense of the word. But, besides Grandfather and Lucas, she'd done more for me since I'd come to Anavrin than anyone has ever done in my entire life. She'd become my mentor.

I grow light-headed from breathing heavily and the bark

bites into my chest as I cling to it. Somehow, I'd always thought there was a limit to my father's power. But, if he's gotten to Audhild this easily, I can't begin to fathom what else he is capable of.

And there's no stopping him from getting to me.

20

A hundred different questions pass through my mind. How did Thoron get to Audhild? Was he hiding, waiting for one of us to come out of the mountain yesterday? Still, how was my father able to capture such a careful dragon and turn her into one of his beasts? Even using the dragon bones, how could he have that much power? What else, then, can be helping him?

The scariest thought of all is, how long before Thoron finds me? The rest of us?

Rekspire has Audhild in a blanket of his power, sparks sizzling off her scales. Audhild shrieks in anguish and it's all I can do not to stop him. She's in true pain. With a blast, Rekspire lights up the area, and I have to cover my eyes. I see spots behind my closed lids.

When I open them, Audhild lies unmoving on the ground. Small spots of Reskpire's residual magic pop across her body. Rekspire lands beside her, his head and tail hung low. His magical web is gone. He changes and treads carefully around the other dragon's body, examining it.

I wait a second to be sure there's no more threat before I change to my firebird form. I let go of the trunk and flutter down to get a closer look, switching back to a girl as my feet hit land. My water-logged feathers are replaced by flourishing leaves that wave about in the breeze. I resemble a cloaked walking bush, but there's no humor in the thought.

Audhild's eyes are closed and her mouth hangs open. She's a shadow of what she was. It truly is as if life has been drained out of her, and I fight to keep the images of the eldrin Garrett's change from running through my mind. My eyes heat up, making the sparkling green landscape in front of me waver. I swipe at the dark, magic sparks which dance upon the dragon's red scales. "What do you think happened? How—?" I clutch the staff and a sob prevents me from speaking. I slap a hand over my mouth to stop the rest from working their way out of the center of my soul. "Why—"

Rekspire's eyes reflect the sadness that weighs on my heart. "I've seen many despicable things done to dragons in my life. I have never seen anything so atrocious. I have no words." He bends over and places a hand on her long neck. "Someone has to stop the death mage before he decimates all dragon life across the broken kingdoms. I never understood until I came here how precious dragon life is. We are the strongest. The Kinsman's messengers, Audhild said. I believe her. That knowledge has been stolen—suppressed to keep us obedient. Unworthy slaves." He spits on the ground and it crackles, killing the grass beneath.

I lift my gaze to the skies, beseeching the Kinsman to show me how to stop Thoron. How can I prevail if Audhild couldn't best him? Doubts build inside me until I'm ready to vomit them out. I crumple to my knees. The staff drops to the ground beside me.

Hoping against death, I place a shaking hand on Audhild's

forehead. It's cold to the touch. Not a good sign for a fire dragon. I mentally reach out to see if I can make a connection. But I find no stirring. No memories. There's only an empty blankness. And an icy coldness. When I try to dig in, to get some kind of reading on the creature, my effort is in vain.

My bracelet rattles against my wrist. I'm startled by a thought. I untie it and place it around one of Audhild's claws. It fits snug, a ring instead of a bracelet. Fire flows hot in my veins, the flames erupting from my hands clasped around the bracelet against the dragon's skin. I'm unsure why, but I repeat the incantation I memorized after creating all the bracelets to protect us. A whisper in my mind tells me it's the right thing to do. I hold their meaning when I say them, pushing them into my intention. The gems meld to Audhild like I'd meant them to do it, though I hadn't. They're a part of her.

Then I picture a light in my mind, like the lighthouse on the island with the Zoe Tree. A glimmer of hope in whatever dark place Thoron's hex has taken her. *"Please, bring her back, Kinsman,"* I plead softly. My energy flickers and then dies back.

It's a silence like the moment after Mother died. Before life changes in a way I couldn't imagine happening before. The expectation hasn't completely died yet, and the pain hasn't fully hit. It's a heartbeat away.

But it isn't the first time I can't tell if my request is heard. I don't feel the Kinsman answering me. I chide myself, knowing it doesn't always work that way. Still, I had a sliver of a belief, a spark of possibility. Instead— "Is she dead?" I choke on the words as I speak.

Slogging footsteps startle me. "Audhild, old friend?" Grandfather brushes past me and scoops her head into his lap. Deep, guttural cries wrack his body. Despair twists his facial disguise. It flickers and drops, leaving his real, beastly face in its place.

My throat aches with the effort to hold my emotions back and not join my grandfather in his grief. If I start to cry, I fear I wouldn't stop. It wouldn't do to have my father find me wrapped up in despair. It would be only too easy for him to capture me that way. I sniff wetly and gather what control and clarity I can manage.

"Tambrynn?" Lucas calls to me in my mind. *"I got lost. Where are you? What's wrong?"*

My heart lifts and then drops as hard. It hasn't even occurred to me that he's still missing. I mentally berate myself. I need to gather my wits, no matter what's happened. *"It's Audhild. Come quickly."* I wipe the tears away, but they continue to leak down my cheeks. I cough to loosen the tightness in my neck and chest.

"I'm on my way."

"Here." Rekspire offers me a leaf. It's big and soft, so I gratefully take it from him. "Thank you," my voice is strangled, but I can't help it. I clean my face with the leaf, managing to blow my nose. It has a cooling effect that soothes my eyes and opens my nasal passages enough to inhale a deep, cleansing breath. "Lucas is trying to find us."

Grandfather rocks Audhild in his arms like a child. The wails are gone now, though his chest rises and falls in silent, desperate heaves. His eyes stare off into the distance, fixed. He doesn't respond to my hand on his shoulder.

I gesture sideways to Rekspire. He follows me back to the tree I hid in. "What do we do now? Is she dead, as in dead-dead? We can't leave her here. Thoron—" I can't say it. It's not something I can imagine—my father desecrating her body for the magic in her bones if there's anything left to harvest. I have no doubt he'd do it.

"She is no longer among the living. However, I cannot say if she is free from the death mage's influence. I put a sleeper spell on her mind, which temporarily broke the link between her and the mage. She could rise up once more when it wears off. And I'm unsure how long it will last." His eyes no longer hold the excited light they had before we started this journey. I'd seen it often in young indentured girls. Life steals their innocence, their joy. And I grieve this loss for him. His tanned skin is pale and drawn. He glances around as if he's lost and searching for something.

I know the feeling only too well. I rub my wrist, praying silently that the protections from the bracelet will keep the dragon safe from my father now, no matter what.

A glance back at Grandfather makes me question Audhild's state of being. "Grandfather becomes ill when he's near one of my father's beasts. Could it be that she's not ... not coming back at all? I don't think he could hold her if it were possible." I rub my arms that twitch with the need to do something. "Besides, there was nothing when I tried to search her mind."

Rekspire is silent.

I slowly breathe in and out several times, trying to clear the hysteria bubbling at the edges of my brain. "Should we go back? Do we continue to try to find Thoron's talisman?" I squeeze the space between my eyes, willing away a headache blooming into awareness. "I'm sorry to ask all these questions. I'm just—" I have to get hold of myself again. "I don't know what to do. I've never handled a dead dragon before."

His handsome face puckers. "I could try to take her with me back to the mountain and chain her up as she did me. Wait and see if she comes back around. Or, because I fear Thoron might find her there, I could chain her up somewhere else. Somewhere safer from his influence, if there is such a place?"

I clutch my still trembling hands and twist them back and forth. I want to make the right choice. But I know Anavrin little better than the dragon. I try to reason through what I know.

The nomad's mountain is a better choice than Grandfather's keep. However, it didn't completely stop Thoron from attacking us from a spot beyond the kinstone. And I don't wish to endanger them should they be there.

What would Mother do? What would Audhild do? "Would you be able to take her back to Far Starl?"

His face scrunches and is unreadable. "Why? To add her, a Sovereign, to anonymity among the bone pile? It's blasphemous."

I fling my hands out, panic igniting in my gut. "If she's there, she won't be influenced by my father if she is still capable of waking up in this undead form?"

"Is that a question?" Rekspire glares at me. He's angry and I'm not sure which part has set him off.

I scream and throw my hands out in surrender. "I don't know. This isn't something that's ever happened before."

I have always wanted to be in charge or at least have a say in decisions. I'd reasoned it would be better than having every choice dished out to me by the unforgiving hands of others. But faced with such a daunting tragedy, I'd willingly give up my freedom right now if it meant Audhild could return to us, whole and undefiled.

"Lucas where are you?" I cry out in my mind.

"I'm coming, my lady. I fear I got blown quite far out of your path and I may have hit my head. It's pounding quite fiercely."

Frantic for too many reasons, I take to the sky to get a better look to see if he's flying nearby. I need his stability to help me think straight. The assurance of Lucas on his way clears the jumble of emotions battling in my consciousness and clarity returns. *"Lucas, there is a path of downed trees by us. Can you find it?"* I spend several minutes trying to direct him before I finally spot his black body gliding on the wind. *"Here, Lucas. We're here."*

He flies a circle around me. *"Tambrynn! I was afraid I wasn't going to find you."*

"I'm so glad you did. We need you." I dart back to the tree and where I'd left the others, drop down, and change back. I land on my feet, something the fire dragon would've been proud of.

Lucas lands beside me. His leafy clothing is bursting with color and life. I'd laugh if I wasn't so scared. "What happened to Audhild?"

"Thoron," I sputter out, hating the sound of his name as never before.

His eyes widen. "It can't be." He moves next to Grandfather, touching his shoulder. There's no response from the old man to his presence. Lucas sends a questioning glance my way.

I shake my head. "Rekspire and I have been trying to figure out what to do."

"There is no good alternative. Not unless there's a healer skilled in returning someone from this state." Rekspire joins us.

Lucas puts his arm around my waist. "I read about one kingdom where the voyants specialized in reversing dangerous mage hexes. However, I wouldn't know how to find the doorway in the Passageway."

"Panacea." Grandfather's voice is rough, gravelly. Tears run rivulets down his nose, dampening the tufts of fur to his neck. His eyes are red, the area around them swollen when he glances my way. "That's Panacea. Madrigal and Cadence did their trials in that kingdom." He glances away from us, continuing his rocking with Audhild's head gently held in his arms.

"How does one travel there?" Rekspire inquires softly, as if he's trying to coax a scared animal.

"The doorway with the sunburst. I have a key at the keep." Grandfather grows silent again.

I worry about his state of mind. Especially if my father is strong enough to turn Audhild, would he survive if they happened to meet each other?

"I'll take her. It's my job to keep her safe." Grandfather finally blinks and lowers his head.

"How?" Rekspire huffs.

Grandfather turns and meets the elemental dragon's stare. "With your help, of course."

"My help? How is that possible? I cannot carry another fully grown dragon, even shriveled as she is, let alone get through the mother tree to another kingdom." Rekspire's neck is strained and a vein pulses on his forehead.

Grandfather ignores him and faces me, his face intent. "Tambrynn, find Thoron's talisman. It's of the utmost importance now. Dragons are among the strongest of the Kinsman's messengers. And if this can happen ..." Grandfather's voice fades away.

My heart seizes, pinching in my chest painfully. "I don't know where I'm headed. I'm unsure how to get there, what to look for." It's not that I don't want Audhild saved. But the task he placed before me is too much. I don't even know where to start.

"You can do it." He answers back as if he knows my thoughts. "You and Lucas came from Tenebris through the Passageway to Anavrin. I have faith you two can finish the job the Kinsman gave us. But I cannot go with you. I must protect the last Sovereign. My life is bound with hers."

Panic and terror, like fire and ice, join forces in a crippling cascade inside me. I grind my teeth together. "A—how?"

"Find the nomads. They know the swamplands. They used to hide out there before they found the kinstone. They can guide you." Grandfather falters as he stands and Rekspire catches him by the arm, helping stabilize him. The old eldrin jerks his pack off his back and digs through several pockets before finding what he desires—two ruby stones with flecks of orange and black. Something akin to relief crosses his face.

He picks the pack up and shoves it at Lucas. "Take this with you. When the load gets too heavy, push the buttons and the pack will lighten for a short period. Use whatever you need." He turns toward me, his eyes wide and glistening as if he has become mad. "Find the talisman, Granddaughter. Destroy it. It is the only way to defeat him now. Please, promise me."

I don't know if I should respond in agreement. He gives me a look, like the first time I met him, as if to say *do you trust me?* I do though it hasn't been long since we met. An unwanted burden is there in his eyes.

I never used to rely on anyone. It wasn't as if I liked it that way, but I can't say it hasn't been nice to have Grandfather beside me. Helping me. I could turn away from him and this mission, even if my gut tells me that would be the way of a coward. I've seen too many in my life. Weak men and women who take the easy path when it gets too hard. It's not who I am, though a small part wishes I could be. Especially now that I've had Lucas, Grandfather, and Audhild believe in me. It's changed me for the better.

My grandfather hasn't steered me wrong so far. It isn't such a hard choice after all. "Fine. I'll do everything in my power to find the talisman."

Grandfather's shoulders loosen as he grips the colorful stones in his fists. He becomes energetic, his grim face altering. As if my answer has brought him back to life. "Find it, Tambrynn. All of the kingdoms are depending on you now. I'd take it away if I could, this responsibility. But it can't be me. I'm not the chosen one. You are. Kinsman help you, but you have to finish this mission or we're all doomed to Audhild's fate."

I sag inwardly. I don't want to do this without him. I don't believe I can, no matter what I said. Especially if I have to rely upon the nomads. But I'm not sure I can stop him. I knew there was something else between my grandfather and the fire dragon. I wish I understood what it is.

Grandfather takes the two bright stones, chants over them, and then smacks them together. The stones erupt in deep red flames, immersing him and Audhild in the heat. I step back from the spectacle. Lucas does the same, shielding his eyes with his arm.

Grandfather stands before me, transformed into a brownish-gray dragon. The scales across his large body are mottled with several shades of both colors, and he has two horns on his jagged head. His wings are leathery and a darker, dusky color. His claws are wicked and sharp.

Audhild is in her female form on the ground, looking shrunken and old instead of the beautiful red-clad woman of a day ago making us blush at her forwardness.

"Keep the dagger close at all times. The bag has many tools, use them wisely. Good luck my beloved ones. Come, Rekspire. I can do this once and only for a brief time. Follow me." He picks Audhild up carefully with his talons, and with a wide arc of his smoky wings, takes flight.

PART TWO

21

I'm more than a little dumbfounded. Did my grandfather turn into a dragon? But, yes. It's true. His brown, mottled body and Rekspire's black one glide through the storm-washed sky away from us.

A glance at Lucas tells me he is as stunned as I am. I reach out and hug him close. "Are you okay? You said you hit your head?"

He touches a spot on the back of his head when we part. "I'll be fine. It's throbbing, but no real damage."

There's a lump when I carefully check it. "It's going to hurt for a bit, I'm afraid." It's a small relief, but I'll take it. I tangle my fingers in the shriveling leaves of my outfit, reminding me once again of Audhild. I suck in an uneven lungful of air. "What do we do now?"

Lucas's gaze is steady and calm. "We continue on. Bennett said to find the nomads and have them help us. I'm not sure they will, but it's a start." Lucas stands tall, his determination clear in the tilt of his head and the tightness of his jaws. I'm thankful for him and his unwavering character. "We were alone in our journey once, my lady. We can do this again."

I know he's trying to reassure me, and I'm grateful for it. But panic is ever-present now. Now each leaf that rattles or every shadow that moves is suspect. "That was before. And how are we supposed to locate the nomads since they're on the move to find where the eldrin have their kin enslaved?"

"I believe there's an encampment not too far from the edge of the swamplands. Let's start there." He hands me the staff, cradles my cheek in his palm, and lowers his head. His kiss is a light caress, more encouragement.

"Thank you." I smile, soaking him in, his scent of home and breeze. It settles the quivering inside me in a way nothing else can.

He gathers the pack, shrugging it on with a grunt. I clutch the Sacratus staff, checking to be sure I still have the Mortifer blade at my side. It's safe in the sheath.

Together, hand in hand, we change.

I follow him as we fly west over the rain-washed land below. We don't speak so I spend the time thinking about the last few events, trying to reason out the storm, the tornado, Audhild's fate, and Grandfather's change.

"Do you see the river and the bridge below?" Lucas asks, breaking through my thoughts.

It's a wide stream with a stone arch bridge, five arches long, across it. Water gushes beneath it and heavy vines cling to the sides. It's tall enough for small boats though not ones with large masts. Birds fly beneath the rounded openings, without any worries. I envy them their carefree life.

I answer Lucas's question. *"I see it."* I survey the area, wondering why he's pointing it out. The banks are steep, which is probably a good thing with the amount of rain that's fallen lately. Muddied water gushes and splashes along the sides and footings of the bridge. Tree limbs bob along with the fast tide. But I see no significance.

"This is the Hevell River which runs from the Bloodthorn Forest. Not far from the bridge going north is another waterfall, the Dragon Falls. The nomad encampment isn't far from there. Even if we don't find Nobbert or Arrin, there should be some nomads who can lead us to the settlement of Lowborn in the marshes."

"You recall all of this from your previous life here?" I ask, amazed at his memory.

Humor rings through our bond. *"No. I was able to find a map in Bennett's keep that listed all of the different settlements, the sanctioned ones anyway, up until Thoron's war. I tried to memorize them all, but I'm sure I won't recall some. This one I do remember clearly, however, because of the falls."*

The sun is warm on my right side, and the wind is gentle now that the storm has disappeared. Nothing darkens the horizon and I have to wonder, since Thoron was already here, what caused it. However, there's no time to reflect as Lucas dodges down and the roar of rushing water fills the air.

Thick trees block my sight of the falls as we get closer, but the spray flavors the air. It's not salty like the North Sea. My body heats in warning and energy tingles across my feathered body. *"Something is here. Be careful."* I caution Lucas.

"Let's find a good tree on the edge, somewhere hidden where we can perch and scout for danger." He darts ahead and I pick up speed so I don't lose him. It's not far to get to the trees lining the rocky area.

We settle into a massive pine facing the cascading water. It's so loud I can't hear anything above the bustle of the river. The drop of the falls is steep and broken up by different ledges, which catch the river's flow and toss it farther down until it all lands in an enormous pool at the bottom.

Out of the corner of my eye, I catch the glimmer of

translucent rocks similar to the stones in Mother's bracelet, except these are a milky color. They cover a great area around the water's edge. *"What are those stones?"* I ask, curious if I should possibly gather a few.

"Legend has it those are the fossilized remains of dragon's bones. But it could be some type of quartz similar to the speckles in the keep's walls."

Muted screams and laughter break through the solid noise of the rushing stream. A glance down reveals that the pool is not empty. There are several water kin swimming among the slapping waves. Mist obscures their features, but they swim too easily to be anything but merfolk, even without their tails. They frolic, some jumping from boulder ridges up toward the top of the falls. They twist and turn, falling so trustingly into the rushing water. As if it holds no danger.

Yet, I recall the surge of cold that battered my skin, sinking into my bones until even moving was painful. That dizzying ride to the froggen's castle is etched vividly in my mind and my body alike, which has tensed at the sight of the playful merkin. I may never be rid of that ghost of a memory. I look away and focus on an empty nest not far from where we are, created from sticks, feather fuzz, and dried grasses until the onslaught of those recollections fall away like water droplets in the air.

Lucas sits unmoving next to me, for once unaware of the turn of my thoughts. *"We'll need to head back west to get around them. Luckily, they're so engrossed we won't have too much problem getting out without being noticed."*

I agree, but before I can make a move, several of my father's beasts break through tall, brushy bushes growing on the edge of the basin and attack four of the unaware merfolk sitting on the edge. While they struggle to get free, others jump into the water and join their kin already escaping downstream.

I step forward, wanting to retaliate against the beasts, and help the captured merfolk, even if their fleeing friends don't try. Mostly I want to tear my father's undead pets to pieces.

"Tambrynn, you can't save them. Not without Thoron knowing where we are." Lucas's concern fills his words and pounds inside my head.

"If I don't stop the beasts, I am no better than Shellsea said I was." But I hesitate. I know Lucas is right. It sits like a hot poker, going against everything that I am.

He squawks, a sure sign that he's as upset as I am with the situation. *"We can't. We have a mission that's more important than saving a few careless merfolk. We will do what we can for their kind when we are able to. Right now is not the time to alert your father."*

I fluff my feathers, irked that he's right again. Even though I've come so far, learning how to control my fire and embrace my inner firebird, it's still not enough to move against Thoron. I'm still as helpless as I was when I was indentured. *"Fine. Let's get out of here before I see more."*

We flutter through the tree until we make it to the other side, away from the view of the waterfalls. With a heavy heart, I follow Lucas around Dragon Falls and away from my father's despicable creations.

The sun has started its descent by the time we reach what we are looking for. However, the smallish houses have been burned to the ground. Charred stones from the chimneys remain like gravestones. It had to have been fairly well established, as the roads are cobbled and worn down. Water trickles not far in the distance. A perfect place to establish a community.

It wasn't a recent destruction, as grass and flowers grow unimpeded out of the blackened ground. Weeds tangle through the spokes of metal wheels from carts or carriages.

Lucas bends down to inspect the destruction. *"It's probably a few weeks old. Maybe more."* He follows the cobbled pathways through the hamlet. It's several blocks wide and double that long, though it's not straight and square as Anatolia had been. The layout is more haphazard and unplanned as if they closed their eyes and pointed to a spot and simply began to build.

"Eldrin?" It's not so much a question as a statement. They're the only ones who would bother the harmless clan. But, why? From what I'd gathered about nomads, they leave all of the other races alone, barring young silver-haired young women they find in forests. They keep to themselves in their mountains or villages. *"What is it about the nomads that make the eldrin target them?"*

"They used to be spurned—treated as unimportant. No one cared about them unless they got in their way. Nomads have to follow the eldrin's rules. But mostly they're peaceful. I'm unsure what's changed since we left. Why they're being harassed now? Or at least since we've returned." Lucas's neck feathers ruffle with a gust. *"Let's fly around to see if we can find them. The eldrin never work too hard to do anything. Perhaps they'll be nearby."*

Lucas is once again correct. We find a sort of prison not far from the burned village.

Metal-linked walls outline an area full of short, hairy nomads—men, women, and children. Eldrin guards stand at equal points along the fence. Barbed wire, which I'd only seen a few times on Tenebris's wealthier farms, is curled along the top of the barrier keeping the nomads hostage. The center, however, is open to the sky. Vultures and other birds of prey circle above the enclosure awaiting their next meal. I shudder at the sight.

There are no trees here, only remnants of them. Like the outskirts of Anatolia, trunks dot the ground of what used to be a forest. So, there's nothing for shade, shelter, or any place to hide if you have a chance to get free. My heart aches at the intentional destruction of what might've been a glorious forest.

We fly a wide arc around the packed prison, secure in the fact that so many other large birds already swirl above the site that we wouldn't be noticed unless one of the guards looked for us specifically. The scent of stagnant water from muddy pools between the prison and the remainder of a forest two stone throws from the fence's edge clouds the air. My eyes water at the pungent stench.

Lucas angles down and lands among the tree's shadows at the forest's border. I follow behind, change, and land. I sink into the deceptively soggy ground. Thankfully, my boots protect my feet. Beyond where we are, where there are fewer trees, it's drier. I have to wonder if the trees were removed to dry out the mucky land.

"What is that smell?" I gag and then cough. Even pigs on the farm didn't smell this bad. I lift the staff and muddy silt drips off it. It doesn't stick to my slick cloak though it hangs past my boots. The vines and leaves on our clothing have shriveled back again.

Lucas's face is scrunched and he breathes shallowly. The pack on his back is taller than his head and thick enough to make him lean forward. "The swamp, I'm guessing. Audhild did try to warn us."

His words about the fire dragon prick my heart. I pray silently that the Kinsman will look kindly upon his messenger. I put my sleeve up to my nose to decrease the odor and ease my watering eyes.

"How do we get the nomads out? Did you see how many eldrin there were?" My footsteps stick and then suck as I pull them free from the sludgy ground. "How do plants grow here?"

Lucas smiles despite the stink wafting around us. "The

ground is rich. I recall some of the shopkeepers selling jars of mud as a beauty treatment."

I gawk at him. "That can't be true."

He chuckles low. "It is. Let's go that way, I think the ground is better there."

I take his hand and we noisily slup our way out of the deeper puddle. "Anavrin is so strange," I mutter.

We locate an area thick with felled trees, a much more stable place to stop and contemplate our next move. I stare at the fence, considering our options. However, there are at least eight eldrin inside, and none of them look too happy even from this distance.

A devious grin spreads across Lucas's face. "I think we're going to need a diversion. Something that will send the eldrin running for the hills and leave the nomads unattended."

I'm a bit suspicious of the gleam in his eyes. I've seen him mischievous. I recall his craftiness when we were children and he'd try to cheat and win. But I can detect a deeper level of his djinn heritage showing. "What are you up to?"

"A bit of a scare should do it. I think you've practiced enough and we're both strong enough to pull this off." He wiggles his eyebrows at me. "We're going to disguise ourselves as your father's beasts. Knowing the eldrin, they'll run off and leave the nomads behind."

At first, I'm shocked at his idea. However, it has some merit. "You think I can pull that level of disguise off?"

His grin is wide and confident. "I know you can."

I glance back at the nomad's cage. There's hardly enough room for anyone to sit down. An eldrin guard yells and cuffs one of the children when she gets too close to him. She doesn't fall to the ground, since there's no room for that. She does knock into another nomad near her, who tips into a third. Anger flares as hot as my ability at the sight. "Let's do this."

22

Scarlet spills across the sky, bathing the area around the swamp in fiery oranges and reds as we prepare to approach the prison. Lucas, as usual, has mastered the appearance of the undead wolf-beasts. I inwardly cringe at the sight, though I'm thankful for how strong he's become. I, on the other hand, am struggling to set the disguise in place. My mind rejects it and blue flames flicker across my skin when I try.

"I know it goes against everything you are, my lady. But it's getting dark, and we might not have another chance until morning."

His implication that we need to hurry only makes it harder for me to take on the role of my father's evil pet. I shake out my hands, which tremble and zing with my ability. My mind knows I'm not turning into one. However, that inner part of me where I believe my spirit resides is appalled at even taking on the image. I'd tasted that evil when I'd connected with Thoron the day before. I take a deep, cleansing breath.

Lucas places a gentle hand on my arm. "Maybe it's too

frightening to imagine since you've seen them attack your mother and watched your father change the eldrin into one? Try instead to find one in your mind that hasn't attacked you personally. Like one that came sniffing around when we were hidden inside your grandfather's shield. Something less threatening."

"I'll try." I close my eyes and try to empty my thoughts of what the beasts represent. I think instead of who they were before their life was stolen so senselessly. I bring my wishes for salvation to them in a silent prayer to the Kinsman, hoping he might hear me and grant my request. My fire warms in the center of my being, bringing with it a blessed moment of peace. In that calmness, I envision the beast.

'*Sluagh redemptió redetis. De veni.*' The words whisper through my mind. It could have been the wind, though, as the impression of the phrase is so faint as not to have been actually heard. But somehow, I know what it means. I'd read similar words when studying with Audhild. *"Redemption comes to the undead beasts."* The slew-ahs, as Siltworth had called them.

Maybe it is my imagination, but tingles spread across my head and down my arms, settling at my feet. Then heat washes across me, settling like damp clothes.

I open my eyes to find Lucas's maw smiling in a grisly fashion. "Did I do it?"

"You did! Outstanding job, my lady! Whatever you did, keep it up and we'll have those nomads out in no time." He takes my hand in his and I'm comforted that I can't feel the sharp claws or the leathery skin.

I hesitate before I confess my thoughts. "I think the Kinsman heard me. Heard my prayer." The ghost of the tingles cling and with it a rightness settles over me.

There's no judgment from Lucas through our bond as I

feared. He squeezes my hand, and together, we head out to confront the eldrin.

We break up when we get closer to the enclosure, where the trunks aren't so thick. Lucas motions to me and then howls. I start snarling and almost choke when I do so. However, it's enough to catch the guard's attention. They shout at each other and point. The nomads are also calling out in fear. They huddle together, shaking and crying.

Lucas circles around and I take the left side, away from the only gate that leads in or out of the fenced area. I howl, focusing my mind on the sound of my voice as well as my image. It must work as two of the eldrin tap their chests and disappear. That leaves six more.

We continue to stumble around and make noise until the last eldrin deserts. I've never been so thrilled to scare another person before. I grin, which must be quite alarming since I bring a wide-eyed nomad child to shrieking tears.

"Tambrynn, come help me with the locks," Lucas calls, voice and appearance normal again.

I drop my disguise, causing several shocked responses from the prisoners. I rush over to Lucas where a heavy metal device hangs from the doorway. I've never seen locks like these. They're shiny and new. "Do you think I can melt them?"

"You could try the dagger. Bennett said it could cut through anything."

Sitting the staff on the ground, I take the Mortifer blade from the holder attached to my waist. It hums in my hand as if in anticipation. I don't question it. I place the sharp blade against the curved bar holding the locking mechanism. It instantly begins to melt away. In mere moments the lock is open.

Relieved, I put the dagger back in the holder.

The gate is double-doors attached by the broken lock.

Lucas swings his side of the gate open and I follow his example and do the same for mine. The eldrin may be lazy, but the doors swing open with little effort on well-oiled hinges. New construction?

Some of the nomads cheer. Some of them cry happy tears. A couple of the older males look at us with suspicion.

I step into the center of the opening and spread my arms wide. "You're free. I have only one request. I need someone to help me navigate the marshlands."

"I told you!" One of the frowning men bursts out. His beard is snarled with weeds and his face is coated with mud. He seems to be the same age as my favorite nomad, Nobbert. "We heard about you. Silver hair, strange eyes. You're the daughter of the death mage. Don't trust her. She's here to take us to her father."

Rage burns in my gut. I'd love to wipe the smug indignation off his face. And how did word about my identity get around so quickly? "I've never worked for my father. I'd rather die. I'm here to save you."

He makes a pashawing noise. "Lies. Look at you, dressed like eldrin, disguised like the death mage's abominations, and changing forms like djinn. Don't tell me you're trying to save us. You're going to lead us to our demise."

"Why would I disguise myself, scare the eldrin away, and then free you if I were working with Thoron? Does that sound like something he'd do?" I ask him, expecting no good answer.

"It don't have to make no sense for it to be true." He crosses his arms over his chest and lifts his chin.

"You wouldn't be related to Nobbert, would you?" I ask, half in jest and half curious. Though there are all quite similar, this one reminds me too much of the grumpy old nomad.

He gives me a wicked one-eyed glare, his squint creasing

the side of his face. It's easy to tell that he's older than the others. "What's it to you?"

Lucas steps up beside me. "It's nothing. Leave or join us. It makes no difference. We're only looking for a small bit of help and then we'll bid you a good life."

"You old cow! You only know what them eldrin a'been saying about the girl." A rotund woman pushes her way through the crowd. "Everyone knows they lie. Besides, how would she know 'bout your brother if she's in cahoots? I say if she's an enemy of our enemy, she's a friend of mine."

The woman turns to me. "The swamp is better than this weltering sty any day. Especially since we lost our village to those warring idiots. Count me in." She wears a dress stained with muck. Her mud-coated feet, unsurprisingly, are bereft of shoes.

Several of the other women raise their hands and eagerly rush to the front, their eyes round with excitement. I have no time to argue with the men, so I shrug off the male nomad's distrust. I move aside, making sure that the staff is away from anyone coming near. I don't wish to lose it.

"Anyone willing to help, follow us. All of the others are free to go." I wave my hand, dismissing the first man and some of the others who frown at me.

"Why're you going to the swamp? It's dangerous, don't you know?" A smaller woman hastens through the gates toward me.

Lucas waves her and the others to a spot beyond the fenced wall. "We go to find the item that will destroy Thoron. We don't ask any of you to put yourself in danger, only that you lead us to Lowborn. Does anyone know the way?"

Several startled expressions follow his question.

The first woman steps up. "I do. But like Tatty said, it's dangerous for true. You sure you want to go there?"

"We're sure." Lucas sounds convinced, though I sense his reticence in our bond. It echoes my own trepidation. He spins and starts walking. "Helpers, follow me."

A few of the nomads still inside take off, running in the opposite direction, dodging stumps as they go. They don't look back. I don't blame them. I rein in my emotions as they leave, giving the rest no reason to disbelieve what we've told them.

I wait as others, almost twenty of them and mostly women, make their way after Lucas. I'm heartened that there are a few men in the ranks, though they seem to be younger since they have no beards. The outspoken one, however, remains where he is inside the fenced prison, his arms still crossed tight over his chest. He glares at me and the others who join us.

When the last one gets into the line to follow Lucas, the grumpy nomad groans and rubs his face. His bristly, salt-and-pepper beard reaches the ground. Five other men, all with beards and with unsure expressions, watch him. He must be their leader.

I don't wait for them to choose, though. They can stay if they wish. I'd set them free and given them the choice to follow or not. I march after the last young male, who rushes to keep up with the rest of the group.

"Hold on." The grizzled nomad sounds pained. "You can't navigate them dark places with just Gebby and the rest. Some ha' never been near Lowborn. They'll get lost or worse."

I turn to see him and the other five march out of the prison. "What's worse than lost?" I have my own opinion, but I'd like to know his.

"There's any number of things worse 'n getting lost. Animals out there are waiting for their next meal, and though you're scrawny, you'd do in a pinch." He huffs as he walks. "And don't forget the witch and her spirits that roam the marshes, not to mention a couple of those abominable creatures you looked like."

"My father's beasts are in the swamp?" I ask, surprised. They normally run in packs searching for their next victim. Or me. Whichever they could find.

He stomps past me. "Are you deaf? Isn't that what I said?" His feet slam down, shlup up, and thunk down again. At this rate, we'll announce our whereabouts to everyone within hearing distance of us.

"Can you walk quieter? Maybe step on the tree trunks instead?" I'm mostly joking as I hurry after him. The ground is getting soggier the farther we head into the marshland. I scrunch my nose against the odor of murky water and rank vegetation. I'm glad now for the boots but have to wonder how deep it gets before we get to where we're going. At least Grandfather had intended to use a boat, not trudge through the mire.

"Not if'n you want to warn off the other scary stuff in this swamp. Most of them won't bother you if they hear you a-coming. They'll fright and run off. They don't like surprises. That'll get you eaten faster than you can blink an eye."

"They who?" I ask, but he tramps away without answering, dodging the impeding stumps with surprising grace. I don't want to leave the nomads in the back unprotected, so I slow down reluctantly.

"There're alligators that swim along the surface of the water. They'll roll you under, drown you, and make you a meal," the younger girl who talked before answers. "Don't step into the water if you see glowing eyes. And if you see flashes flying around, it's the sprites. Mostly harmless unless you pull on their wings or some such. Don't follow them, though. They love to lure anything into the water and sing to you as you sink."

"Sprites?" I ask, cringing at the idea that there are animals big enough to drown and eat you. But, then again, Siltworth had been big enough to do so. A tic starts in my hands and expands until I'm full-on trembling.

"Oh, yes. The swamp is home to many things that want to be left alone," the girl continues helpfully. Other nomads murmur in agreement. "It's also a haven to those creatures who aren't welcome anywhere else. That's why our kin used them for so long. Nobody wanted us around." Her round face is earnest. "But it also means there are more dangerous things skulking in the water and darkness."

The grumpy man reaches Lucas in the front and, with some wild gestures and words I cannot quite make out, takes the lead. With a swing of his arm to follow him, he dodges right and along some path only he understands. And since it's dusk, I'm hoping the man knows where he's going.

A 'creek-ka' sounds to our left, too close for comfort, and then a splash of water makes me jump. It's followed by a couple of other swishing noises and splutters of water.

And it's as if I'm back in the stream, pulled along to the froggen's castle. My chest compresses, restricting my airway. I can't breathe.

23

The young nomad girl touches my arm. "Those are toads. Nothing to worry about. We're not close enough to deep water to be in true danger yet." She must sense my panic. Her voice is soothing.

With her assurance, the panic eases and I can inhale past the fear that clogs my throat. I try to not make it obvious, but my chest heaves as I regain control of my senses once more.

"Be careful where you're walking. Roots grow out of the water and you can trip easily. Many a'nomad have broken bones not watching where they're going." It's a male's voice.

"Sh—should we be going another way?" My tongue is tied and I struggle to sound normal, not spooked like I truly am. Will the fear of that abduction never leave me?

"I trust Debbert to take us along the safest path," the same man says. I find him—he's one of the first who volunteered to go with us. He doesn't seem to be concerned. "The dark is our worst enemy now, though the eldrin won't pursue us at night. Watch where you step. Gliding your feet is best."

My foot hits something hard and I stumble. So much for

gliding my feet. We need light, even a little. So, I tap the staff twice on a stump. Blessed light glows around me in a circular halo. At first, I'm comforted. However, shadows move and dart around as creatures flee from our presence or the light. Luckily, none are big.

To our right, the silhouette of the prison is in the distance. I use my staff to keep myself from becoming too entrenched in the slick mud that grows thicker, and deeper. It is getting harder to pull out as we move further into the bog-like area. Audhild was right when she said the swamp is wet and muddy. I don't dwell on thoughts of the fire dragon or, in my ragged state, I'll be shedding tears in front of everyone.

"Lucas, are you okay with him leading us?"

"He says he knows a shortcut that should avoid most of the nasties. He seemed to be telling the truth, and if he isn't, we can always leave. However, I don't think a nomad would risk the lives of his fellow kin just to scare us," he replies.

"One of the other nomads said the same. I hope you're both right." I help one of the women who has gotten stuck in the mire to pull her foot out. I brace the staff on a protruding root and yank her free.

"Thank you, miss. I'm Lolla." She smiles up at me. "And don't mind Debbert. He's been crusty since the day he was born."

I can't help my laughter. Her levity breaks through the funk that's settled around me since I heard the toads jumping. "Sounds like Nobbert. I'm Tambrynn." Lolla hadn't held out a hand as Arrin did, so I don't either. I'm relieved she doesn't. I also decide not to hide my name like I had when I'd met the first nomad group. They already realize who I am, so it doesn't seem worth the effort.

"Ach! Terrible twins, the two of them." Lolla chuckles with me.

"Twins!" I exclaim. "I knew it."

"Brothers, yes. Not actual twins, though. It's a competition for being the worst churlish curmudgeon. So far they're nose to nose. Even, don't you know?" She waves her hand and giggles as if she'd told a joke. She turns serious and gives me an appraising look. "We did hear the enforcers talk about you and that Councilmaster Nyle. They were amused that Nyle lost the Eye of Fate, but not thrilled it's out of eldrin hands now. Serves them right, far as I can see. Doesn't seem right to wield that kind of power when you're selfish about it. By their own laws, it should serve the good of the kingdom, not the eldrin alone."

"Hush, Lolla. This attitude is what got you snatched to begin with." The older woman drops back to walk beside us.

"And what got you snatched, eh? We're all here for the same thing, standing up to those infighting fools." Lolla huffs. "It ain't right how they treat us. Raiding our village. Burning it to the ground. I'm not going to keep my mouth shut about it. They can lock me up all they want."

"So, you want to go back, then?" the older woman responds sharply. When Lolla says nothing, she tsks. "That's what I thought. I'm Tibby, by the by, Debbert's wife. But don't pay much mind to that. Nomad men are impossible on the best day."

The mud clears up for a short distance and trees stretch their branches above our path, throwing deeper shadows over us. My staff lights up, staving off the worst of the darkness and giving us a small circle to see by. "I'm glad you both joined us. Nyle's been making a nuisance of himself over by the kinstone mountains where Nobbert and Arrin live."

"What's he doing now? It's been a cat's age since I saw them." Tibby lifts her skirt and crawls over a stump, or is it a root growing out of the ground? I can't tell. The landscape is getting rougher.

Some of the others move closer to me, possibly for the light, until we're all walking in a huddled ring.

"The eldrin there have taken all of the women except Arrin," I explain, keeping the staff tipped to make the sphere of light ahead of us as large as possible. Even so, I catch movements out of the corners of my eyes. When I face it, I see nothing to be concerned about. I check my energy, but it's resting peacefully inside me. No shoots of alarm. No zip of heat. "Debbert knows where he's going, doesn't he?"

"Aye, he does. He might act it, but he'll not lead you wrong. He don't like doing something that wasn't his idea, that's all." Tibby grabs my arm to make it over a waist-high log that spans into the depths in both directions. Moss grows on top of it in a thick blanket, keeping it soft as we crawl over.

The trees are thicker here. Water now sits atop the sucking mud below. It's almost up to my knees, waist high for the nomads. I'm unsure how we're going to continue when Debbert steers the front of the group around a large tree and heads left. I turn the corner myself and am surprised to see a wooden boarded walkway emerge from the slog. It's attached to two sturdy trunks and suspended above the muck by ropes strung from the trees.

It must've at one time been longer because I step on sunken boards as we enter the boarded path. The ropes are soaked and grimy with silt and slick with slimy plant life. However, the other ropes which hang above the swamp are clean, giving me hope that the pathway is at least partially safe.

"Mind your steps, it can be a bit frightening at first. These swinging bridges were made for us little folk, though some of the exiles came out here, too." Tibby warns me from behind.

I wait for a couple of the others to go across before I dare place a foot on it. The root at the end of the wooden boards is worn smooth. Muddy water glistens a couple of finger widths below the makeshift, flattened step.

I place one booted foot and grasp the rope on both sides, my staff held tight under my arm so I can still see by its shining orb. The bridge sways with my movements, making me dizzy. I stop, my hands fisted at my sides, until the movement ceases and the spinning in my head ends.

Muted laughter breaks my concentration. A glance around verifies that the nomads are laughing at me.

"Go on then, it won't bite you," Tibby tells me while Lolla pushes at my backside.

I fight off the prick of embarrassment that makes me want to snap back in response. However, my stomach decides at that moment to roil dangerously. I can't chance taking a hand off the rope, so I hold back the bile rising in my throat by sheer will.

"My lady? Are you all right?" Lucas's concern breaks through my paralyzing fear.

"Fine," I say through gritted teeth. I'm not sure where it's coming from, but all of my instincts tell me to turn and run. I don't sense any magic. My necklace remains dormant on the chain and my hands are not lit up with blue energy. I breathe shallowly to allay the unease raising havoc in my gut.

I take another tentative step forward, slowly, so the bridge doesn't move too much. Another step. And then a third. Another foot and I'll be over the water's edge, which gleams like spilled oil beneath the moon's light, the dark liquid wavering at the corners of my sight.

An illusion? I hesitate. "Did djinn live in the swamp?" I ask no one in particular.

"Sure, some," Tibby speaks from behind me. "There's been any number of miscreants and undesirables that have taken to the swamps over the years. The last time I stayed here there was a large group of djinns, which is unlike them. Djinn prefer solitary life, you see. But they'd been targeted by the eldrin for a time after one of their Council had a particularly nasty run-in with one of their kin."

I glance around once again and do a gut check for danger, but besides my upset stomach, everything appears to be fine. And if the djinn were here once, that might account for the illusion that wavers on the edge of my sight.

On my next stride, my necklace heats up. Air pops and there's no time to react before I'm lifted off the wooden walkway into the air. My staff drops from under my arm, landing on the wooden planks below. Lolla and Tibby jump to grab hold of my boots, but they're still slick with sludge. The women fall to the walkway, shaking the swinging bridge violently.

"Who disturbs my peaceful slumber?" The voice is inside and outside of my head all at once. I can't tell which direction it comes from.

I try to change, but I can't. I'm held in a spell. Pressure blooms in my head. It was the same as when my father tried to invade my mind. Panic grows into hysteria and I grab the dagger Grandfather gave me. With a thought of *'reveal,'* I swing the blade, and the illusion breaks, falling around me like leaves. And then I am dropping down.

I don't know when I closed my eyes, but when I open them, I'm back on the swinging bridge—alone.

The nomads are gone.

So is Lucas.

The figure before me is dark and fierce with piercing red eyes. Mist surrounds us. "Only fools ignore my warning." I can't tell by the voice whether it's a male or female. It makes a sweep with a bony arm encased in a tattered long sleeve and the ache in my stomach is gone, the dizziness disappears.

I blow out a relieved breath. "What—who are you?" I ask carefully, reverently.

"I am the Hulda, the swamp witch, crypt keeper, and spirit guardian for the lost souls." It clacks as it advances with jerky movements. The hooded cloak it wears covers all but the hands and feet, which are bones, no flesh. I can't see its face. Only the red, glaring orbs penetrate the shadows. There's a heaviness to its presence. It is prominent—formidable.

Though my necklace remains cool against my skin, every inch of my body is tense, warning me. My ability rests, aflame and ready in the center of my being. When I try to call on it, however, it slips through my intentions like liquid dripping through my fingers.

The Hulda walks upon white stones. Except, they're not stones. One rolls, and instead of a smooth rock, it's a skull. They all rotate to stare at me with their empty eye sockets, their jaws hanging open in silent screams. I swallow back a lump of revulsion.

When the being doesn't say anything more, I try to be courteous. I've gotten out of many tight situations with good manners. "Pleased to meet you, Hulda. I am Tambrynn."

"Do not try to flatter me with your mortal courtesies. You have trespassed in the gravest fashion. The living do not dwell with the dead, though you should know that well enough, daughter of the death mage." Mist, which starts upon the water rises, separates into shapes. Light flickers inside them. Like shimmering ghosts, they surround the Hulda.

I open my mouth to speak and taste bitterness, despair, and anger. I gag and it takes me a moment to regain my composure. "I meant no disrespect. I have come to find something that will put an end to my father's reign. I only wish to search for it. I'm not here to harm you or anything you guard."

"You. Are. Not. Welcome. Here." The mist whirls about the Hulda as if caught in the wind. Yet, there is no wind.

The words knock me back against the back ropes of the bridge. Vines and limbs shake. An unseen force pushes at me. I clutch the rope tight, my muscles straining against the onslaught. I'm not near strong enough to hold on for long. My ability churns in my gut, but I'm not able to pull from it. Water slops below me, and I catch a glimpse of glowing eyes and something wide snaking along the surface.

More power hits me, stealing my breath. I'm bent over with my back against the rope. My hips distend and muscles along my spine ache as if being pulled apart. My ears fill with cotton, dimming my hearing as I strain against the force.

"Stop!" another voice breaks through the charged air. It also is neither male nor female in nature. "Stop this right now." It's not demanding like the Hulda's words, but the pressure releases, and I drop to my knees on the hard boards of the walkway, panting.

Spit flies from my mouth as I exhale the breath I hold. My chest heaves. Could it be? *"Lucas?"* I call out with my mind like a child crying for its parent. It's desperate, I know. But I've grown used to not being so helpless lately. I almost forgot how terrifying that feeling is.

There's no answer. Reaching out with my mind to find him reveals nothing. Silence. I am well and truly alone here. And I am no match for whatever the Hulda is.

24

"Calling for any living being will do you no good in the spirit realm. The Kinsman himself has set my sovereignty. Only he is stronger than I here." The Hulda's voice has moved, making me more nervous. "You should not have come here."

The Kinsman? Her words frighten me on a level I can't explain. There's a surety, a finality to them that rings true. "I'm unsure how I got here," I wheeze out. I want to stand to face the Hulda, but I'm not sure I can. My pelvis aches as if I were the short end of a turkey wishbone after it's been snapped in two.

The Hulda rises out of the water in front of where I lay sprawled on the bridge. The hood is gone now, and wild, dark hair waves around the skeletal head like snakes.

Instead of jerky movements, it, for I don't know if they are a she or a he, glides over the fog that clouds the top of the marsh below. I squint. Or is it the smoky mist that's transporting the being? "You used the Mortifer Blade to cut through reality and enter the Betwixt, my territory."

My nerves snap with alarm at her declaration. Grandfather had said I could cut through the air, but I'd never considered it could do this. How do I get out of here? I glance around for the dagger, but it's not within eyesight, and I'm still in too much agony to move and see if it's beneath me.

I need to appeal to this Hulda if I want to make it out of here alive. "My deepest apologies for disturbing you. I had no idea—"

The Hulda laughs, a terrifying, deep sound that echoes around the swamp like a fog horn. "Mortals with their paltry ignorance. I should snap you in two and add you to my collection." The specter-like mist crowds close around her, the lights inside of them throbbing like a single heartbeat.

The wind blows against the swamp witch, drawing its attention, and I notice the hair is more like black seaweed. "Who challenges my authority?"

One of the wavering shapes moves toward the witch. Blue orbs face off with the Hulda's red, glowing eyes.

"Kinsman-selected you may be. But your oath is to do no harm to the lost souls. His law, the one you protect so rabidly, forbids you from striking one of his messengers, or your reign shall be put asunder." The specter's light blue eyes brighten and blink with each word. "Whether this child meant to or not, she is lost. It is your job to help her find what she seeks."

I'm unsure whether I appreciate the entity calling me a child, but I suppose if you've been dead for years, anyone alive would be young. I say nothing, praying silently that the Hulda will listen to them. Help is better than being battered by the witch.

"Do not use holy words to persuade me! The Kinsman sentenced me against my will. I will do as I wish. For he does not listen to the cries of the cursed." The Hulda moves and bends over the rope railing, the skull inches from my face. I expected the odor of rot and death. But it's nothing like I imagined. There's a tang of bad choices, regrets, and loss. It's an innate knowing that passes across my mind.

Tears sting my eyes. I'd lived with people telling me I was evil all of my life. But now I know differently. And though terrified, I'm not going to be pushed around by some malevolent swamp witch, powerful or not. "I am not accursed. I am the Kinsman's messenger, as they said. I'm a firebird sent to save the living from my father, the death mage." As I speak, my abilities flare inside me, warming, heating. My hands glow blue. "And you will not stop me from finding Thoron's talisman so I can destroy him."

The Hulda screams and jerks away from me. "Don't say his name!"

I call out to the dagger, which I can now feel beneath my leg. In an instant, it's in my hand and I drag myself up on throbbing legs to face the Hulda. "The Kinsman may have locked you here, but it was surely your own actions that sealed your fate. Who are you to pass judgment on me when the Kinsman alone can do so? When I do find the talisman I seek, I will send my father here to spend the rest of his eternal death with you."

A roar fills the air with an ominous pitch. The Hulda's eyes grow until they are lamps, burning and engulfing the very air around them. In a blink, the witch rises and rushes at me.

I raise my arms to protect my head, the dagger held firm in my hand. Anger, hate, and every ugly emotion I have ever experienced wash over me. They're the deepest sins, ones a person never admits. The Hulda's intention to kill me sizzles against my consciousness, penetrating my bones like needles.

All I know is pain and fury. Cold flames lick across my body, numbing me until I am frozen. My flesh is sealed in a brutal, frigid state.

How can this be? I am a fire and flame. A firebird. I open my mouth in a soundless squeal, a plea for my fire to rekindle. For the Kinsman to hear me and release me.

A spark, a flash of red among the icy blue of my soul, and pain explodes all across my body as I blaze back to life. My veins fill with liquid fire which crackle and snap like a pyre.

I am light. I am fire.

Screaming fills my ears. Bubbling, gurgling death cries. Skulls and bones melt before my eyes, scoring the area with a charred blackness. The swamp witch shrieks as the wrath of my inner flame engulfs her. My veins are ablaze. It flows hot, comforting in the warmth that spreads like a wildfire through me. I don't fight it. I close my eyes and accept it as who I am.

"Tambrynn." It's the voice I heard opposing the Hulda.

I blink. All of the cloudy haze is gone. What's left is an indecipherable shadow person. It's not the Hulda. There is no heavy weight of power or anger. No red, piercing eyes.

"Yes." I simply state, uncertain about what is happening.

The shadow reaches out toward me. The blue eyes have lightened to a glimmering white. "I am Astralee, your father's mother. It is my honor to meet you."

I'm stunned into silence. After a few moments, I raise my hand to the shadow. All I sense is a chilled welcome from it. That's not right. The coolness is healing me. Air, like a breath, bathes me in incandescent light, which gleams and then dies.

"You were close to death, as close as one gets before you cannot go back. The witch is not sanctioned to do that. It is a trespass. I am simply restoring what she took and giving you back your life." Gently, the shadow helps me to stand, the hands solid as any real flesh would be. At that moment, I am surrounded by her essence. Sadness, grief, and joy are intertwined in a bittersweet perfume.

"You—you're my grandmother?" I ask a bit dumbly. My

heart races, warring with my head which tells me that can't be right.

"Yes, that's the word—grandmother. I am as you say." She moves back and settles on the bridge as if standing before me in person—if that person were a featureless shadow. "I have few minutes to help you. The Hulda will return angrier than before. She is intent on stopping you. You must listen carefully."

The shock wears off and I have questions for her. "But, why are you here? Are you a lost soul?"

"I chose to be here. That is why the witch has no power over me. And my story is a twisted and sad one, I'm afraid. I am the reason your father is bitter and hate-filled. After Jarmon deserted me, I resented the child we had. Thoron was teased and harassed because of who I was, who he was. They called Thoron a half-breed from the moment he was born. In death, I can see how it wounded his spirit, twisted his soul."

She continues, "I raised him bathed in my own hostility, both for his presence and his father's rejection. Soon, he became what I was, furious at everyone and everything. We were two of a kind until he found dark magic. All of the suffering he has caused is my fault."

"How did he get into dark magic?" I'm cut off by her raising a shapeless arm.

"There is not enough time." A square object appears in her shadow, radiating with a silver-white sheen. "This box is made of silver mixed with dragon's tears, a toxic poison fatal to all who touch it in its melted form or breathe the fumes it emits. There is no key to open it, so melting the metal is the only way to get to the talisman inside."

She goes on. "Inside is a special gastrolith, a stone from a dragon's craw, which Thoron used in his first black magic ritual. You cannot destroy the box without risking your life.

You cannot get to the stone without destroying the box. It's called Memento Mori, an old saying that means, 'remember you die.' Only by sacrificing yourself will the curse be removed. It can't be forced upon one to break, for their life would be at risk, but by natural actions through free will destroyed. Do you understand?"

It fits in the palm of my hand. The sides of the metal square are carved with symbols, not unlike the sigils on the cavern walls and Grandfather's displacement rocks. These, however, are more jagged. Her words soak into my consciousness and the answer comes to me without much thought. "Someone has to sacrifice their life to get to the stone. Then someone else has to destroy it. Why are you giving it to me?"

"Not just anyone can destroy it. It has to be someone worthy. I died trying. I was not worthy enough." Her ghostly hand raises to my hair. Unease wraps frigid fingers around my spine. "I sense you are worthy."

My heart stutters with her admission. Tears gather behind my eyes.

"Don't cry for me. I have what I deserved. Weep, if you must, for the innocent boy Thoron could have been had I not been such a vengeful mother. He never knew true security or a loving hand at his brow. No one should ever grow up like that."

My heart breaks at the picture she paints of my father. Though I suffered as an indentured servant, I had known love. If I hadn't had mother and Lucas as a child, I shudder at what I would've been.

Astralee moves suddenly and darts a glance over her shoulder. "My time is almost up. You need to know that your father is not the only threat to your life. The froggen have unleashed a—" the sound of water rushing drowns out the sounds around me and I can't hear what she's saying. "—affects all the kingdoms. You must stop them before they—"

noises of waves crashing assault my ears. "—the Zoe Tree. You must be vigilant."

"Grandmother? I can't hear you." I reach out to touch her, but there's nothing there.

She reappears and covers my hands in both of hers. The Memento Mori hums as I grip it tight. "Be fierce, my dearest girl. I believe in you."

And she is gone. I blink my eyes and I'm back. The Betwixt is no more.

Nomads dart up and down the bridge, leaning over the sides and calling my name. Lucas flies above, screeching frantically.

Any energy I might've still had disappears. My bones are jelly weak and I collapse, landing hard on my backside. "Lucas?" I mutter wearily.

"My lady! What happened? One minute you were there and the next you were gone." He flies close enough that his wings graze my head.

"I—" I'm cut off by a roiling sound that invades my hearing, like a furiously bubbling stew. Voices burble, but I can't make out what they're saying. My back stiffens. I've heard this before. The voices are frantic. I clutch the talisman to my chest. Even in the shade of the massive trees it glimmers and hums with magic.

"What are you holding?"

I don't want to talk to him where I may be overheard by the froggen. "We need to get out of here before I can explain. We can't risk being overheard." I tuck the metal box in my pocket for safekeeping.

"Tambrynn!" Tibby runs over to me, rocking the swinging bridge perilously, and hugs me. Her arms are tight around my neck, bending me backward.

I squeal in pain while bracing myself against her embrace.

Though small, nomad women are quite strong, and my bones already ache from my encounter with the Hulda—my hips in particular.

"Let the girl breathe, woman." Debbert grumbles. I notice, however, that he doesn't seem to be quite so contrary toward me.

I squint at him. He's acting a bit too guilty to not confront him. "Did you know there was a swamp witch?"

He wrings his hands. His beard has moss and twigs in it. Had he been searching for me also? Why? "I didn't know she'd call you out. No one's ever crossed over and come back before."

I keep the anger that flares inside me in check, though the heat of my fire burns in my veins. "But you've seen others cross over? You knew there was danger and you didn't warn me?"

His eyes glance left and right, anywhere but directly at me. "It's not a common occurrence. Very few cross over." He shrugs his wide shoulders and a stick from his shirt falls into the water. "I thought sprites or alligators would be the worst we'd run across. And you were warned about them."

Tibby clicks her tongue. "What he's trying to say is he's sorry. Truly, it never occurred to me, either. The Hulda doesn't stir often. Only when fates are turning."

"What's that mean?" It's Lucas, who landed not far away and is pushing toward me. He takes my hand, kisses it, and presses it tight to his chest.

I lean my forehead against him, thankful to be back. His scent of home washes over my senses, comforting me.

"Ach. It means that something big is afoot. Bad magic. Death of leadership. The Kingdom ending. The last time she showed herself was when Risan, the eldrin sanctuary, was attacked by Thoron. Nothing's been safe since. We heard her from our village shrieking in the dark several nights before it happened. But even then, no one was taken," Tibby says.

Lolla's round face is earnest. "I heard she was a voyant in her previous life which explains why she knows things before others do."

"Voyant or not, she was quite powerful. I'd prefer we move along before she decides to return and crush me with her magic again." I ignore Lucas's sharp gaze and grab the staff that had rolled, landing by my feet. The gems are dark, so I tap the handle once on the wooden planks. Welcoming light shines again.

Lolla hands me the dagger with a sad smile and an awkward curtsey. "Glad you're back, my lady."

I jerk at her use of Lucas's endearment. His narrow eyes are crinkled with a smile. *"She means it as a true honor. You fought the Hulda and returned. You are now elevated in their eyes,"* he speaks in my mind. To them, he states, "Yes, we are glad Tambrynn is returned."

The nomads form a line and continue trudging in the direction we'd been going before I'd entered the Betwixt. Debbert takes the lead, as I expected. I'm unsure if I can fully trust them, but reason tells me that even if they had mentioned the swamp witch, it probably wouldn't have changed anything.

They talk about how their kin found the sturdy cypress trees and chose to build their huts high away from the interference of the magic folk. I half listen to them as we trudge on, my mind going back over my interactions in the land of the dead.

The wood walkway becomes a bridge as the planks rise. Soon we are suspended far above the water. The path meanders from one massive tree trunk to the next, braced between with thick logs. I squeeze Lucas's hand, which I still hold. I will probably never let it go again. There's only enough room for us to walk single-file, so we walk slightly offset with

Lucas leading me. However, I'm not complaining. I'd rather be close to him in this awful place. Audhild was right. Too many things are hidden in the depths of this marshland for comfort.

"I'm sorry to have given you a fright," I tell Lucas in a low voice. "It wasn't much better on the other side." I wonder about how the Hulda ended up stuck as the keeper of the Betwixt by the Kinsman. What had she done to deserve that punishment? And why did she want to stop me from getting the talisman? It hums in my pocket, but I say nothing yet.

"A fright is too simple a word." His voice is tight. "I didn't sense you at all. It was more than unnerving. I was terrified."

"As was I." We walk on for quite a while without speaking. I watch the play of the moon and the shadows across the trees and the marshes below. The fog of rot clears as we move upward. This high, it's more open, the trunks and limbs shrinking toward the tops of the cypress trees. It is curiously beautiful among the branches. Moonlight reflects off the feather-like foliage.

The swamp below us is like a grouping of large puddles with weedy vegetation growing in between and along the edges. Some pools are larger than others, their centers reflecting the moon's silver cast like a mirror.

My mind jumps back and forth between what Astralee told me and wondering about my grandfather, Rekspire, and Audhild. The bulge in my pocket assures me the talisman is still safe. Now I have to figure out how to get to the stone.

It's simple, really. All I have to do is not get killed trying to destroy it.

25

"Welcome to Lowborn." Debbert stands in front of a large hut. It is a split log constructed and attached to the cypress with braces. Several of the houses are scattered among the large trees, the wooden paths dividing and leading right to the front doors.

I turn in a circle, taking it all in. Below, the marsh pools spread out in abundance, though from our position it's hard to see. The mounting heat from the sunrise churns the air with a soupy warmth, but a breeze rustles through the higher branches giving us relief.

"People-sized bird houses." I muse quietly to Lucas who grins back. He is bent with the weight of Grandfather's pack. He shifts it off and drops it to the walkway with a grunt.

"The eldrin won't bother us here. Too crude for their spoiled tastes." Tibby pats my arm.

"Yes, I can see that." I walk over to one of the buildings and rap on the side. Weathered though it is, it's firm. Sturdy braces hold fast the room-sized house to the trunk. The surface gleams with a coat of some sort of aged lacquer. "They look well made."

"Oh, yes! We nomads are competent craftspeople. Whatever we make lasts. And cypress is a hearty wood." Lolla smiles brightly. Her face is red with the heat, and moisture dampens her soiled dress.

Sweat trickles down my hairline as well. "Is there someplace to rest? I think we're all quite exhausted." I ask not only for my and Lucas's comfort, but to also get him alone so we can discuss what happened with the Hulda. I want to show him the talisman and ask his opinion on what we should do.

Tibby takes charge easily. "They're all empty for the picking. Let Tambrynn and her man have the largest, mind you. Otherwise, everyone spread out and find a place to claim." She points several of the younger nomads to houses farther down the path while Debbert pokes his head in and out of others, inspecting them.

"A few cobwebs, but some of the furniture remains. I'm surprised." Debbert shuffles past us to hurry down another path. The lines on his face are creased less and his voice is devoid of the sarcastic grump he'd had earlier. "I claim my old home."

A look I can't interpret crosses Tibby's face. She smiles at us when she turns to glance our way. "I'm going to help him inspect the rest of the area. The lodge should be along this pathway." She points to our right.

Lucas grabs the pack and dragging it, leads the way past several crooked trees which grow across the bridge and tangle in other tree limbs. The shade is a welcome change, though the breeze is stifled here.

The lodge is bigger than the others. It is attached to two trees that grow side by side and is much larger than the ones before. Unlike the others, it has a chimney that pokes out of the roof, its stones blackened. Lucas sets the pack down and opens the door. He swipes away dusty cobwebs.

There is a dresser with a half-full lantern on top, several dusty, melted candles in holders, and a couple of books on the left side. Running down the longest wall is a bed frame with no mattress or any kind of bedding. It's long enough for both of us to lie on, which is a relief. Most of the huts aren't big enough for Lucas and me to fit in. I'm grateful for Tibby's forethought.

To the right is a fold-down table with two chairs. Flat stones are mortared into the back floor and wall surrounding the small fireplace. It's big enough to cook a small meal or heat the building. Two pans hang from hooks on the walls above a small countertop. Sitting alone on the counter's shelf is a hollowed-out chunk of wood with several crudely-carved utensils sticking out of it.

The hut's width is narrow but wide enough for necessity, and almost big enough for comfort. "Why would anyone leave everything?" I ask as I run a hand across the well-worn counter. It must've once been sealed, but the wood no longer holds a smooth sheen. I clap the dust from my hands.

"Perhaps they had no choice? This place may be safe from eldrin, at least to some extent. However, other beings wouldn't have such misgivings."

"Like djinn?" I say, half teasing.

"Yes. Djinn, however, don't care for community much. They're much more inclined to settle in places alone if they can, or they'd be a bigger threat here." He picks up some debris from a corner and studies it. "I have to wonder if it's safe from some of the waterkin?" He holds out a scale that covers his entire palm. Even in the dull light, I can see the reflective iridescence of the item. Too big for a fish but about the size of the mer-girl Shellsea's scales.

My chest tightens. "You think it might be froggen?"

He drops the rubbish outside the door and scrubs his dirty hands down his leafy outfit. "It could be any of them. You heard what they said. Many outcasts and criminals have come and gone from here. Living above a marsh would be grand for anyone seeking shelter from their crimes. We'll have to be careful. I don't wish to run into any of them again if we can help it. Now, tell me about your encounter with the Hulda."

I close the door, which shuts solidly but leaves us in the dark. He fumbles on the dresser with the lantern and some sort of lighting stick. The familiar tang of lantern oil hits my nose and I sit on the wooden logs which make up the bedframe. It reminds me of the small cottage on Tenebris, though it is much smaller.

Lucas sits next to me, breaking my musing. His eyes are serious and I take a deep breath and tell him everything from the moment I started to feel unsure on the swinging bridge until the moment I returned from the Betwixt. Lucas's hand is warm on my arm, comforting, as I end my tale.

"So, the froggen have unleashed something?" He asks about the last information I give him that my grandmother stated, brokenly. His fine eyebrows furrow. He holds the Memento Mori box, my father's talisman, in his hand. "It sounds like it involves the Zoe Tree."

"It does. And I recall seeing something in the visions I got from Rekspire. That presence shouldn't have been in the passage. What if it was the froggen? Could they have found my ring and entered?" The idea chills me.

"It's possible," Lucas murmurs. "What would they be doing in the passage that could affect all of the kingdoms? Destroying the doorways?"

"Or destroying the passage? Did you come across information on the passageway when we were in Grandfather's keep? Perhaps if we knew more about it, we could figure out what might be happening." I rub my face. I'm so incredibly tired I could fall asleep sitting up.

Thumping sounds outside the door. We stop talking and wait.

A minute later another thunk rattles the lodge.

Tibby knocks, opens the door, and sticks her head in. "Ha-loo! Sorry for the noise. I drug a couple of extra mattresses down in case you need any. I remembered you were pretty sore when you returned from dealing with the witch."

Four, square pillow-sized cushions are leaned against the handrails outside of the lodge.

My back twinges as I shift to face her. "Thank you, Tibby."

She shrugs. "We're all settled in now. I wanted to check on you two and make sure everything's comfortable." She glances around the space, curiosity shining in her eyes.

"This space is quite accommodating," Lucas assures her.

She lugs in the sewn square mats. They're a muted gray color, making me think they're fairly worn though they look to be in serviceable shape. "I patted the dust out already, so they should be ready." The door rubs as she closes it behind her.

Lucas chuckles. "I think she was more than simply checking on us."

I grin back. "You think she was spying on us?"

"Nomads are curious folk." He takes the cushions. Instead of placing them on the bedframe, he puts them next to the rock flooring in front of the fireplace. "I do apologize for this, but you may need to sleep on the hard floor, my lady, so we don't burn the kind nomad's hut-house down." He lies on the edge of the soft-looking bedding.

I groan but understand. "Maybe I'll be too tired to even flicker a flame today." I lay down on the cold surface, my hips and back protesting. "I wish we had Grandfather's hot water springs right now. I could fall asleep in them, work out my tender flesh, and not set anything aflame." I yawn.

Lucas makes an agreeable mumble. It only takes a couple of moments for him to close his eyes and his breathing deepens into slumber.

I'm not far behind him.

———

I dream of eyes watching me, falling from the swinging bridge into the murky swamp, and of dozens of grinning froggen dragging me to a watery death. Vaguely I hear Lucas singing to me, and the nightmares recede and I fall into a comfortable sleep.

It's dim when I wake up, and no candle burns, but it's warm and cozy on the floor. I grab at a blanket tucked around me and jerk my eyes open. I move my head to see how that's possible. The cushions are gone, but someone has put a quilted spread across me as I slept.

"How?" I move to sit up, but my backside protests. I groan back at it.

Footsteps plod against the wooden flooring and I turn to see Lucas. Except it's not Lucas.

"Ye're alive!" Arrin grins at me from one of the chairs that have been dragged to the opposite side of the room. She leans against her bone-white walking stick and stares at me.

The door is open, allowing some light in. A breeze swirls through a window I hadn't realized was there. It flips the ends of Arrin's long gray hair. She is fresh and clean and smells like a flowery soap.

As soon as I comprehend she is there in person and not a dream, my heart lifts. "You're a most welcome sight! How'd you find us?" I can't help the delight that's reflected in my voice. "And where do I get a bath, too?"

She cackles out a laugh. "I'm afraid the rainwater bins are emptied out already. We do enjoy our baths."

"Is that why you were swept up in the illusion so easily?" I ask, curious.

Her wide grin is my answer. "Now, as for the other question, *ye* found *us*. We've holed up not far from here, regrouping, you might say, before we take on the eldrin and free our kin." Her eyes twinkle. "One of our young'uns heard a ruckus and found all ye here, sleeping like the dead."

I cringe at her words. The dead hadn't slept in the Betwixt. "I'm glad you made it here safe and sound. I've been worried about you since the dragon scattered you to the winds."

"Aye, it did, the beast. Took us a day or so to find each other. That dragon is why we headed here. Dragons don't much care for swamps, they're haunted ye know. So Nobbert and I figured we'd be safe enough until we freed the rest of the captive nomads. Tibby told me ye were here, so when that Watcher of yer'n left to scout, I told him I'd take watch until ye woke. Ye were quite restless. Was it nightmares?"

"Something like that, yes." I look all around, trying to focus on anything but the images from my dreams.

She takes out a pipe and tamps in some leaves. When she's satisfied, she lights it and takes a long drag, letting the smoke curl around her face when she exhales. The scent of dried apples soaked in strong liquor fills the air.

"I didn't realize you smoke." I shift so I'm on my knees and then use the other chair to help me stand. Then, I sit and face her, waving the fug away.

"I found a stash in the hut I'm staying in." Smoke from her pipe drifts out the door. She smacks her lips together. "It's a bit old, but I'm not complaining." She gives me a one-eyed, squinted look. "I heard ye took on the Hulda and lived to tell the tale." Her laugh is a cackling sound, bright with amusement. "If'n that doesn't convince Nobbert ye're the prophesied one, nothing will."

I roll my shoulders, hoping to stretch my tense muscles. "He has reason to distrust me. Trouble does seem to find me easier than most." My grin is sheepish. "I am sorry for that."

"Pshaw! Trouble finds us all at one time or another. Now," she claps her hands, "tell me what ye learned from that old windbag."

26

"You know the Hulda?" I ask, surprised, though I probably shouldn't be. Arrin seems to know quite a bit about everything.

"Knew her once a long time ago." Arrin puffs and her face is obscured behind an aromatic cloud. When I don't answer, she waves her pipe at me to keep going.

"I didn't learn much from her except to fear her. There was another spirit there. Her name was Astralee." I explain to Arrin about my grandmother and the Memento Mori—my father's talisman. When I come to the last part where I couldn't hear her, Arrin tilts her head my way.

"Blurbing water, ye say? It's them froggen, I tell ye. After they took me to that ridiculous castle of theirs, I figured out they'd been using the streams and such to listen in on everyone. Despicable creatures." She points the pipe at me. "Do ye think they heard ye in the Betwixt?"

"I'm not sure how that's possible. The Hulda made it clear no one living could be found among the dead." I ponder that for a moment while Arrin puffs. "It couldn't be the opposite, could it? The dead can't cross over to the living, could they? Would there be a dead froggen that would be spying on the Betwixt from that side?"

"Heh." Arrin frowns, her lips tightening around the end of the pipe. "Or a voyant who speaks with the dead. I've known a few spirit talkers in my life. My grannie always warned me about such things. Said it was abhorrent to call on the souls, crossed over or not. Ye probably noticed yerself how dangerous they can be."

I rub a hand across my eyes. "I did."

She *tsks*. "Water surrounds us here, though we're pretty far above it. I'd still be pretty careful spilling secrets if I were ye. Don't trust anyone ye're not completely sure of."

"Tambrynn?" It's Lucas calling from outside the small hut. There's not enough room for all three of us, so it must be a warning in case Arrin is still here.

She takes a small stone implement and grinds the fire out of the end of her pipe. Smoke curls and dies, leaving behind a thick, but not unpleasant scent. She pockets them both and stands. "It was good talking with ye. I'll be around." She limps out, walking stick in hand.

She and Lucas greet each other before he ducks into the hut. "How are you feeling?" Though his words are light, I can sense his concern through our bond.

I stretch. "Rested. Sore, but glad to be out of danger for the moment."

He takes the seat Arrin deserted. "Supper will be ready shortly. I caught a couple of squirrels to add to a smorgasbord of other squirrels." His chuckle is a welcome sound.

"Not much to eat up in a tree?" I ask, humored as well.

"No birds. They disappeared after we moved in." There's a

certain twinkle in his eye as if to say birds are too smart to linger where they might get eaten. "A few mushrooms. But I guess this isn't the season for most of them. And they don't have any stores left from the last residents. It's all been scavenged by other creatures. Debbert mentioned it's been quite a while since anyone's been here." He pulls a finger through a thick line of dust and then taps the back wall with his hand. "They're remarkably sturdy even if they are a bit small."

"Did he mention why they stopped living here?" I ask, curious. If it is so safe, why would they leave?

He rocks back, leaving two legs of the chair on the floor. "He said the swamp became restless. The residents would have nightmares, and some of the nomads said they 'sensed an unseen presence.' It scared them, so they moved to land and built the village there. I wonder if it was the Hulda they were sensing?"

I consider that. There'd been several spirits, including my grandmother, in the Betwixt. The Hulda was certainly strong enough to make her presence known. "If it was the witch, I don't blame them for leaving. It might not be the best idea to stay this close to her. But, I'm not sure we have any safer options at this point." I recall the bubbling water and Arrin's warning. "Grandfather's keep has been the safest place on Anavrin so far. I'll be glad to return and figure out how to destroy this talisman."

The chair drops down and Lucas leans forward. "So, tell me about the Hulda. We've got some time before the supper is called." His eyes are too perceptive. He knew I only told him the parts I wanted him to know.

I take a deep, balancing breath. "It was the Mortifer blade." I recount how she was able to stop me so thoroughly and had me bent almost in half. "She's strong enough to scare me, that's for sure, and not a being I want to come into contact with again." I pick at one of my fingernails. "When I used the dagger, I meant for the presence to be revealed, not to enter the Betwixt."

I struggle to remain composed. "It's terrifying. A place where lost souls are left behind. It wasn't a happy place." I continue, explaining to him everything that happened and then my conversation with Arrin.

He stares at the silver box. He turns it over, studying the markings. "She died trying to destroy it?"

"That's what she said. She didn't have time to go into details."

His hand fists over it, his knuckles whitening. His face darkens. "You're not sacrificing yourself to get to the stone."

My heart pinches at his anger. His hair spills like ink across his forehead and I long to run my fingers through it, assure him that I'm not going anywhere. I hold back, knowing I can't promise anything. My father must be destroyed. "I didn't say I was going to sacrifice myself—"

He shifts in the chair, sitting on the edge closest to me. "Good. Because you aren't going to. We'll find another way. Maybe Astralee didn't know everything about it. We'll find something in Bennett's library to help us."

Pain rocks me and I soaked it in, knowing it's only his fear for me coming through our bond. I brush my fingers through his silky hair. I close my eyes, remembering each time my father's magic hit him—every time he was injured for helping me fight back. It was agony.

When I look back at him, there's a longing in his gaze that mirrors my desire to keep him safe and by my side. I'd do anything for him, for his safety. I know he'd do the same for me.

The moment is interrupted by voices.

I wipe my shaking palms down my viny pants. Mud flakes off the boots I still wear, leaving a trail on the wooden floor. I shuffle my feet together, leaving a larger pile as I let the tendrils of our shared intimacy go. "I wish Grandfather and Audhild were here to help."

"I know." Lucas hands me the Memento Mori back. "Keep that safe. We don't want Thoron to get it back."

A shriek rents the air, something only a dragon might make. Lucas jumps up and is out the hut door before I grab the staff and make sure the dagger is at my side. I stuff the box in my pocket and join him on the swinging bridge a couple of moments later. With all of the foliage, it's hard to see what made the noise.

Arrin limps her way across the planks to us. "It's another dragon," she wheezes. "Take cover."

I glance at Lucas, and in an instant, we are both airborne. We weave our way above the limbs and leaves. The treetop canopy is thick when we reach the clear sky. From up here, I can view the breaks in groups of trees which goes on for as far as I can see. Light from the lowering sun colors the foliage a richer shade of green.

Another shriek comes from our right. I catch the flash of a dark tail whipping between pines, snagging and breaking a tree top.

"Rekspire?" I call out in case it's him. I pray silently it is and that my father hasn't hurt him. *"Nomads are living in the trees."* It's a subtle warning.

"Tambrynn? I've been searching for you."

I sense nothing wrong. No ill will. Nothing like I had with Audhild. *"Yes! Climb above the trees. We're here. What is going on?"*

His black form shoots out of the branches like an arrow. His body spins until he locates me, and then his wings take hold of the wind and he darts toward us. *"There's something wrong with the Zoe Tree. There's water everywhere. The kingdom is flooding."*

"Flooding?" It's Lucas, his voice strained.

"Come. You have to help me close the doors. I can't manage it on my own. Bennett told me you could help pull the door closed."

Pull the door closed? I'd only be able to pull if I were in the passage. Wouldn't I? Could I? Questions swirled in my head. But there was one I needed to know the most. *"Where are Grandfather and Audhild?"*

"He had to take her back to the keep. We couldn't get through to the passage to get her to another kingdom. He'll have to lock her up there, he said, until you kill Thoron. When Thoron is dead, he's hoping she'll be released from the curse." He swings over us, his lengthy wings blocking the sun. *"The island is almost gone. We must hurry!"*

"Let me warn the nomads." I dart back down, with Lucas on my tail. It takes me a moment to orient myself since there are layers of huts built along the wooden bridge strung for miles along the forest of swamp trees. But I catch the sounds of some of the nomads arguing, which leads me to them.

Arrin, Nobbert, and Debbert are having a loud discussion. I hear my name, but I don't have time to worry about the men's latest complaint about me.

I swoop down and land behind them. Lucas stays in his bird form and lands on the rope handrail beside me.

Arrin is the first to notice. "What's wrong?"

"Rekspire, the rogue dragon, has returned with a message. The Zoe Tree is flooding. Lucas and I have to go back and seal the door."

"Flooding? What do you mean flooding?" Debbert barks.

Arrin smacks him in the arm. "What do ye think it means, ye ninny? There's water that's flooding." She turns her puckered face my way. "Don't worry none about us. Go save the kingdom." Her hands shoo me away. "We'll spread the word best we can. Hopefully, we're all safe up here for a while at least."

Relieved, I take off once again. We rejoin Rekspire. The heat of the day is waning as the sun goes down. It's dark in the distance, which is strange, but I can't worry about that right now.

"*Let's go,*" I tell the dragon, and prepare to follow after him.

It isn't long before I realize that Rekspire is holding back to let us keep up with him. "*Rekspire, we're slowing you down. And you said it is urgent. Is there a way to ride on your back so we get there quicker?*"

There's silence for a moment. "*Unlike the other dragonkin on Far Starl, I am unused to bearing a rider. But, yes, it would be faster. You'll have to change back. Settle between my spines and hold on. Without a saddle, I'm unsure how steady I will be.*"

I dart over his back and drop to the biggest space I can find between his flat spines. They remind me of bent elbows and poke out from his scaly back. Lucas is right behind me. He flits around my head, chirping, until my feet land and I change. Luckily, his scales are slick enough to slide my boots down without hindrance.

I grip the spine, as air rushes over me. A glance over my shoulder assures me Lucas has done the same.

Rekspire's long neck stretches to look back at us. "*I will now go faster.*"

And true to his words, his speed picks up. The wind burns my eyes, so I hide my head between my arms. The air shifts from a warm moving breeze to whipping past us so quickly I'm chilled. I call on my fire to warm my body, but not injure the dragon I ride. "*Are you warm enough?*" I ask Lucas.

"*It could be better, but I'm fine. I'm not sure I would want to be a dragon rider, though. I prefer flying under my own power.*" Humor laces his words, and I have to agree with him. It's a bit unnerving.

The massive wings push up and down even as his body moves side to side—different than a horse, which is my only riding experience. Though I know I can change into a bird in the air, it's still disconcerting to not be in control. I'd rather not revisit my jump from the eldrin sanctuary where I almost died. Had it not been for Audhild, I would've.

"Yes, this is different from what I imagined, too." The wind's current breaks, which causes the dragon to jerk down to catch the next one. I hold on tighter, sure my hands are white with the effort.

"It might be better had we the right equipment. I read that Dragon riders use saddles and headgear that keeps the wind from their faces." There's a tightness in his voice now that wasn't there a moment ago.

"Hold on." Rekspire breaks into our conversation and we shift forward. He darts downward, through some wispy clouds.

Had he not warned us, I would fear he was falling, the descent is so quick. However, he levels out closer to the treetops and the air grows warmer.

We cling for what seems like an hour when I catch the first echo of panicked voices. Raising my head, I see them. People with loaded carts, horses laden down with items, and people with makeshift bundles are all headed away from the direction Rekspire is taking us. Children cling to their parents.

And then it hits me. They're traveling as night falls. I did believe Rekspire, but now it feels more real than it had before. How far has the flood gotten if they've organized this well and they haven't stopped yet?

"*Who are they?*" I ask.

It takes a bit for Lucas to respond. "*Mixed-races mostly. A few djinn, you can tell by the different creatures traveling alongside the others. Animals won't do that without being driven. Djinn will. There may be some voyants as well, but they're harder to spot.*" He waits a bit longer before continuing. "*What I don't see, however, are eldrin. They may have transported to mountains or somewhere safer.*"

"*Is that good or bad?*" I ask.

"*Bad, maybe? They wouldn't stick around to try to save the doorway, which should be their job as the leaders of Anavrin. But sadly, it isn't surprising.*"

From the glimpses I get, I see no actual flooding. Until we pass the crowds clamoring not only on the roadways but also along the pastures. We swing over emptied villages, doors stand ajar, and cottages abandoned. Animals roam freely without a care. What of their fate?

I can smell the water before I spot it. It's not deep. Yet. But it's spreading.

The moon is full in a sapphire sky. Its reflection glimmers in the wet expanse where tall grass pokes out like bristles on a brush. There are no travelers now, no animals here—their instincts have taken them to higher ground.

"*We still have a distance to go before we get to the Mother Tree.*" Rekspire finally speaks up. "*I may need to stop and take a short break before it gets too deep.*"

In an instant, I am once again in my silvery firebird form with my magpie Watcher flying beside me. Our reflection ripples in the glassy water and is highlighted by the glowing night sky. It would be beautiful had the situation not been so dire.

Rekspire, in his dragon form, drops to the ground and lands

knee-deep in the flood. He takes a long drag of the semi-clear water. Settling on a bush, I take a drink myself, finding the water still fresh, not salt water. There must be a stream nearby filling and overflowing first. After drinking my fill, Lucas and I find a tree nearby and land to wait for the dragon to rest.

Murmuring fills the quiet landscape. Rekspire still drinks, unaware.

"Do you hear that?" I turn my head back and forth to search for the source. Lucas is on a branch above mine and to my left. Blue energy snaps around my feathered body. The fire inside me kindles and heats quickly.

"No, but you're lit up with your blue magic," Lucas confirms. *"And my feathers are tingling with warning."*

"Rekspire, be careful. I think something's in the water." I hope the dragon is paying attention to our conversation, but he seems intent on getting his fill before we hit seawater.

The water ripples and swells. The dragon shifts backward, but a group of fishkin jumps out of the water and onto him. They grasp his legs and tail and try to climb up his body.

I shriek, angry at the attackers, though I trust the drake can handle himself.

Rekspire roars, knocking the offenders away. White lightning flashes in a wide arc around him. Several creatures fly off, landing and jerking in the rolling water. They bump a few more clambering creatures down, but more come after them, determined on harming the dragon. However, it's futile, since dragon scales are thick and hard to penetrate.

The flood is bubbling now, almost frothing. It's almost as if the water itself is rabid. Scents of fish and saltwater saturate the air. The moisture rides the breeze that picks up, building, and clouds darken the sky to our right, in the direction of the Zoe Tree. Gusts shake the limbs and rattle leaves, blowing cold. I shiver against it.

I take to the sky to see what's happening. There are water kin of all kinds swimming around. Though Grandfather spoke of fishkin and fin folk as being different, I can't tell which are which here. A few too many of them remain in their froggen form, something I'd thought had been destroyed when I broke Siltworth's pearl. I'm worried about why some remain as their frog selves and some don't. I pack that question away until we're all united.

As I realize the full extent of the threat in the flooding expanse below, blue fire surges through my veins, overwhelming me. I scream, and my bird squawk echoes, booming around us. The few remaining birds flee from the noise. To my surprise, my scream is accompanied by fire shooting from my beak.

Though shocked, I don't fight the heated rage that pours through me like molten metal. Arching my wings up, I aim the stream of fire at any of the waterkin that dares to get close to the drake. He tries to beat them off, but there are masses of them climbing up others to get to him. He can't use his lightning as creatures swarm him.

Rekspire rakes his claws over some who try to climb up the smoother scales on his belly. Lucas darts in and pecks at them, jerking back when they try to retaliate. The water continues to rise, coming up to Rekspire's lower belly now. If I land as a girl, I'd have to swim, something I don't want to do. Water and fire aren't a good mix, and I need my ability.

The dragon does manage a web of lightning, but the water now dampens his ability to strike with force. The energy fizzles and dies when it hits the water. He's powerless against what is coming up from the depths, and I have to wonder how many fish kind there are. Have they all come here at this moment?

I direct my fire at the throngs on the black dragon, which have reached his wings and are actively holding him back from flying out of the burgeoning flood. The last of my flames flicker and die. Out of fire, I'm chilled and pull back to wait for my energy to rekindle. Several charred water kin float in the water, some still alight and smoking. The acrid smoke joins the briny scent, clogging my nose and turning my stomach at the stench.

Should I stay a bird or should I change back and use my calling ability? I hesitate, unsure.

A loud splash startles me. Clouds churn over the moon, swirling and obscuring the light for a long moment. When the moon is freed from the assailing storm, I finally see what rose out of the water, standing tall and confident like a regent in the glowing moonlight.

A bulbous-looking man with a pot belly and thin limbs stands atop something—a strange sea creature. The being's body is shapeless, almost gelatinous in form and movement. And then I see the numerous legs. It's an enormous octopus. The odd man's mouth is overly wide, though his lips are thin. His bald head sticks out of a nonexistent neck, like a lump on top of his body. He stands confident on the octopus.

I narrow my eyes, hoping I'm wrong. It can't be, can it?

"Ah, good. I see you got my calling card." He coughs, and I cringe at the phlegmy sound of it. It's nightfall now, and his overlarge, feral eyes glimmer green-gold. Several other fishkin gather around him. One jerks a female out of the water, her greenish hair and skin familiar. She's yanked, kicking and fighting, to the froggish man. "Welcome, Silver Mage with the star eyes, to my new sea kingdom. I have a new proposal for you." He holds his thin arm out toward the girl, Shellsea, who is gagged and thrashing in the hands of her froggen captor.

Siltworth.

I hadn't been wrong.

Shellsea had warned me. Astralee's words should've clued

me in. Cold sweat breaks out across my already chilled body, and I fluff my feathers to rid myself of the sensation.

I had hoped he wouldn't still be dangerous since I'd destroyed his pearl talisman.

Yet here he is, right in the center of the flood.

It wasn't a coincidence. Nothing ever was with the fallen froggen king.

27

I fight down the bile that wants to crawl up my throat. It burns different from my firebird ability, scalding me with its fervor.

Siltworth's long mouth tilts up in a smirk. "You can speak to me if you open your mind to it."

Lucas screeches. *"Don't do it, my lady!"*

Enough of the froggen have come to stand by their leader that Rekspire is finally able to break away. Streaks of blinding lightning flash from the dragon in an unorganized shower. Those who the magic touches, fall away to spasm in the water, dead almost immediately. There are still too many uninjured bodies accumulated in a crowd to take on by myself.

"I don't plan to open my mind to him. But what are we to do? We need to get to the passage and he is threatening another creature. Look at her," I tell him with strong conviction, *"She's terrified."*

Shellsea's memories sing through my mind. Though she's as evil in many ways as Siltworth, she'd been his victim. And she might not be here in his control had she not stopped me and tried to get me to help her, help her kin—something I haven't had time to do anything about.

Rekspire floats over us, water running off him like rain, breaking my musings. *"We need to get to the Mother Tree before it's too late."* His voice is stiff and angry.

"I can't leave the girl in his hands. He'll kill her and rejoice in it."

"I make you a deal. I will spare this girl's life and stop my flood if you destroy Thoron's talisman which you now possess." His voice still croaks, though it's not as deep as it once had been. He is less like a threat and more like a sad, misshapen creature. However, I know he is not harmless. He's quite the opposite.

But how does he know I have the Memento Mori? Astralee warned me about the froggen. Shellsea had as well. The froggen were spying on us from everywhere. There is no way I'm giving it to him, Shellsea or no.

"You don't have forever to choose, and I have no talisman left to destroy." His smirk creases one wide cheek. He splays a lumpy hand across his sunken chest, showing a ring around one of his fingers.

My ring! Siltworth *had* stolen it. Is that how he's been flooding the kingdom? Had that been his plan all along?

My ability flairs to life once more, covering me in comforting warmth. The blue of my fire darkens until it is almost as dark as the night sky. It dims my eyesight with its intensity. My hands, no my wings, itch to wipe Siltworth's grin away for good this time.

"Burn him. Drown him. Let him rot in the Sunkin Forest." The voice in my head screams with a vengeance.

The Hulda. It's the witch's voice!

How does she have access to my mind? As I take in the feel, sound, and taste of it, reaching out as I had done with the stones when I connected with my father, I see how she is linked to my father and he to my grandfather. Both of them have links to me. How? By the Mortuus Irrepo curse? It was the only explanation.

How do I stop it?

"My lady, do not give him the satisfaction of thinking about his request. You know he will turn on you faster than you can change." Lucas's words batter my mind. He's upset and worried.

I shake my head, the feathers lifting from my neck. I ignore the lure of violence in the invading voice and answer Lucas instead. *"I know that. Truly, I do. And even if I wanted to, I have no idea how to break the box to get to the talisman. And Astralee said I'd die if I try."* I pace back and forth on the limb, wanting to act but not knowing what that action should be.

"Exactly so. Don't even consider it."

Siltworth moves his head in a silent signal. The froggen who holds Shellsea draws out a wicked-looking blade. It's curved and jagged, and I catch a glimpse of the edge. It's sharp.

Before I know what I'm doing, I change. "Stop!" I push my intent on the mergirl's captor. My staff falls into the murky depths below the oak I settled in. I call for it, but several fishkin pounce on it, fighting for it. Water churns in their frantic battle.

My flames drip on the branch I balance on, but I'm too occupied making sure the dagger and talisman are still safe in their respective places, which they are. I'm angry at myself for not thinking of the consequences of changing. However, of much more concern is that I am now too large for this branch to hold me for long. It creaks under my boots. I slide sideways, closer to the trunk, where the limb is thicker.

The froggen holding Shellsea, those around it, and Siltworth, are frozen in place. Long arms curve around Siltworth from the multi-legged monster beneath him. In a flash, the creature dunks the froggen-leader, bringing him back up sputtering and angry.

"You will regret that Silver Mage!" he shouts, water dripping off the tattered clothes he wears. "Get her, my pet."

Rekspire darts down in front of Siltworth. The drake shrieks, lightning crackling from his body. The octopus ripples and disappears beneath the flood, the water rushing around them, allowing the froggen to evade the attack.

Something hits my tree. I stumble and cling to the trunk when another blow crashes against the solid oak. Leaves rattle all around me. The wind picks up again, swaying the limbs.

"Change back, my lady. You need to get out of the tree. The kraken is trying to knock the tree over so you'll end up in the water." Lucas squawks and joins Rekspire in his assault. He knocks over the motionless froggen holding Shellsea, and together they fall into the writhing sea.

"You mean the octopus?" I shout to be heard. The rough bark pricks at the viny outfit I wear and I hope it isn't putting any holes in the fabric. The wind whips through my cloak, tearing at it as well.

"The monster Siltworth rode in on, yes. Kraken are larger than octopus and vicious," he says.

Shellsea escapes her frozen captor. With a last glance my way, she swims off, leaving us to handle the rest of the mob.

I yell "Release." The froggen's head bursts through the surface, and he chokes on the saltwater. Though I'd saved him, he does not look as if he was going to thank me anytime soon.

My hand tightens around the dagger, ready. Grandmother's warning comes back to me. Siltworth is up to something pertaining to the Zoe Tree. I won't play into his game. "I don't make pacts with madmen," I call out over the noise. With a single thought, I change back to a bird.

I fly directly at him. When I'm almost on top of him, I

change back and drop as soon as I no longer have wings to support me.

He grabs at me. His hands encircle my neck, choking me. I swing the dagger and slash. It digs easily into the flesh of the froggen king's chest, slashing down as easily as warm butter. Red blooms dark in the water. A surprised gurgle erupts from him and he releases me to clasp at the wound. But it's no use. The dagger is sharp and has dug in deep. No amount of magic can help him now. His soul is a ghostly stain as it leaves his body.

I gulp in as much air as I can before I splash into the water. My legs kick against the deluge, but something wraps around my waist and yanks me down. Without thinking, I scream, expelling the small amount of oxygen I inhaled. I grimace at the foul-tasting seawater and snap my mouth shut.

My fire is ready when I call it, but I'm unsure if anything happens because whatever is wrapped around me doesn't let go. No light ignites. No warmth comes forward. I'm at the mercy of the monster and the sea.

My chest is tight and I work not to panic. I swipe the dagger across whatever holds me and bubbles burst around the roundish, gel-filled part—the head, or possibly the body. I'm unsure which or if it's both. Another arm grabs my right leg while another gets hold of my left arm. A fourth arm swipes around my body as if trying to search for something.

Thoron's talisman?

I jerk around, trying to free myself. I slice at one of the arms, cutting it off, then work at the one around my waist. More bubbles and a shriek spew from the creature. It's a strange sound, mournful and muted. I try to reach where it holds my leg, but I'm growing weaker. It takes more energy to fight in the water than above it.

My necklace is the only warm spot on my body, and the

bitter chill of the water is starting to numb my feet, legs, arms, and hands. Again.

Sheer fear spurs me into motion. With one last effort to attack the arm around my leg, I stab but miss again, luckily not stabbing myself instead. The monster swings me around, throwing me backward. My lungs are burning. They spasm, wanting to breathe.

Fish and other sea things flow past us as we battle. Memories of my trip upstream to the froggen's castle invade my mind. *"Help!"* I *call* out. *"Kinsman, please save me."* My mouth opens without my consent.

Blessed air fills my lungs.

My body tingles and I realize it's the clothes helping me to breathe. The vines and leaves wiggle around me as if in a jovial dance, thrilled to fulfill their purpose. I'm invigorated. And somehow, I don't have to inhale or open my mouth to get oxygen, though it doesn't hurt if I do. It's incredible!

A flash of light temporarily blinds me. Fish dart in groups, swimming freely as the water spreads openly. The light blinks across my sight again.

The lighthouse!

Something dark swims by us, and the creature holding me jerks as if hit. I take that moment to slash around, trying my best in the darkness to find its arm. I make contact with something.

Light bursts, and I catch sight of what is battering the giant octopus. It's one of the seahorses Siltworth and his attackers rode in Shellsea's memory. The head is fierce, its dark eyes sparkling with promised violence.

28

Darkness creeps across my portion of the sea as the lighthouse's light disappears, making another circle around away from me. I'm tossed sideways as the kraken holding me is pummeled again. There's a watery squeal of pain and it lets go, finally.

Freed, I start to kick and swim my way back to where I think the surface is. But it's dark and I can't tell which direction I'm going. I'm going on instinct only.

Something swims beneath me, the lighthouse revealing the seahorse. I grab on. The skin is rough, bumpy, and not at all fish-like. Within a moment, we're above the surface. Though I was able to breathe underwater, it is still a relief to breathe through my nose, using my lungs. Salt and the pungency of fish taint my tongue and nose. I gag and spit.

The seahorse bobs as it holds me up, waiting for me to gain my bearings. "Thank you." I struggle to catch my breath.

It makes a whinnying sound. Its teeth are wide, long, and blackened.

A head appears in front of me, startling me and I squeal.

It's Shellsea. She may not be able to dive into the depths, but she is an adequate swimmer. Her head barely moves as she stares at me, while I thrash around like a fish out of the water. "I saved you," she says. "You owe me."

I don't answer her. I don't fully trust her. And with all that's been happening, I'm not completely sharp enough for this kind of conversation. So, I take a moment to consider my response.

"Your seahorse did. And I saved you first. I killed Siltworth, which I believe truly frees you from his hold." Saltwater sputters from my mouth. It's not something I can control, treading water as badly as I am. The seahorse is beside me, helping keep me afloat, but I am not as skilled as she.

The mergirl frowns, her long, green hair wafting around her like the seaweed it is. She's silent long enough to make me wonder if she'll respond. "Fine, understood. We're even on that account. But because you murdered the frog king, now we may never know where he hid his treasure, our crowns."

I shake my head. This one is easy. "He wouldn't have told you even if you tortured him. You and I both know that. He would've laughed at you while he died." I wait for her to react, but she says nothing. "I promised you I will try to find it. As you can see, I'm busy at the moment, and I am a novice at sea swimming." Frolicking in a stream I could do, especially if I could touch the bottom. This was beyond my ability, even with the suit.

"What if I tell you how to destroy the death mage's talisman?" Her stare is steady and truthful.

My eyes narrow. "How do you know about the talisman?"

Her cheek twitches. "Siltworth talked about it for a long time. Ever since the talisman was created. The froggen used to openly spy upon the bogs and the Hulda. They made a blood oath. The witch agreed to hide the talisman in exchange for the mage releasing her from her cursed reign in the Betwixt once he becomes the ruler. The witch believes he delays making his move."

"Why would he delay? Isn't that what he wants?" I ask.

One bony shoulder shrugs out of the water. "Who can tell with mages? Their pact shut the froggen temporarily out of the swamp. He regained access, but the witch is vigilant. She spreads lies among the truth. Too often, Siltworth would act upon his intelligence and be humiliated. He was incensed and swore vengeance against the death mage and the witch, vowing to gain the talisman and gruesomely destroy them both."

"Why does she reign there? Why is she being punished?" I ask.

Shellsea bobs then, as if considering what to say. "She betrayed the Kinsman who placed her in charge of the oceans across all kingdoms. It wasn't enough for her. The sea is lonely. Isolated. She wanted to rule the kingdoms as well. So, she called on the dark magic of her kin, those who betrayed the Kinsman and fell."

"Sounds like she wanted to be the Kinsman." I keep an eye on the sky, worried about how far the kraken had dragged me. How long before Lucas finds me?

"Her motives were inspired." Shellsea's dark eyes gleam in her grinning face. It's terrible and fierce. It reminds me of the Hulda.

I'm taken aback. "Inspired? How can you say that?"

She hisses. "I wouldn't be here without her. She spawned the mermaids. Changed the fishkin into the magical creatures they are today, empowering the finfolk. It was her spell that helped create the first froggen. She was our ruler until the Kinsman punished her—bound her powers. Now none of us are safe on land or in the sea." Anger and disgust radiate from her voice.

Understanding dawns on me. I knew the Hulda was powerful. I hadn't understood why. That's why she tried to stop me from getting the talisman. She'd be stuck in the swamp forevermore. "Why would Siltworth want Thoron's talisman if you have to die to get to it?"

Her grin is menacing. "He was going to have you break the enchantments, die, and then take the talisman for himself. He would've flooded every kingdom and become the greatest king who ever lived. But you did stop him. The question is, can you stop your father?"

In the distance, I hear Lucas shrieking. I get one final look at the mergirl, her green seaweed hair drifting around her head. Her worship of the Hulda has unnerved me. I won't repeat the promise I made her before. "Good day, Shellsea."

She dips down beneath the surface of the water and is gone.

With a thought, I change and flap messily in the saltwater before catching the air with my wings correctly. I'm airborne and searching for my Watcher.

I find him and Rekspire not far away.

"My lady! I thought I'd lost you again!"

"The mergirl found me. Her seahorse freed me from the kraken's grip. We talked for a short while." We fly in circles over a flooded landscape. Only the tops of the trees are visible now. And I can't spot the lighthouse's flash any longer. The water is too dark and deep.

"What did she say?"

I inwardly groan. *"Too much to explain. But she confirmed the froggen are behind the flooding. And I'm not sure how to find the Zoe Tree to stop it."* A thought pops into my mind. *"Rekspire, are you all right? Can you swim?"*

"I'm unharmed. Swimming is not a dragon's best skill, but I can for short periods. However, I am not able to use my magic underwater. And as tired as I am, I don't know how long I can help do anything." His inner voice is raspy.

"I'm unsure my fire will work underwater. But we have to try. If Siltworth succeeds in flooding the whole kingdom, we are all in grave danger." Though it was stating the obvious, speaking the danger out loud helps me to reconcile the possibility I will die trying to stop them. I have as much chance of that as I have of destroying the talisman.

And I am pretty sure I can't die twice.

I keep my thoughts about dying to myself. Lucas would never agree to it. Not without a fight. And I'm too tired to fight at the moment. "I wish we had a suit for Rekspire to be able to swim with us."

"Maybe we do, my lady." Lucas dips around me. "We have your grandfather's mantle."

29

I could hug and kiss Lucas for thinking of the selkie's mantle. *"What do you say, Rekspire? Would you like to help us fix the flood?"*

"I can try." His uncertainty leaks through his tone.

"I'm sure you'll take right to it. It's like flying in water." Lucas encourages the dragon. I know what he is trying to do. We were both uncertain of how to fix the flood.

"So, we'll all go together," I say. "I caught sight of the lighthouse not far from here. You and I should be okay with the clothes Audhild gave us. I had no trouble breathing. They helped me survive the kraken's battle. Together, we can go check it out."

"Use my back." Rekspire offers. *"There are no more trees close by. And I will soon have to go find a spot to land. We need to hurry."* He sighs audibly. *"I hate water. Far Starl has few rivers and seas. I long for my home and its dry land."*

I land on his spines as before, only a few notches back, remaining in my bird form. It allows Lucas to land where there's more space so he can change and get the mantle.

He lands gracefully, balancing himself between the spines. He digs through the pack. "Here it is!" He brings out the mantle at the same moment Rekspire dips into the wind.

The mantle falls from Lucas's hand into the rolling sea below us.

"Oh, no!" he cries out.

I fly off and circle around the area it fell in. It's dark and I can't see anything beneath the surface. *"I fear it's gone."*

"It's all right." Rekspire sounds relieved. *"I'll go back and find Bennett and Audhild. Call out to me if you need something and I'll come to you."*

"Rekspire, could you take this with you? Give it back to Bennett?" Lucas asks.

"I can do that. Be careful you two. Good luck."

Lucas drops the bag, changes to a bird, and together we fly off, watching the black dragon disappear, the pack clutched in one talon.

"Let's go." I dart down, changing right before I hit the water. I go in feet first and take a deep breath to ease the shock of the cold water. We move together.

Grasses tickle my arms when we sink to the bottom. Breathing is still a bit of a challenge, but the lively tingle of the oxygen the leaves give me is refreshing. *"How are you doing?"* I ask Lucas.

"It's fascinating." Lucas lands not far from me. *"I never would've thought I'd be on the bottom of a sea inhaling air from the water like a fish."*

"We need to find the lighthouse."

"Okay, which way?" Lucas paddles toward me. I catch a slight glimmer in the vines holding the leaves to his clothes.

I hesitate, not wanting to admit I'm lost. But there's nothing for it. *"I'm unsure. I got turned around as we swam for the bottom."*

Dark shapes flicker at the edges of my sight. *"Do you think we could use disguises down here? We might not be alone."*

I think of Shellsea. Her motives were never clear, and I didn't fully trust her to be on my side. *"It doesn't hurt to try."*

I recalled mermaid tails, the shape, and how they helped the creatures navigate the water efficiently. I also envision the webbed fingers. My legs tighten and my hands prickle, the only indicator the illusion might be in place.

"I think it's working." I try it out, and I'm able to move my body like I'd seen Shellsea do.

"I believe you're right. Let's search. The Zoe Tree's island is south. If I use my instincts, that would be ..." He stops for a couple of moments, his body swishing circles in the dark expanse. *"This way."* He grabs my arm and we're off to my right.

We swim longer than I anticipated. However, I no longer see the light. *"Has the water doused the light?"* I ask, unnerved. If we can't find the Zoe Tree, there won't be a kingdom to save. My body strains as though we're traveling against the current, in the right direction. It's a small relief.

"It can't be much farther. I bumped into an anchor from one of the boats. It probably rose with the sea. Keep searching."

"If only we could see better." I start to wonder if we are swimming in circles. It's too hard to tell in our murky surroundings. Possibly we are swimming closer to the main shoreline where I'd seen other boats before I'd drifted off into the Sunkin Forest.

I hadn't meant to think the last part. The remembered terror grips me and I freeze. A minute ago I hadn't paid attention to the frigid water, but now my legs cramp.

"My lady?" Lucas's concern reaches out, trying to comfort me.

His voice grounds me. I clear my mind of the memories. I can't lose control like this. There's too much at stake. *"I'm okay."* My voice is shaky, I know. I've sunk so I tread water. *"I had a flashback of our boat trip. That's all."*

"Ah, yes. Who could blame you? It was not our finest moment." His chuckle is heartening, allowing me a moment to regain my composure. His chilled arm snakes around my waist, assuring me.

"You were fine. I was a mess," I admit. His arm tightens, wrapping around me. *"Lucas?"* I ask, alarmed.

It isn't Lucas's arm.

I'm being dragged through the water once again. At first, I'm too shocked to react. When my necklace heats up, my stupor is gone. I refuse to let another creature lead me on a watery death ride.

I tug at the fire inside me, uncaring if it will work. If nothing else, I might stun my captor. I open my mouth and shriek, *"Let go!"*

Flames, scalding and ready, shoot out of my mouth, catching the octopus by surprise. Its pained cries blurb around me in a whirling fury as it races away.

I'm not alone. Other eyes glow from the abyss surrounding me. Friend or foe, I'm not sure. And I'm not waiting any longer to find out. I call my flames around me, warming me. Water bubbles around me, turning hot—boiling. Nothing approaches me.

Through the wavering flames, I see the flicker of silverfish and other creatures, fleeing.

I turn and head back to Lucas.

————

I find him not far behind me, his crazed, darting lumber through the water less than effective for swimming.

His eyes widen when he catches sight of me. He'd taken on

the form of some large fish with fins along his wide, pale side. Dangerous looking. *"Tambrynn! What happened? Is that your fire glowing around you?"* His relief is matched by an equal amount of disbelief. He swims a circle around me to verify what he sees.

"Yes. I tire of water rides and creatures trying to capture me. So. when I grew angry, my fire came to life. I'm done being scared." Between the light and the warmth, I'm much more comfortable with the task ahead.

"It's ..." he hesitates. *"You're beautiful and terrifying. I didn't know you could hold your ability like this in the sea."*

I bask in his compliment. *"I didn't either. But we need to find the Zoe Tree. We should have an easier time if my fire doesn't flicker out."*

As he had before, I seek out my instinct for direction. I find north first, which is the easiest with its pull. Then I turn and go the opposite way.

Lucas follows me silently. We scare several groupings of fish before we get close to trees that have been swallowed whole by the flood. One tree sticks out among the others, the Zoe Tree. The doorway is wide open, and though there's no light, a radiance shines through the abyss, drawing me closer.

I circle the tree before settling down in front of the broken doorway. The doors have been blown apart, similar to the way my father tried to gain entry into the cottage when I first met him. Pieces lay on the ground, but I'm sure with the flood, there are some missing. The doors sag inward toward the passageway where the ambient light originates.

"Ready?" I ask Lucas.

"As I'll ever be."

And we're swimming through the battered doors. Inside the passage doesn't look much better. Trees are uprooted. Chunks of ground have been torn open, leaving chasms.

The water is heavier here. Putrid. Like the essence I'd experienced from my father.

"Can you taste that?" I ask Lucas.

"I can tell something's off. And the bracelet you made me is tight on my skin. What do you sense?"

"My father." My necklace is still warm against my skin, my ability still burning around me. *"I thought it was the froggen. What if I'm wrong and Thoron is waiting for us?"* My flames flash from blue to silver, not with a warning, but in time to the fearful beating of my heart.

"Then we'll handle him like we always have," Lucas speaks confidently. Either he doesn't remember me running from my father at the nomad's mountain, or he's fooling himself.

Audhild's emaciated form flits through my mind. The glow around me turns silver, though thankfully it remains. I say a silent prayer that the Kinsman will help me fix the doors and the passageway. The farther we go, the more rancid the water becomes. No fish swim here. No creatures darken the pathway.

"Lucas, do you recall the story you told me when we entered the passage?"

"Which story, my lady? I told you several." He swims beside me, floating over downed trees, through their submerged limbs.

"The one with the water funnel." I tried to recall what he told me.

"The icy brinicle," he replied. *"The Kinsman used the water funnel to steal the unfaithful away to a realm where they can't return. I warned you if you got too near it, you might be sucked into it."*

We pass another doorway, still safe and shut. Maybe the other kingdoms were okay. I pray that to be true. *"What if it's the opposite? What if someone, the froggen or my father, has tampered with the river there."*

"The River of Life, Cadence called it, though there were other names in the books I read in Bennett's keep." He's quiet, contemplating. *"The books state that the river connects each kingdom and feeds the Zoe Tree, the tree of life, which keeps the doorways open."*

"We know that Siltworth wanted to flood Anavrin. I saw my ring on his finger, so he had access to open the tree. Could he have known about the River of Life?"

We come upon the bridge, the carved wood still slick and graceful underwater. I follow Lucas beneath the curved ceiling. If the rest of the passage had been rank, the potency here reeks enough to curl the leaves on our swimming outfits.

Haunting cries echo from somewhere I can't see. High-pitched clicks and calls break out in random, uneven bursts. All noise stops, however, when I draw near, bringing with me a silver firelight.

Though the passageway is flooded, there is no sign of the brinicle. However, there must've been a battle. The area is littered with dead water creatures of all kinds.

And floating right where the water funnel should be is a large snake-like fish. Its body slides through the sea with easy grace, moving in circular patterns. Spots pock its greyish-brown skin, which curiously isn't scaly but smooth. The head is flat.

"Watch out, Tambrynn. That is the deadly shocking eel."

30

Lucas's words catch the eel's attention and it slithers to face us, the golden eyes watchful, alert.

"Shocking eel? Is that what killed all of these creatures?" I push away several silverfish floating belly up.

"Most likely. And it doesn't look like it's going to let us go any farther. Something tells me this is Siltworth's work. He must be hiding something."

A faint light breaks along the eel's skin as a wave pulses from his body. My necklace is alive with heat. Before it can hit us, my protective shield wavers around me. The swell of electrical current, much like the kind Rekspire uses, hits my wall and crackles and dies.

The creature bobs its head and swims closer. Smaller pulses flow from the creature across my shield, which blocks it. I can tell, however, the power of the surge as it washes across my protective sphere. It's significant. *"Why would it attack all these other water creatures, though?"*

Lucas grabs my arm, his illusion drops, and he paddles

backward, away from the eel. *"It could be here to guard whatever Siltworth was doing."*

"How do we get past it to stop the flood?" I keep my eyes on the massive being. It's longer than a man would be tall, wider than my waist at its center. Though it couldn't gulp me down in one bite, it wouldn't take much work to have me for dinner.

It advances again, its body and tail slithering through the sea.

"Do you still have the dagger, my lady?" Lucas is tense next to me, his feet kicking hard to keep him afloat and facing our newest enemy.

I check my side where it rests safely in my sheath. There's still a bulge in my pocket—the talisman. *"Yes."*

"You may need to use it so we can get past. Like you did with the froggen king." Lucas's chilled hand rubs the small of my back.

Instinct tells me to turn and swim away. It's all I can do to advance instead. I swim crookedly around the eel, and it turns to keep me in its sights. There are more pulses, some small and some stronger that rush toward me.

Lucas, taking advantage of my distraction, darts off the backside of the bridge and out of view.

The eel jerks its flat head away in a sudden move, toward the bridge. Toward Lucas.

I take that moment and lurch toward the creature, slashing the Mortifer blade.

Electric power bursts from the eel, blasting me backward. It squeals in agony and the tang of blood scents the water.

The power overwhelms my protections and the hot zing of the eel's shock devastates me. My body jerks wherever electric energy hits, shocking me with the same intensity my father's hexes had. My heart stutters painfully in my chest. I choke on agony, biting my tongue and drawing blood.

It seems like hours, though I'm sure it's only a few

moments before the pulse is gone. The pain isn't, however. My side is seared, the pain unimaginable, making my head spin and my stomach twist. The last of the heat brands my flesh like melted metal on skin. As fast as it burns, the cold water seals it.

Lucas rushes to me. *"Tambrynn. Are you all right? Where does it hurt?"*

His fingers are icy on my shock-sensitive cheeks. The leaves on my outfit are shriveled. My mouth is open wide but I can't breathe. My muscles are still frozen. Lingering snaps of icy fire pip and pop along my nerves. The dagger is clutched to my chest tight, but my fingers are unable to move. I realize the talisman is on my injured side. Bone-deep agony spreads down my leg. The intensity draws tears that disappear into the saltwater.

Lucas's hands rub at my arms, shoulder, neck, and across my face. His lips are puckered with desperation, his hands shaking and unsure. Silver locks of my hair float around his beautiful face.

Maybe this is it. If the eel has damaged the talisman, I'm sure to be dead within moments if I'm not already so. I try to smile, but my muscles don't respond. I'm left staring, unblinking into my Watcher's dark eyes. The same eyes I smiled into as a child playing with him in the fields near our home on Tenebris. The memories had come back to me before we crossed into Anavrin, they are some of the most precious treasures I hold. Mother is smiling. Lucas is laughing. And I am happy. My fire winks, flickering uncertainly.

High-noted clicking calls have Lucas twisting away from me. I can't see what is happening.

"Wha—" Lucas shrieks.

I'm smacked from beneath, a hard slap on my upper back.

I convulse, inhaling the briny water, flavored now with the eel's blood. I choke, coughing and sputtering. The leaves on my clothes unfold and come to life once more, blooming and sending tingles across my arms, torso, and legs. I heave like I've run a race, grimacing at the pain.

And then I'm smiling. The trauma from the eel was dispelled. I'm alive! *"Lucas, I'm okay. Whatever that was, it helped me breathe."*

Lucas embraces me in a tight grip, and we drift downward. *"Oh, thank the Kinsman! I didn't know what to do."*

A chittering call, not unlike a bird, but different in a strange, underwater echo, startles us both. It's a gray sea animal. Much bigger than a fish. It has a long snout and a rounded head with a long, sleek body.

We break apart to face it.

It bobs its head in an adorable dance.

"Is it smiling at us?" I ask Lucas.

"It's a dolphin." He reaches over and rubs the rounded head above the eyes. Like a puppy, it rolls over and Lucas's bubbling laugh accompanies his scratching of the dolphin's white belly. Several more dolphins join us, their chittering, high calls filling the area with sound. They squirm around us in excited circles, their flipping tails moving the water in clashing waves. *"I've heard they can be quite helpful to people lost in the sea."*

A couple of them bounce the eel back and forth as if rejoicing over its death. Maybe they were—some of their brethren's corpses are victims of the eel's shock. I'm unsure what happened here, but it was messy and violent.

One noses my arm and takes off swimming into the dark depths below the bridge. *"Should we follow it?"* I look at Lucas, who watches the antics of the creatures with a small grin.

"I've heard stories of them, but I've never seen one until now. They don't seem to be a threat. Maybe they'll lead us to the source of the flood."

Together we follow the dolphin, the others forming an arc

around us. When we don't swim quite fast enough, two bump up beneath us. Like the dragon, I grab the fin and am in for a ride. Water rushes past me in a bobbing dash through the saltwater. I realize with relief that I'm not afraid like I had been with the froggen or the kraken. The eyes of the dolphins are dark but have a kindness that resonates, though it could be because they look like they're grinning and happy. Regardless, my necklace doesn't heat up and I don't sense any ill intent.

Our rides pull up, and water pressure hits us from behind as they stop. Lucas and I tumble off the animal's backs and onto a beach.

"What is this?" I choke out, staring at the water above me in stunned confusion. I'm not used to breathing in air now and it takes me a moment to transition from breathing with the help of the water outfit. The leaves, true to form, shrivel again on dry land.

Numerous dolphin heads poke out of the water as if the world is upside down. They're above us and we're below them on land.

Dry. Land.

"This is absurd." Lucas's voice is hoarse as he regains his bearings. He turns in a circle.

I follow him. It's not a huge area, but large enough to house a barn. My fire still radiates from me in a bluish light. Though the water was cold, the air is worse. My side aches with the sensitivity of burned skin without the cold water to ease the pain. I pull my arms across my chest and gently call my flames to help alleviate some of the discomfort.

Fish bones and shells are scattered across the sand. Dried seagrass is sprinkled along the shore that leads to a wall that extends up into the water. It's dark, and I can't make out what it is, but it hums. When I reach out with my ability, I sense a power behind the buzzing darkness.

A doorway.

Rattling from my left makes me jump.

"Who's there?" a man calls out. He steps out of the dim recesses and into the furthest reaches of my fire's light.

It's Councilmaster Nyle.

His face spreads into grin. "Have you come to rescue me?"

31

Lucas steps in front of me. "Rescue *you*? Wasn't in our game plan, no. I'd love to hear why you're here, though."

My side, which had ached so badly in the water, is beginning to thrum without the sea to keep it cool. I reach inside my pocket and find ... something roundish. I pull it out. It's an uneven stone. "Lucas." I nudge his shoulder, whispering.

He glances sideways at me. "What's wrong?"

I hold my father's talisman up. "The eel broke the curse."

With a last, menacing glance at Nyle, Lucas spins to see. He takes it in his hand. "Is that magic I sense?" His voice is low.

Nyle's neck is strained as he tries to catch what we say.

"I believe so." I grit my teeth against the agony of my wound. Though I didn't die taking the curse off the box, I am assured it left a mark behind that isn't going to be easily dealt with. I work to ignore the pain and face the eldrin, trying to catch Lucas's reaction.

Lucas palms the stone, brows furrowed. "You didn't die. I

thought you said your grandmother told you a sacrifice was needed."

"She did." I don't want to tell him about my leg yet because Nyle doesn't need to know any more than what he's already heard.

Whatever I say, or how I say it, makes Lucas glance over me. *"You're injured?"* He knows this, but he says it more as if questioning what it means.

"Yes, and I'd rather he not know about the talisman. Besides, I'm still alive, right? It can't be that bad."

I'm not encouraged when he says nothing back.

More rattling echoes in the small space and another man steps out of the shadows. He's tall, white-skinned, and has scars that cover every inch of his body. Pale gold hair runs down his back in an untamed mane. His eyes are so light they appear almost colorless. He has a warrior's body, wide and strong.

Dangerous.

He's shackled with something similar to Nyle's manacles. Heavy chains wrap from wide metal bands, which almost seem to be part of his body instead of resting over his skin. They lead to more bands around his ankles. Thick chains run off them into the dark.

"Who are you?" My voice wavers, but I stand firm. I bite back a cringe as the wound in my side flares.

"Theocles, guardian of the doorway to Hevell." His voice is hushed, but his words buffet us like wind.

I step back, uncertain.

Lucas reaches behind me and squeezes my arm. "If you are guardian, who do you serve?" he inquires.

"The one and only Kinsman." He bares sharpened teeth as he speaks with a grimacing grin. It isn't humor. So, is it anger or menace he exudes?

"Then why are you locked up?" I ask despite my fear. Thankfully, I'm standing too far for the chains to reach.

I turn my head, studying him. His shoulders and body are relaxed. His face is intense as he contemplates us openly.

Is he like the Hulda, stuck guarding a realm because of some misdeed?

He purses his lips, moving them strangely as he must decide how to say what he's thinking. "It is my fate. Better question, why'd you fall through the trap door?"

Trap door? I glance around.

Nyle laughs at my confusion. "A doorway to a hidden space, in this case, one you cannot easily go back through. It seals the door to Hevell. Without the brinicle, its lock, the banished will escape." He jerks his head toward the darkness. Energy pulses there, along with pounding that I imagine are fists on the other side of the door.

I glance at Theocles. "Yet the guardian is shackled?"

"The sea monster," he shakes his head, "kraken—tricked me. Puffer poison. When I came to, I was chained." He lifts his arms and the thick metal clanks.

Nyle sneers. "Some guardian. Fooled by the simplest creatures."

How long has Nyle been down here? I send him what I hope is a haughty look. "Seems to me you were tricked by the same group."

"Yes, but I was taken in by the king of the deals. I was supposed to receive his deep-sea treasures in exchange for my knowledge of how to break the brinicle's power. This buffoon was poisoned and duped into a false friendship. I was under no such illusions in my dealings with the froggen king." His grin is calculated. "Poor froggen idiot. Didn't realize a thimble of poison isn't enough to take a guardian down."

I frown. There is more the eldrin isn't saying. "So you *had* a bargain with Siltworth. You may be comforted to know he is dead." I watch his expression closely and am not disappointed.

He pales, his imperious humor gone. "Good riddance," he spits out, his voice strained. His scowl changes almost as immediately, however. Gone is the derision, and in its place is a practiced smile. "Since that is the case, and he won't return to do so, can you set me free? The key is over there."

As if I could trust him.

Theocles spits in Nyle's direction. "Scum eldrin. False cleric. He lies."

They stare at each other, their shared loathing evident in the tilt of their chins.

My shoulders pinch. I don't have time to haggle. "I'm only here to reset the brinicle and stop the flood. Can either of you help me with that?"

They both turn to look at me and I can almost feel the heat of their gazes.

"I can." Theocles says as Nyle demands, "Break my chains and I'll help you."

I turn toward the guardian. "How can you help me?" After a thought, I add, "Specifics, please."

His shoulders droop ever-so-slightly as his throat moves with a swallow. "The doorway needs to be resealed. Pull the water back. The Kinsman's protections will immediately recreate the brinicle." He waves his hands in a circular motion and his chains rattle and clink.

"No, no!" Nyle asserts, panic clear on his too-eager face. "Don't do that. At least not before you let me go." When he doesn't get the desired response, he continues to appeal to me. "You're not a murderer. I promise all charges will be dropped and the eldrin will leave you both in peace if you use the key and unlock these chains." He holds his cuffed hands up in a silent plea. They are red and puffy, likely from attempts to gain his freedom.

"Shameful," Lucas growls. "If you had said anything else besides that, I might've tried to believe you," he points a tense finger at the eldrin. "You dare to try to reason with Tambrynn after what you did to her and the nomads? Continue to do, as I understand it." His laugh is full of contempt. "Do you ever think of anyone but yourself?"

Nyle's shapely mouth pinches tight. His silence is hot and telling.

I fully turn my back on him. "How do I call the sea back?" I ask Theocles.

"Chosen of the Kinsman, you hold his light. Your gifts hold the answers you seek." He sits on the sand, his legs crossed. Only now do I see gills set in his neck. They're closed, possibly to allow him to breathe without water. It's a curious sight. I haven't seen anything like it on the other water kind.

"Are you finfolk or fishkin?" I ask, curious.

His face is stony. "I was before them. All things and none. I am Guardian."

I catch the emphasis he puts on the last word.

"You won't drown in the sea? What of the chains?" Lucas asks him, pointing to the shackles.

Theocles's white grin is wicked. "I am cursed. My place is here." He rattles the metal shackles. "These will not hold me when I regain my full strength. Until then, I guard the door and wait for the Kinsman to reset the One World. Only then will my redemption be achieved."

"So, you're like the Hulda?" I ask, curious. She hadn't seemed so redeemable.

Scars on his face whiten as the skin beneath reddens. "I am not my sister. I betrayed first but repented." He fists his hands until they turn white. "My cup is bitter, but anything else is—"

He stops speaking. His face contorts. "Unworthy. I accept my fate."

Unworthy? I can't imagine something more deserving than what he is currently doing—guarding a doorway to the forsaken kingdom. If the others behind the door are as powerful and great as he and the Hulda, what else could lay beyond its border?

But I'm also torn. I can't leave Nyle behind when I try to pull the water back. I also can't let him continue to rule over Anavrin as he has, and I get the impression he still would.

The throb in my leg grows. I need to make a decision soon. I'm getting woozy from the pain.

Theocles grunts at me. "Finely crushed fire rock. Paste with blood thorn sap for your wound. Apply until healed." He then jerks his head in Nyle's direction. "His path is fixed, unchanging. Not ours to direct." He points his bound hands at my hip. "Use the Fate Sealer with a blood pact."

"Fate Sealer?" I reach for the dagger. "You mean the Mortifer blade?"

The giant man squints. "Fatal blade? Maybe so. There were twelve." He spreads his hands, the chains clinking. "They hold many names and great power." He waves to the dark shadows where the doorway supposedly is. "One served my defeat at the hands of my sister Hulda. She evades its touch. For now. She's genial, yes?" His laugh is barking and deep.

Horror ripples over my body. No, the Hulda isn't genial whatsoever.

I shake off the awareness that this guardian has voyant abilities. He's already scary enough. Luckily, he appears not to mind helping me. "How do I make a pact with the dagger?" I ask. "Though he doesn't deserve it, I can't leave Nyle here."

"Cut your hand. Blood is magic. Spoken words of power will seal it. Make the bargain smart and binding."

Bargains. Deals. Pacts. I can't get away from them no matter how I try. A dolphin chatters at us from above as if encouraging me. Or telling me to hurry.

"You can do this, my lady. Use your insight to guide you." Lucas's demeanor is neutral, but his words are the confidence I need.

I pull the dagger from the sheath and stalk toward Nyle, Lucas close by my side. My hand is steadier than my knees. "Hold him, please."

Nyle gathers his hands against his stomach. Confusion darts across his smooth face when I reach for his head instead.

Nyle's life explodes in pictures and images in my mind. He was an amiable child. Charismatic. His handsome features and charm along with an ability to spin a tale in his favor follow him from his youth to his adulthood. He finagles information about the holy articles from his mentors, eventually using that knowledge to steal the Eye of Fate and the apatestones.

He becomes Councilmaster, a self-proclaimed title, in the aftermath of Thoron's battle ending the eldrin's unopposed reign. Then his charisma changes. He can't stand the people he manages to deceive. They aren't strong enough or smart enough for him.

Worthless, his spirit whispers to me. Only those who oppose him are worthy, a challenge.

Others like me. Like the nomads. He can't fool us. Like the strategic games he played as a child, he plans each move carefully. Removing obstacles. Making pacts. Plans for the ruination and destruction of any foe.

His compulsion is much like Shellsea's, though it involves less violence and more manipulation. His spirit is incredibly proud. Instead of using his abilities of coercion to unite or help others, he uses them to elevate himself.

I see Nyle meet with Siltworth shortly after I broke the

pearl. He arrogantly makes a deal with the former frog king believing he will regain his control of the scepter. He's smug and confident until the froggen betrays him. He spirals in disbelief at first. How could such a lowly creature get the better of him? Then, his rage spears my mind with its hunger for revenge.

I tear my hand away, leaving him breathless on the ground. I pray I'm making the right choice because I don't see Nyle changing. Quite the contrary. Lucas's words about Farmer Tucker's son come to mind, how his fate is the best revenge. Leaving someone here to die would be something Nyle would do.

I don't want to be anything like him. Nor do I want his death on my conscience.

"Nyle, I will agree to set you free if you in turn denounce your position as Councilmaster, and never hold another position of power within the eldrin ranks. You'll give up all the holy items you stole. You'll agree to make restitution to the nomads you have taken and imprisoned. And lastly, you will agree to never make another pact with any creature, friend, or foe, under penalty of death." I prick my thumb.

"That's not a fair trade. What do I get in return?" Spit flies from his lips and his cheeks turn a bruised shade of blush.

"You get your life, you slimy snake." Theocles ridicules him.

32

Nyle turns icy blue eyes on the guardian. I don't doubt that if he could, Nyle would gladly end the guardian's life.

My finger stings from where I pricked it. Nyle begrudgingly holds his hand out. Luckily for me, the blade is deadly sharp and it takes little effort. There's no doubt the eldrin will try to weasel out of our deal as he has so many other scenarios I viewed in his life.

However, I do uphold my promises.

Once Nyle's blood touches the blade, we both bend over as the magic takes hold of us, binding my words to our future, whatever that might be. My gut is locked up and twisted tightly for a moment before it's gone. Lucas's hand on my back is reassuring though not warm. The chill reminds me I need to hurry.

Since I trust Nyle as much as I trusted his partner Siltworth, I take the blade to the chain far enough away that it weighs him down still. I wouldn't want him to get away before I'm able to restore balance in the sea.

"What're you doing? You promised to set me free." He sputters as he realizes what I'm doing.

"Yes, I will. When I'm done resetting the sea." The dagger cuts through the metal like slicing through ripe fruit.

When I finish, I replace the dagger in its sheath and stand facing the edge of the sea above us. With one hand, I call to it, pulling, tugging away the border of the air bubble we stand in.

"Return to me." I send a mental picture of the sea around me, beckoning it to listen and obey. The sea, though, is wild. It has a consciousness. I sense dark secrets in its depths. Things it doesn't want to reveal. I push those aside. Except for Siltworth's treasure, I don't wish to know anything else.

Thumping like a drum thrums from behind me. The doorway. They are close to getting the doorway open. Unholy shrieks and howls filter through the barrier, igniting me into deeper action.

Fear invigorates me. Sweat breaks out across my brow. The first drop hits my scalp.

I ignore Nyle's blustering, hysterical commentary behind me.

A few more drips. Yes!

I use both of my hands, ignoring the stinging that digs into my leg's nerves with an unrelenting ache. I beseech the creatures of the deep to return, for the depths to reclaim abundance. I sense other doors other than on Anavrin which have sprung leaks.

I go deeper. Light blazes in my mind—the Zoe Tree's guardian. She speaks to me without words, showing me how she's divided, a piece of her spirit set inside each doorway. She is the mechanism for the doorways to work. But her pathways have been abused, her roots are suffering. In Anavrin they are almost dead. If I don't stop the flood, she will perish. With her death, each doorway will be closed forevermore.

Even to the Kinsman.

There will be no reuniting of the One World. Grace, goodness, and mercy will fall. The times of evil will never end. I see the darkness in my mind. It's the same bleak venom that inhabits my father's soul. But this is much worse.

I can't fail.

I double my effort, giving all that I have. I'm breathing heavily, my strength stretched thin. It starts to rain, gentle at first.

"Deep breath, eldrin. You're going to need it." Theocles laughs, a deep hearty sound.

Nyle's shrieks drown him out.

Hand over hand I pull. The leaves on my outfit dance in the shower coming from the trapdoor.

More pounding, frantic this time, beat against an unseen barrier. It matches my stressed heartbeat. My strength is waning. I rally the last hum inside me for one final yank. Like falling into a lake, the deluge comes. I'm choking as I adapt to breathing in the water once more.

I quickly swim over to a panicking Nyle, his cheeks puffed out with the last breath he took. I slice through his manacles, trying not to cut him in the meantime, but I fear I nick him as he struggles to get free.

Unsurprisingly, Nyle races off. He swims better than I can, and he's making good progress until one of the dolphins pokes him from the side. It's playful, but it gets his attention. I continue to pull, and only when I can't pull any more weight, arms shaking from the effort, do I stop.

Water spins at my feet, sucking at me. I kick, jerking back quickly. The spiral grows and grows, the tail pushing against the darkness of the doorway. The brinicle reaches upward, growing wide as it goes.

Lucas pulls me back from getting dragged into the funnel.

I'm so tired. I float back to gaze at it. Power radiates from it, drawing in the eel's victims, probably the eel itself, ripping, tearing, ravaging until they're gone.

The water clears, the reek of death absent.

It's the work of the Kinsman, I know. The truth of the thought settles in me, assuring me. His power has reset the sea.

With a small wave at Theocles, I swim off, Lucas beside me. I pat the first dolphin on the side and settle myself on its back. We're off. They're faster than Nyle, and we're beside him within moments. We slow and I grab hold of one of Nyle's arms. Lucas grabs the other. We tap the dolphin, and we're off again. Frigid water sluices over us, and I'm thankful to have the outfits which help us breathe.

Nyle, as expected, thrashes, his face darkening with the need to inhale. He's spasming when we break the surface.

He's furiously sputtering and choking, cursing us.

I ignore him and scratch at the dolphin's head and belly. It cackles at us and then swims away.

"How're we supposed to get to land?" Nyle's head bobs as he struggles to float.

The water is shifting, moving toward the center of the brinicle. The dolphins have brought us to the other side of the bridge, out of danger of being dragged back down again.

I try to change, but I can't. I'm much too tired to wait for the water to recede. The top of the bridge is not far, so with a knowing glance at Lucas, we head in that direction.

Lucas shifts. He flies off to the wooden structure and waits for me to make my way there. The top is a couple of feet from the surface. I don't think I can climb up the side, which I'd have to swim to.

"Tambrynn, here." Lucas offers his hand.

I take it gratefully, not looking back at Nyle. I did my part of the bargain, freed him, and helped him out of the sea's abyss. It is up to him to be smart enough to follow. He certainly isn't as exhausted as I am.

Luckily, the roof of the bridge is covered with boards, and the area is wide enough for all of us to rest comfortably side by side with room to spare. I lay down wearily, my arms and legs no more than jelly, and stare off into the endless sky with no sun or moon to distract me. I do wonder what time it is, however. How long has it taken us? I've lost track of it all. It seemed like weeks, not hours. Maybe it has been.

I close my eyes and hear, rather than see, Nyle groan as he hefts himself up not far from Lucas and me, Lucas between us.

"Rest up," Lucas tells him. "We have doors to fix before we can enter Anavrin again."

I'm too tired to discuss the Zoe Tree's guardian. I fall asleep immediately and am not surprised when I wake up to find Nyle gone. I gently remove Lucas's arm which rests heavily across my throbbing side. I check the flood.

Bushes poke out of a muddy wash below, the water still swirling in places as it continues to return. Did Nyle slip away before the water fully subsided, or did he wait until he could climb down and slop his way off the bridge? Will I ever see him again? It will be too soon if I do.

I have no interest in following or trying to find him.

Lucas rests peacefully on his side, one arm behind his head as a pillow. I wipe a lock of his hair that's stuck to his forehead to the side and he stirs.

"Wake up, sleepyhead. We have more work to do."

His dark eyes open and he grins. "I had *some* dreams last night. Involved a killer octopus and," his mouth twists, "Nyle."

He's so handsome in his sleepy state. I kiss his cheek and the seawater's saltiness makes me grimace. "Gah. Awful."

"Kissing me?" Lucas shifts so he's half sitting up.

I laugh. "You taste like seaweed. We must stink." There's no lingering sweetness of the flowers that once filled the passage. No scent of trees and grasses. The brackish sea scent is all around us. I run a finger down his cheek from where I kissed him to his neck.

"Stink, huh?" A dangerous glint sparkles in his narrow eyes and one side of his lips crooks upward. My pulse speeds up as desire ignites inside me. However, I know that mischievous look.

I try to move, but he catches me and holds me, gently, and kisses me. He's tender. I press myself closer, deepening the kiss. Passion, like a fire, ignites inside me. I run my hands across his chest and back, my body tingling with delight.

He shifts closer, accidentally touching the wound on my side. I jump back, grimacing at the renewed pain.

"I'm so sorry." He's panting, as am I. "How bad is it?"

I don't want to discuss the pain. "It is what it is." I sit up. "And we have things to do." I gaze out over the passageway.

Lucas moves his arm behind me and I rest my head against his shoulder. I take solace in the strong and steady beat of his heart. "I'm so glad that's over," I breathe out. "Siltworth is dead. The flood is stopped. The Zoe tree is saved."

"We still have your father to face." His voice rumbles in his chest. "Wait, did you say Zoe Tree?"

I tell him briefly about finding the tree's guardian as I was reestablishing the brinicle. "It seems that the tree is also a key. Without it, the Kinsman won't be able to unite the One World again."

"So you're the key to saving the key." Humor laces his words.

I teasingly bump him with my shoulder. Thoughts of the keys remind me of the valuable item I'm carrying. I search my pocket. Fiery pain zings down my side when I get close to the wound. The pocket is empty.

I panic. "It's gone. The talisman is missing."

Ignoring the agony, I pat my body frantically to check, but it's not there. "I can't believe he did it! Nyle took the talisman," I moan, lying back against the bridge's roof. I rub my hands over my gritty face, disbelief making my heart stutter.

Lucas raises a fist and opens it to reveal the stone. "He didn't. I never gave it back to you when we were under the sea."

Sweet relief washes over me and I drop my arms to the boards. "You are infuriating, but amazing." I reach out to caress the side of his face, glorying in the gift of my Watcher.

He preens, his chest puffed out, and his face lights up with delight. "I am." He runs his hands across the tangle of my hair. "And so are you, my love."

I smile and drink in his kisses. Playful at first. And then more urgently, until we're left breathless once more. My side aches and I'm gritty with salt residue.

So we remain still, holding hands and enjoying each other's company until the water is gone.

———

The doorway is a disaster.

Since there's no real tree on the inside of the passage to check, I rest my palm against the rough bark on the Anavrin side of the Zoe Tree. I detect a small light inside, faint but present. I pat it and look around at the chaos left behind.

"I don't know if I can fix it." I'm no Kinsman who can split kingdoms and set enchantments over magical doorways. I stand with my hands on my hips, the crinkled leaves of my outfit tickling my hand. I favor my right side, where the curse injured my leg. Unable to walk the whole way through the passage, we'd flown. But the wound still made it hard to travel. None of the trees had made it; they were all broken or uprooted. And a thick layer of silted mud cakes what bushes and plants remain. I could never have made it out on my own.

"Not all of the pieces are here and the tree is leaning precariously toward the cliff." I don't say that the roots are pulled slightly on one side, though they are. "Can we fix that?"

"I'm unsure. But we have to at least try to block the doorway, or every creature will be traipsing hither and yon. You mentioned the tree's guardian spoke of being abused. Maybe that's because they've been used too often lately. Or because the eldrin use them for treasure-hunting reasons. Either way, we need to seal them back up. Somehow." Lucas's no-nonsense attitude helps me brace against my doubts.

I certainly don't want the froggen to come back and tamper with the doors or the trees. Too much is at stake for that to happen. I take a breath and puff it out. "Okay. Let me try."

I close my eyes, hold out my hands, and *call* all of the pieces of the door to me. It isn't like it was in the blizzard or with the sea. My senses are heightened as I feel the residue of magic on the shards, the strips, and the pieces. They come to me and I see them as the puzzle they are, wanting to be returned to their place. They're eager to be whole.

Lucas's warmth disappears as he moves out of the way of the scattered debris flying toward us. A few jagged pieces nick my arms and face. I try to slow the progression for safety, but they zip and zing, coming to rest exactly where they need to go, no matter what's in the way.

Some fragments are lost beneath the grimy layer in the passage and the flattened island hilltop, scattered everywhere. It takes a fair amount of concentration to draw them all. I stop and take a break.

The trees here are battered, but I think many will survive. The lighthouse still sits on the cliff's edge near the small beach, but the light no longer shines. I'll have to find another bone to light it again. It's on my list of things to do. It's all a bit overwhelming, so I focus on the task at hand. Which is enough by itself.

Back at it again, I move my arms, pulling the pieces as I had with the brinicle. At last, I yank a large plank that had been stuck under a fallen tree limb. It comes at me fast, and I duck in time for it to miss and bounce off the side of the Zoe Tree's trunk.

My leg burns at the sudden movement and I suck in a breath.

"Magnificent job, my lady." Lucas strides over. He picks pieces of bark from his hair, still stiff from the seawater.

I chuckle and brush my fingers through the tresses. "Let's see if I can seal it back together now." I tap the pile with my boot.

"Tambrynn?"

Audhild?

33

I trip over a chunk of wood and almost fall upon hearing the fire dragon's voice. Lucas catches my elbow before I go down to my knees.

My eyes dart to him, my heartbeat thrashing in my chest. Has she gotten free? I glance inside the passage, wondering if we have a chance to enter before she gets to us.

"It's okay, Tambrynn. She's with me." Rekspire's words are strong. Confident.

Still, I'm unsure.

Lucas and I tuck ourselves behind the tree as the female dragon's red form flutters into sight. She's still not plump, but her flight isn't as crazed or crooked as during the storm. Rekspire is indeed with her.

I squint to try to make out what's on his back.

Grandfather!

"We're so proud of you. The flood is gone." Audhild's words are humble and low. They don't have the blasting power they once held.

I mourn even as I hope.

"Come out, youngling. I mean no harm. Your grandfather can explain."

Slowly, I creep from around the tree, limping into the open. Bright rays from the waning sun light up the trio with bold, golden light. They've landed not far from the charred path of Audhild's fire.

The first time she saved me.

Rekspire lays down on the ground, allowing Grandfather the opportunity to dismount. It's still a drop to the ground from his back, which the old eldrin makes, though he grunts when he hits land, sodden though it is.

"How is this possible?" I ask her.

"There was hope that came to me in the darkness. A light that showed me my way back to myself. I believe you know something about that?" She raises her claw, the one I'd placed my bracelet on. The gems are there, glittering in the sun's glow. *"I cannot change back yet, but I am no longer bound by your father's magic. At least while he is away."*

I understand what she didn't say. Like my grandfather, who is fine until the beasts arrive or Thoron appears, the fire dragon is not fully under his Mortuus Irrepo curse.

"We figured you'd be here trying to put the door back together." Grandfather walks beyond the other two. An almost imperceptible gimp mars his smooth gait.

My hand twitches. I wish I still held the staff he'd given me. It was lost to the sea now, along with his mantle, the ring remaining on Siltworth's finger when he died, and probably numerous other items. I'm not even sure where to start looking for any of them.

"Tambrynn?" Lucas nudges me.

"What?" I ask, realizing Grandfather has asked me something while I haven't been paying attention. "My apologies. What did you ask?"

"How'd you end the flood?" A smile splits his disfigured face. It is a most welcome sight.

I pull at the leafy fabric. "It was because of Audhild's gift. Without the swim clothes, neither of us could've delved to the bottom of the abyss where Siltworth had drained the sea."

Lucas and I had tried to piece together the reasons for his actions but hadn't come up with anything that made sense. Why would the froggen let the inhabitants of Hevell free? Had he truly done it on purpose? Did he, like the Hulda, have other grandiose plans for taking over more than one kingdom?

"*Ocean.*" Audhild corrects mildly.

I blink at her response.

"*The sea cannot hold the brinicle of justice. It's placed beside the River of Life and leads to the ocean floor, which connects each kingdom's water source. It is also the only doorway into the accursed kingdom of Hevell. There the Kinsman can monitor it.*"

The ocean floor is like the Zoe Tree, then—the key to the seas and rivers everywhere. Despite what I know of the Kinsman, I have to wonder at his ability to create such marvels. "If the Kinsman watches over it, how did the froggen get there and flood the passage and Anavrin? Why would he allow it?"

Her tongue clicks, and smoke curls over her scaly upper lip. "*Why does anything bad happen to good creatures? Free will and choices. Did you meet the guardian there?*"

"Theocles, yes." I lift my chin, unsure why I feel attacked by her words.

"*And you met the swamp witch?*"

I grit my teeth. "It was quite a meeting, yes."

"*I believe we had this discussion once before. The Kinsman's creations all have the gift of free will. To live and to love as they will. Right or wrong, they can do as they wish. There comes a day, however, when judgment falls upon us all. For some, it comes swiftly. For others, it feels too delayed to bear.*"

I think of the difference between the two guardians. One accepted his fate, and one fights against hers. They both rebelled. Only one was repentant.

Audhild bows her head as if she understands where my thoughts lead. *"You were there and chose to serve, to save Anavrin from the flood. You will be rewarded for that, and I pray you accept your reward."* She opens her dragon mouth and smiles. *"Like the strange outfit, yes? It, too, is a blessing. Probably not one you'd envision when it first showed up."* She's teasing now. However, her point has merit.

"Are you all done mindspeaking now?" Grandfather grunts, his disfavor evident in the tilt of his head.

"Yes," I reply unapologetically. I'm grateful to have Audhild back, even if she is weakened. And no matter how grumpy he sounds, I know Grandfather is as well.

"Let's get this doorway back and operational. We don't want everyone wandering in between kingdoms." He pulls a bag out of his pocket and empties it to reveal large stones with fresh runes carved on them. They're larger than the ones we'd used before. "These more powerful shifting stones will help hold it until a better doorway can be built."

I take in my companions, all beloved by me in some strange way. Somehow, I knew they were sent to me by the Kinsman. His ways might be beyond all I can understand, but at that moment all I can do is utter a silent prayer of thanks to him for placing them in my life.

Grandfather hands me the first stone, and together we begin to seal the doorway.

EPILOGUE

Thoron laughs at the eldrin caught in his trap. Poor idiot. Did the fool really think he could try to enter *his* dragon kingdom without being noticed? His spies, beastly and other, are everywhere, after all.

Besides, this man has enemies quite willing to spill their guts. Literally and figuratively.

"Please, don't hurt me. I can offer you information about your daughter." Nyle sputters and spits like a cornered cat.

Probably partly due to three of the monstrous pets surrounding him. They stare blankly at the man they hold tight, waiting for Thoron's command.

This! This is the best part. The power to make others squirm. He knows the feeling intimately.

Relishes it.

He'd grown up being called names because of his rank. *Half-breed. Mongrel.* He was nothing of that sort. However, he couldn't prove it. Too many people laughed at him. Treated him differently because of it.

He sobers for a moment. No one laughs at him now.

A smile curls across Thoron's face, taut from the newly-ingested power. Stupid Far Starlians. They don't understand the treasure they have in the dragons, both dead and alive. Like his weak mother, who had lived there most of her pathetic life.

Her actions led to her desertion in a kingdom she didn't know. She'd raised him to despise the eldrin, hate their kingdom, hate who he was.

She realized too late how that hate empowered him to become what he was today.

The most powerful mage ever to live.

Thoron twists his neck, trying to ease the haze the power makes him feel.

It's a delicate balance—how much to take in without becoming drunk on it. There were so many bones, though. He could feast until he burst if he wanted to and then start over again.

A squeak tears him away from his languid musings.

One of his pets has too tight of a hold on the eldrin's collar.

Imbeciles! All of them. It's a good thing they have him to think for them.

"Not so tight!" he screams at the sluagh's mind. The beast releases his grip, stumbling away from his master's ire.

Frail, these eldrin. Soft from their elevated status and meager understanding of magic. They wield it. He runs his hand across the Eye of Fate lovingly. His hand lingers near the gauntlet on a shelf next to the scepter. What the Eldrin couldn't fathom with all their training was that you must *become magic.*

What had they been talking about?

Oh, yes. Tambrynn.

"What do you know of her?" he asks, not inviting the power of her name.

"I know where she is right now. She'd be easy pickings. Her

and the other one with her. The djinn." The scent of ambition and greed permeates the air around him in a green haze.

Again, Thoron grins. He never used to be able to sense these things. Only after the dozenth bone or so had he begun to read intentions and desires. The delicious development he consumes, welcoming it into his being. His stomach distends, but he ignores it.

The eldrin hangs dully as Thoron feeds off him. His sight becomes unsteady, doubled until everything is blurry. Too much too soon.

He can't speak, so he uses his mind control. *"Lock him up. I'll use him later."* Thoron waves a hand at his pets. They jump to do his bidding.

The eldrin screams and yells, his voice hoarse. He fights against the beasts, but it's no use. Thoron boosted them with his newly found power earlier. Enough so they didn't become sentient again. It takes a lot of power to suppress their spirits, implanting his will upon them instead.

He knows the others thought his pets dead, their spirits missing. They weren't. He didn't have that kind of power yet. But he would. It is only a matter of time before he becomes a god himself.

The door shuts on the eldrin's pitiful wails. Though he enjoys the power the eldrin bring, they aren't full of light like the dragons.

Or his daughter.

The plan for her is already in play. Luck had been on his side when the fire beast stumbled across him, her ire raised enough she didn't sense him fast enough. She'd been a wonderful addition to his resources, though siphoning power from a live dragon isn't the same as using bones. Bones don't resist him.

His steps aren't steady. A belch explodes from his mouth,

and he balances himself on the wall until the wooziness wears off.

Ugh. The eldrin's power isn't settling.

Thoron would take care of him later. Besides, he doesn't need an eldrin to tell him how to find his daughter. He knows her location. He'd waited for her to set the flood to rights. Stupid fish playing games in a big pond. They were no match for her or him. Lucky for them, he didn't have a taste for tadpoles. Too dark and greasy. He preferred creatures of light.

Ah, but true to form, his daughter didn't disappoint. She saved him from having to act before Far Starl became flooded and he lost his boneyard.

Then he would've been furious. He'd have had to seek more revenge as he had with his weak father. And his bitter mother.

Astralee had taught him to hate and then rejected him when he became a hate-filled mage. He'd done it to make her proud. To take her back home to Far Starl. She hadn't been impressed as he'd hoped.

So, he'd made her pay.

Satisfaction flushes through his system as he leans back against the plush bed covered with red satin sheets.

It wouldn't be long now. With the fire dragon out of play, it was only a matter of time before he worked his way to his daughter. One by one, he'd pick them off, consuming them. She'd be his, all of her power at his fingertips.

And then nothing could stop him.

To be continued …

SPLIT KINGDOMS OF THE KINSMEN

- Anavrin
- Tenebris
- Panacea
- Hevell
- Zoar
- Emporium
- Risan
- Benario Vale
- Pseminia
- Iolneo
- Far Starl
- Trithis

CREATURE RACES IN THE KINGDOMS OF TENEBRIS AND ANAVRIN:

Nomads – non-magical people. Small and stout in stature, they are creative and industrial.

Eldrin – a noble, holy race charged by the Kinsman to guard and care for his holy writings and relics. They are an ethereal-looking people but pompous and condescending at heart.

Mages – dark magic users, can be any race. Evil resides in their hearts and souls.

Djinn – shape-shifters who can change into any living creature on demand, often mischievous and tricksters.

Voyants – telepathic beings able to communicate with other creatures in their minds and can sense other's emotions.

Sluaghs – (pronounced: Slew-aws) the undead creatures hexed by dark mages with a mortuus irrepo curse into becoming part-beast and part-person. Evil permeates their beings and they are controlled by the necromancing mage.

Froggen – a cursed race of fishkin. Genteel in manner but swindlers at heart, they are untrustworthy. Hexed into creation, they live in waterways and seas which permeate

Anavrin and rule it as a watery kingdom. They desire ultimate rule over Anavrin.

Trellers – non-magical lumberjacks who work in the forests of Anavrin.

Finfolk – water kin that are warm-blooded, air-breathing mammals (pinniped or fin foot) and have developed flippers for legs/arms. They are more communal than the fish folk.

Fishkin – the more self-serving of the water races. They were more easily persuaded to become froggen due to their anti-social behaviors.

Merfolk – Mermaids and Mermen. Are social, but like animals in the wild when they get a taste of blood, or in merfolk case, the life force of other creatures, they are addicted to it. Have amazing voices and use them to lure the unsuspecting to their deaths.

Dragons – holy messengers of the Kinsman, they are magic incarnate and sought after by mages for their blood and bone which hold magical properties. Their gift of fire burns away that which is corrupt. They are a rare and endangered species.

Firebirds – AKA phoenixes, also rare and endangered. Born healers, they are the protectors of the righteous and guiders of the lost and downtrodden. Their gift of fire heals rather than destroys.

ABOUT THE AUTHOR

Winner of the 2016 ACFW Genesis Award and finalist in the 2018 Grace Award and the 2020 Great Expectations Contest, Dawn has been recognized for her published and non-published works. Her flash fiction stories have been published in *Havok* magazine under both her real name and pen name, Jo Wonderly. Her debut novel, *Knee-high Lies*, was published in 2017.

As a child, Dawn often had her head in the clouds creating scenes and stories for anything and everything she came across. She believed there was magic everywhere, a sentiment she has never outgrown. Nature inspires her, and her love for the underdog and the unlikely hero colors much of what she writes.

Dawn adores anything Steampunk, is often distracted by shiny, pretty things, and her obsession with purses and shoes borders on hoarding. Dawn lives in Iowa and helps her husband run their foodservice and catering business out of Omaha, Nebraska. When not reading, writing, or catering, Dawn loves babysitting her grandchildren, is parent to Snickers the Wonder Beagle, and can usually be caught daydreaming.

ALSO BY DAWN FORD

Woodencloak by Dawn Ford

The Band of Unlikely Heroes - Book One

Thirteen-year-old troll princess Horra Fyd's life changes forever after
an unexpected visit from the fairy queen and her two daughters.
Tales of fairies gave Horra nightmares as a young troll. Before
evening falls, however, a real nightmare unfolds. Horra's father, King
Fyd, goes missing. Her woodgoblin instructor is poisoned and uses
his magic to revert to a seed. And a mysterious, gaunt man wearing a
cape and playing a panflute joins the fairies in trying to capture her.

Horra flees but is instantly lost in a world she's never had to travel
alone. A letter hidden in her knapsack from her late instructor

informs her that a power hungry Erlking seeks revenge against her kingdom and their allies for a two-generation old war. She is tasked with getting his seed to the Weald, a magical forest. There it can regenerate into a druid, the only creature with the power to hold the balance between good and evil, and who is able to defeat the Erlking.

However, the Erlking is always one step behind her. Horra must fight to protect herself, but she has no magic. She accepts a gift from a dead druid spirit of a charmed woodencloak to disguise her. But magic failed her mother, how can she possibly trust it?

Can Horra have faith and courage enough to trust a power she can't see, and become a warrior heroine her foremothers can be proud of? Or will she allow fear to rule over her and lose everything that matters—including her life?

Get your copy here:

https://scrivenings.link/woodencloak

———

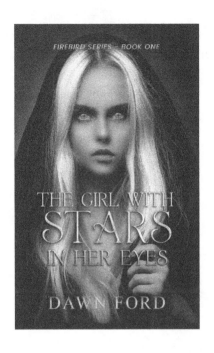

FIREBIRD SERIES—BOOK ONE

THE GIRL WITH STARS IN HER EYES

DAWN FORD

The Girl with Stars in Her Eyes

Firebird Series—Book One

Eighteen-year-old servant girl Tambrynn is haunted by more than her unusual silver hair and the star-shaped pupils in her eyes. Her uncontrollable ability to call objects leads the wolves who savagely murdered her mother right to her door.

When she's fired and outcast during a snowstorm, her carriage wrecks and she's forced to find refuge in an abandoned cottage. There, her life is upended when the magpie who's stalked her for ten years transforms into a man, Lucas. He's her Watcher and they're from a different kingdom. His job is to keep her safe from her father, an evil mage, who wants to steal her abilities, turn her into one of his undead beasts, and become immortal himself.

Can they make it to the magical passageway and get to their home kingdom in time for Tambrynn to thwart her father's malicious plans? Or will Tambrynn's unique magic doom them all?

Get your copy here:

https://scrivenings.link/thegirlwithstarsinhereyes

MORE FANTASY FICTION FROM
EXPANSE BOOKS

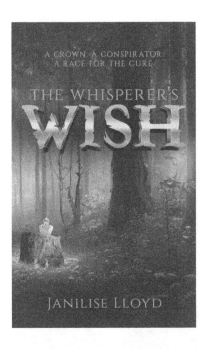

The Whisperer's Wish

by Janilise Lloyd

For sixteen years, Laurelin Moore has been keeping a secret. She is a whisperer, and she knows that to reveal her gift now is a dangerous risk. Past whisperers have been exploited for their power. But Ausland's queen is dead and acknowledging her magic is her only chance at becoming a Rook in the Pentax—a competition that will decide the kingdom's next ruler.

Laurelin isn't in it for the crown, though. She's after the wish that will be granted to the victor. A wish that would save her dying brother, Pippin. But there are dangerous undercurrents to the competition, and Laurelin finds herself at the center of it. She begins to search for answers and discovers a secret with the potential to shatter the entire kingdom.

Get your copy here:

https://scrivenings.link/thewhispererswish

———

The Near Distant—Novella Collection

by Brett Armstrong, Erin R. Howard, and

C. Kevin Thompson

2023 Selah Award Finalist

On a day trip into the wilderness around Lake Tahoe, college students Ned, Tyler, and Everly stumble upon a monolith. No one knows its origin or purpose, but structures like this one have popped up all over the world, making national headlines. While not the local legend the group hoped to find, they decide to investigate, only to be engulfed by a blinding, powerful pulse of light. Instantly, the three friends find themselves in separate and drastically different worlds. They must quickly adapt to their new surroundings or perish.

Get your copy here:

https://scrivenings.link/theneardistant

———

ExpanseBooks.pub (an imprint of Scrivenings Press LLC)

Stay up-to-date on your favorite books and authors with our free e-newsletter. Sign up here:

https://scriveningspress.com/newsletter-signup/